# THE
# COUNTRY
# GIRL

A heartbreaking and powerful WW1 saga

# SALLY TARPEY

JOFFE
BOOKS

Joffe Books, London
www.joffebooks.com

First published in Great Britain in 2023

Cover art by Jarmila Takač

ISBN: 978-1-80405-820-6

*For my sister, Geraldine, my children,*
*Luke and Kate and my grandchildren.*

For you to find
Some quiet, peaceful
times — for yourself.
Enjoy this.

Love — always.

J xxx  6/23

## AUTHOR'S NOTE

This novel began with research into a lost part of my family history and evolved into a work of fiction. The discovery that my grandfather had a previous wife and a child in 1918, led me to research and imagine what happened to his first family. I became fascinated with what might have befallen this young woman and her son.

In creating the story of *The Country Girl*, I followed a trail of investigation which led me to several unanswered questions. As with all works of historical fiction, therefore, the resulting story is a blend of real events and invention.

Many of the details of village life are based upon my own experiences as a child growing up in the countryside and the stories my parents and grandparents told me. Micklewell is a fictional village, although it has geographical and historical links to many places in Hampshire.

Kate and Dot Truscott's stories continue to absorb me and I am currently working on a sequel to *The Country Girl*.

# PROLOGUE

*Sweat trickled into Kate's eyes and yet she was shivering. The throbbing in her temples made it difficult for her to raise her head. Her body twisted and turned, trying to find a position where her bones didn't ache. Lying on her back made it easier to breathe, but if she stayed in that position for too long, it was agony. Her throat was dry and she was constantly thirsty, but when she tried to reach for some water, her hand shook so much that she couldn't hold the cup. She floated in and out of today and into tomorrow on waves of pain that made it impossible to distinguish day from night, wakefulness from sleep, presence from absence.*

*Life was going on around her, she could hear voices. The clatter of pans told her that food was being prepared and the smells of cooking reached her nostrils, but when Albert tried to spoon soup into her mouth, her tongue couldn't taste and her throat wouldn't swallow. His gentle words of encouragement urged her to try to eat, but her appetite had left her, along with her ability to decipher was what real and what was an invention of her fevered mind.*

*In this world of drifting, she clung on to the threads of her life that wove in and out of her consciousness. She heard her child crying, but couldn't go to him, her limbs weighed her down. She felt the touch of her husband's lips, but could not kiss him back. Always there for her, she was so grateful for that, but his face was no longer clear to her, she was slipping away from him.*

*Where was she? Micklewell, her Hampshire home? Was this her sister, Dot, bending over her or her mother, Ada? Whose was this face? Then she remembered. She was in a lodging house in Fareham. She'd left her village home in 1912 and so much had happened to change her life since then. She had to fight this. Please God she would survive this illness. She had so much to live for.*

# PART ONE

# CHAPTER ONE

*September 1912*

Kate Truscott removed her muddied shoes, rinsed the dirt from her hands and wiped them on the rough towel hanging beside the kitchen sink. She smoothed down her rumpled skirts and sighed.

'My back is killing me,' she moaned as she sat down opposite her mother who had her breast bared, feeding her fourth child. 'I'll be glad when there's no more spuds to lift in that field. Seems like we've been digging and bagging forever.'

'You wait 'til you've birthed a few babes, then you can complain about backache,' her mother replied.

Kate was fifteen years old and her intention was not to become a mother just yet. She had more important things to think about, dreams of a different life, a life that did not entail grubbing around in the dirt on a farm. The money she earned was a feeble amount, but at least it meant she was contributing to the family income. She just didn't want to be doing it for the rest of her life.

'I've brought back a bag of potatoes,' she said. 'The ganger said I could take the ones that were scabby or spoiled by the fork. They'll last us a few days.'

'Well they've kept you late today,' Kate's mother, Ada, said.' You'd best get upstairs to your sister now. She wants you to tell her a story. She won't go to sleep without one.'

Kate smiled to herself as she opened the door at the foot of the stairs. Her sister, Dot, was as dark as she was fair but they shared the same spirit. The difference between them now was that Kate was on the verge of womanhood and Dot was still a child.

Kate's light-brown hair fell down her back and she flicked the loose strands away from her face and out of her deep blue eyes as she concentrated on navigating the turning stairs. She remembered to duck her head to avoid the beam, for she'd grown to be taller than her mother now. Her courses had started and she felt within her a surge of energy that she sometimes found it difficult to contain. Her breasts were filling out and she was aware of attracting the attentions of the young men of the village. She had a boldness in her expression that spoke of her growing confidence in herself.

Dot was sitting up in bed when Kate entered the room. 'About time too,' Dot said wrinkling her nose at Kate.

'Just you wait 'til you have to earn your living, Dorothy Truscott,' Kate said. 'You don't know how lucky you are. Now, which story is it to be?'

'The one about the two mice.' Dot grinned, nestling down under the covers.

As Kate told the familiar story, she looked down at her sister's sweet, freckled face and smiled. When she spoke the final words, she kissed her lightly on the forehead and rose up from the bed, trying not to make the metal springs complain with their usual squeak. She turned towards the door only to hear a pleading voice whisper, 'Tell it again, Kate, please tell it again.'

'But I've told you it so many times, Dot,' Kate replied, 'and there'll be trouble from Ma if you stay awake any longer. It's Sunday school tomorrow morning.'

'Oh Kate! You know it's my favourite story,' Dot whined. 'What sort of mouse are you, Kate, a town mouse or a country mouse? I'm definitely a town mouse. I can see myself drinking from fancy glasses and eating off the best china.'

'I've told the story and now I'm going downstairs. I've got the washing-up to do and then Ma has given me a pile of darning — Dad's work socks. Just be grateful you're eight and not fifteen,' Kate replied.

'Phew!' said Dot with her fingers clamped to her nose. 'I hope she washed them first.'

Kate picked up a cushion from the chair in the corner and threw it at her sister.

'Cheeky,' she said, suppressing a giggle. 'Don't let Ma hear you casting doubt over her homemaking skills or there'll be trouble. Now, night, night!'

Kate returned to the kitchen, the main family room in the house where they ate, drank, gossiped and sewed. She looked at her mother and wondered how she coped with bearing so many children. She was beginning to show her age and she was often tired. Many of the daily tasks fell to Kate. There was always plenty to do. She washed and cooked and cleaned as well as working in the fields at Wellhouse Farm. It was nearing harvest time and there was a deal of picking and gathering in to do, so there were not many of the daylight hours that she could call her own. Her brother, Fred, did little to help around the house, as he was out labouring long hours. Together the family managed to feed and clothe themselves and keep warm in the winter, but there wasn't much left at the end of each month.

The kitchen was warm from the range which had been stoked to cook the family meal. The stew had boiled over and the smell of burnt gravy filled the kitchen. Kate's nose wrinkled. That would be another job to do, cleaning that up before the blacking, which was long overdue!

There was still the washing to get in and the chickens to put away for the night and she must try to get that darning done before the light faded. Kate could see through the kitchen window that Pa was still outside trying to mend the puncture on his bike. She wanted to talk to both of them about what Maisie Harwood had shown her in the *Hants and Berks Gazette*, but she knew better than to interrupt him when he had a job to finish.

She sat down opposite her mother, in the only other comfortable chair in the room, shifting the large black-and-white cat as she did so.

'Go on, Jimmy, go and find some mice to catch,' she said, moving him from his favourite spot.

'Talking of mice, how many times did you have to tell it this evening?' Ada Truscott asked Kate.

'Just the once but she tried to get away with more,' Kate replied.

'She's a bright spark that one,' Ada said, moving Henry from her right breast to her left. 'And so are you, Kate. There must be something better for you out there than digging spuds, it's a waste of your talents. Miss Clarence always said that you were her star pupil,' Ada added.

'Mmm, well, as you mention it, there's something I want to talk to you and Dad about,' Kate began.

'Sounds serious,' Ada replied. 'He must be nearly finished now. Go tell him the tea's been poured and it's getting cold, that'll shift him.'

By the time James Truscott had put his bike away in the shed and cleaned himself up, Kate had rehearsed what she wanted to say several times over in her head.

She determined the best way to approach it was to come straight out with it. 'I've been thinking,' she said, 'now Dot is getting a bit older, she's able to do much of the work I do about the house.'

Her parents looked at each other and raised their eyebrows. Although Dot was an intelligent girl, they all knew that she was not the best at carrying out instructions. Her mind wasn't always on the task.

'Well . . . what I'm trying to say is . . . I think I would be better use to the family if I earned a bit more. Maisie

Harwood gave me this. She cut it out of the paper.' Kate read slowly and carefully:

> WANTED, *clean and presentable girl to work as nurse-maid in family home of respectable businessman. All domestic household duties pertaining to care of five well-behaved children. Apply, in writing, to James Winton Esq. Woodland House, The Crescent, Andover.*

'It sounds just perfect, don't you agree?' she said. 'I think I should apply.'

'But Andover's miles away and it's a town, a very busy town,' her mother replied. 'Could you not try for something closer to home?'

Kate was aware of how much her mother relied upon her, but she also wanted to feel what it was like to be independent. She loved Micklewell but she knew that there was a wider world beyond it and lives that must be lived in a completely different way to her own. Being in service would not be a life of ease, she knew that, but a voice kept whispering that there was more to be discovered about herself. If she didn't try she would never know what that thing was. She had to find her own way, besides which they needed the money and she would be one less mouth to feed. She crossed her fingers and came out with it, hoping she sounded calm and considered.

'You know as well as I do that there's no decent paid work to be had here in the village, Mother. Come the winter I could be out of work for months,' Kate replied.

'The girl's right,' Kate's father agreed. 'My earnings at the forge and Fred's at the farm add up to barely enough, once the rent's been paid. And now young Henry's here, we've another mouth to feed. If she wants to apply, I say we should let her. She needs to take any opportunity she can. She needs to earn herself a better living, Ada.'

'What's this about earning a better living? Nothing wrong with getting your hands dirty.' It was Fred arrived home from his work, covered in dust from the haymaking, his hands scratched and his hair matted and stuck with bits of straw.

'Well don't you look the scarecrow,' Kate teased him. 'Better get yourself cleaned up if you're going to the Queen's Head tonight. No young woman's going to look at you twice with that hair. Looks like you've been pulled through a hedge backwards.'

Fred threw the cap he'd removed from his head at her and she dodged out of the way.

'Our Kate's applying for a job,' their mother said. 'Nursemaid at some posh house in Andover.'

'Oh, is she? Well, little sister, and how do you think you'll get along with all those ladies and gentlemen with their fancy ways?'

'I'll learn to do what's expected of me. I can read and write and I know more about looking after children and housework than you do,' Kate said, defending her decision.

'You're right there,' Fred said and then, softening his tone, he added, 'And they'd better appreciate what they've got or I'll be over there to sort them out.'

Kate laughed, her brother had always been there to stand up for her, from the time they were in school. He'd ducked Gilbert Tucker's head into the horse trough, outside the pub, when she told him about how he'd taken her skipping rope and tied her up to the school railings at playtime. Earlier that summer, he'd warned off Bert Butcher, at the village barn dance, when he kept pestering her. He threatened to hang him by his braces in the oak on the village green.

'Hold on there, Fred. I haven't got the job yet,' Kate said. 'I haven't even applied. I've only just shown Ma and Pa the advertisement.'

'Well, best get on and do it, then,' Fred replied.

Kate was pleased that she had the family's support and set about writing the letter that evening.

# CHAPTER TWO

*October 1912*

Kate Truscott closed the gate of the only home she'd known for fifteen years and waved goodbye to her parents, her brothers and her sister. She was leaving the tiny village of Micklewell to become nursemaid to five children she'd never met, the offspring of the wealthy James Winton Esq and his lady wife. This was the first time Kate had travelled such a long way from the village and on her own too. It was going to be a long walk to the crossroads where she would be able to pick up the carter's wagon on its daily route to the railway station. For this reason, she'd been careful with her packing and only allowed herself one treasure, a book that her teacher, Miss Clarence, had given her for helping the younger children with their reading. Her bag was light and so was her heart. She told herself that the flutter in the pit of her stomach was more excitement than nerves.

She paused at Wellhouse Farm and looked at the image of the Soldier on the Wall. She was going away but he would remain, standing to attention in his black bearskin, larger than life! Someone had painted him in his scarlet and blue during the time of the Crimean War. Kate had grown up with him and she nodded to him as she made her way down the village street.

She glanced at the field where she'd picked and bagged potatoes. No more dirt under the nails, she thought, and no more muddied skirts. Life in the town was going to be so different. She hummed to herself and strode out towards the crossroads where she would meet the cart. It might be months before she would see Micklewell and her family again. That seemed strange now, but she had made up her mind, she was ready for something new.

On reaching the crossroads she knew that she'd allowed herself plenty of time but even so, she couldn't help continually glancing up the road. She breathed in the cool morning air and listened to the trilling of a blackbird in the hedgerow. Would there be birdsong in the town? She hoped so, for it always lifted her spirits.

The clip-clopping and trundling in the distance made her stomach flutter. She was on her way. No going back now!

'Morning, Miss,' called the carter as he reined in the horses, 'you'll be wanting a ride. How far are you going this morning?'

'The station please,' she replied. 'I'm starting a new position today, in Andover.'

'Ooo! Andover, is it? Watch out for them town folk with their hoity-toity ways,' one young man with a mud-spattered jacket and rough, chapped hands teased.

'Move over, then,' the carter called to the other travellers. 'Let the young lady on and make sure none of you spoil her nice clean clothes with your dirty boots. We can't have her arrive covered in countryside muck now, can we?' He smiled, winking at her.

Kate was not offended by the banter, for she felt pleased with her appearance. She'd wanted to make a good impression with her new employers and so had taken special care in her preparations. She'd brushed the cat hairs off her coat and darned the holes in her woollen stockings. As the wagon joggled along, Kate recalled the wetness in her mother's eyes

11

as she'd let down the hem of her best green dress with its high neck and buttoned bodice.

'It suits you well,' her mother had said, 'but perhaps a little too short now for a young woman about to go into service.' She'd brushed Kate's thick, light-brown hair with an extra thirty strokes that last evening to make it shine and told her to pull back her shoulders and be proud of herself.

Kate had become a little self-conscious of her breasts since her courses had started. She was aware of the changes in her body and knew that they drew the attention of the local boys. Her friend, Maisie Harwood, often said that she wished she was tall and elegant with blue eyes like Kate, not short and dumpy with plain old brown eyes. What Maisie lacked in good looks, however, she made up for in good sense. She gave Kate all sorts of advice about the train journey and Kate followed her instructions precisely.

'Make sure you ask at the ticket office how many stops to Andover and be sure to sit near some other lady travellers. Count the stations and ask someone before you get off to make sure that it's the right place.' Kate kept all this in mind.

The arrival of the train at the platform was noisier than she'd expected, but she resisted the temptation to put her hands over her ears. The squeal of the brakes and the rush of steam escaping from the engine startled her, but as soon as she got on board, she enjoyed the sensation of moving along at a speed far greater than even the fastest horse and cart could achieve. She settled to looking out of the window at the passing countryside and listening to the conversations around her.

At the first stop, she retrieved a letter from her coat pocket. It was her letter of acceptance for a trial period with the Winton family and instructions on how to reach The Crescent and Woodland House. She read it over to herself. It was really happening! She was not only travelling many miles from home, she was going to live in a big house in a town. She was starting a new life and she would make a success of it. She would make sure they liked her. She would work hard.

In Andover, the streets were full of people and she had to take care to watch out for carriages when crossing the road. She wasn't used to such hustle and bustle. She passed some fine shops, milliners with such hats on display as she had never seen before. Feathers and finery! She paused while crates of wines were unloaded from a cart and asked if she was going the right way for The Crescent. Her feet were beginning to ache as her best shoes were old and had a thin sole and, as she looked down, she noticed mud on the uppers. She stopped beside a wall and, when no one was coming, took out her handkerchief and spat on it to remove the marks.

When she finally arrived at her destination, she stood for a while before the three-storey house and counted the windows. She had never seen so many, not even on the manor house in her village. She tilted her head back and looked right up to the attic windows where she supposed the servants' rooms would be. Her legs wobbled and her head swam. Lowering her gaze, her eyes settled on the biggest window downstairs fringed with heavy curtains, behind which glowed a warm light. That must be the sitting room. She wondered if her employers were, at this moment, sitting beside the fire, taking tea. Her letter of appointment had directed her to enter through the small gate to the right of the main entrance and take the path which led around to the back of the house. She should report to Mrs Bowden, the cook and housekeeper.

Kate felt an inclination to turn and run but she gave herself a stern talking to. This was what she had wanted, wasn't it? A different life, more than just lifting and bagging potatoes. *Come on, Kate*, she whispered to herself. She gripped her bags and proceeded to follow instructions when a voice behind her called, 'Can I help you?'

A short girl wearing a buttoned-up coat that looked two sizes too small for her was struggling with a huge crate of groceries. Her hat had fallen over one eye and the other peered over the top of the overflowing cabbages and leeks. She blew out of the corner of her mouth and then complained loudly, 'Blasted delivery boy forgot nearly half of what we ordered, 'scuse my language. So, I got the job of retrieving the rest. General dogsbody, I am. Looks like you've come to stay. You must be the new nursemaid then. Follow me,' she said, nudging her head and walking in front.

Once they were inside the girl placed the box on the table and sighed. She turned towards Kate, rubbing her arms and saying, 'Blooming heavy, that is, me arms are nearly dropping off. What's your name then?' she asked, examining Kate as if she was a joint of meat. Kate was astounded at the array of pots and cooking vessels around the kitchen and the open pantry door revealed more bottles and jars than she had seen before in her life.

'I'm Kate,' she said, managing a nervous smile. 'I was told to report to Mrs Bowden, the housekeeper.'

'I'm Eliza-Jane, kitchen maid, glad to make your acquaintance, I'm sure,' Eliza said, wiping her hands on her coat and extending one towards Kate.

'You can call her plain Eliza,' a voice said from inside the pantry. 'Now, young lady, step down off that high horse and don't be getting above yourself,' the older woman added as she entered the room. 'Thinks if she speaks like them she'll become like them, but it takes more than fancy talking to make a lady. Get yourself down to the cellar, Eliza, and bring me up two bottles of brown ale. Steak and ale pie tonight and we'd better get busy or it won't be baked in time for dinner. I'm Mrs Bowden, cook and housekeeper. You can call me Mrs B, pleased to meet you.'

'Pleased to meet you, too,' Kate replied.

'About time we had a new nursemaid. Those twins have been running riot and giving the mistress all sorts of head-aches. They need to be more occupied. I'm sure you can manage them though, a strong girl like you,' Mrs B said with a smile.

Although she displayed plenty of bluster, Kate believed that beneath that stern exterior, the housekeeper probably had a soft heart. The folds in her arms, that squeezed beneath her rolled-up sleeves, looked as though they had comforted many a lost soul. The way she tucked in her double chins and smoothed her reddened hands over her apron made Kate feel that she had a secure hold over all that went on below stairs, and probably above stairs too.

'Now, let's get you settled and you can tell me a bit about yourself,' continued Mrs B. 'Just leave your bags there. Eliza will show you to your room later. You look tired. Let's get you a nice warm cuppa.'

Mrs Bowden moved to the range that dominated the vast kitchen and slid the lightly steaming kettle onto the hot plate to bring it to the boil. The red glow of the coals, behind the huge metal bars of the grate, spread their warmth throughout the room and made Kate feel immediately at home. But this kitchen was very different to the one she had left behind. Their little kitchen at two, Mead Cottages would fit into one small corner of this one. The wooden-armed chair beside the range reminded her of the one her mother sat in to feed her baby brother Henry, and the soft cushion, the same dark blue that showed all of Jimmy the cat's white hairs. She could almost hear his purrs.

Everything in this room was multiplied four times bigger than anything she had ever known. The vast array of pans, hanging beside the blackened monster of a range, lay ready and waiting for the next boiling and steaming and the oven door, on heavy metal hinges, held back a blast of heat that could produce a roast dinner for an army. The dresser that stretched along most of one wall was much longer than the one in the kitchen of Wellhouse Farm, the biggest house she had ever been inside in Micklewell. Blue-and-white patterned plates stood in rows reaching up almost to the ceiling and beneath them an array of serving bowls with lids. Cups dangled on hooks and neat piles of saucers and tea plates were stacked on the lowest shelf.

Kate ran her fingers over the worn surface of the wooden table which was scrubbed within an inch of its life. There were knots in places and the one in front of her reminded her of a girl's face edged with tousled hair, just like her sister,

Dot. A dull ache rippled through her chest. She was going to miss Dot especially.

A cup of hot tea was placed before her. Kate had taken only a few sips, when Eliza returned with the bottles of ale. Eliza poured herself a cup of tea and joined Kate and Mrs Bowden at the table.

'Let's give Kate a few minutes to recover from her journey,' Mrs B said, smiling at her. 'Tell me about your family, dear. You have brothers and sisters, I assume?'

'Yes, an older brother, Fred, a younger sister, Dot and little Henry, he's only a few months old. I did have another sister, Ellen, but she died,' Kate replied. She didn't know why she was telling her about Ellen but there was something about Mrs Bowden's kindly face that made Kate trust her.

'And this is your first time in service?' Mrs Bowden asked.

'Yes,' Kate said, 'I worked on a farm before.'

'Well, looking after those twins will be just like trying to herd a bunch of animals.' Eliza grinned. 'Just you wait and see.'

'That's enough of that,' Mrs Bowden interrupted. 'Don't you get yourself too comfortable, young lady, there's work to do. Drink up and go and tell the master and mistress that Kate's arrived.'

Kate continued to answer Mrs Bowden's questions about Micklewell and life in the country until Eliza reappeared to take her to the parlour where Mr and Mrs Winton and the five children were waiting. As she closed the door behind her, Kate's spine locked and her face froze. A sudden desire to run out of the room and through the front door overtook her. She felt comfortable in the kitchen with Mrs Bowden and Eliza, but the luxuries of these surroundings were totally unfamiliar to her. Mr and Mrs Winton stood poker straight in front of the fireplace with the three youngest children in front of them. The older girl was beside her mother and the older boy beside his father; they were almost as tall as their parents and more like young adults than children, Kate thought. They were all smartly dressed. Mrs Winton's hair was swept up and her dress had a high neck edged with delicate white lace.

It was Mr Winton who spoke first. 'Now, my dear, don't be shy,' he said, his gaze straying from her face across her entire body. 'Come and meet the family.' His invitation had the effect of unsettling rather than reassuring her.

Kate bobbed a curtsey and moved cautiously further into the room. Her attention was briefly drawn to a huge china vase that stood in the corner; it was almost big enough for her to climb into.

'Come and say hello to the children,' Mrs Winton said. 'Kate, isn't it?'

'Yes, madam,' Kate replied.

'As you will see, our eldest two are quite grown up. You will be spending most of your time with the three youngest,' Mr Winton explained. 'Let me introduce you.'

'This is our eldest son Philip,' Mr Winton continued. 'He's eighteen and studying hard for a place at university. He takes the Oxbridge entrance exam in September.'

Philip smiled broadly at her, a gesture that put Kate more at ease.

'Our eldest daughter, Clara.'

'I'm fifteen and will soon be studying to go to university too,' Clara announced.

Same age as me, Kate thought, but she seemed older. She glanced at Mr Winton who cleared his throat loudly and said, without even looking at his daughter, 'Clara has much to learn about becoming a young lady and we are looking for the best place for her to complete her education.'

Mrs Winton cast a sideways look at her husband and took over the introductions. 'This is Thomas, he's seven.'

Thomas looked bored by the whole thing and fiddled with something in his pocket.

'And the twins, Simon and Sophie.'

'We're five,' they chorused.

'Pleased to meet you all,' said Kate, bobbing again.

'As I said, you will work mostly with young Thomas and the twins,' Mr Winton continued in a brisk, business-like tone. 'The older children have a tutor. Their education is of the utmost importance, particularly Philip's.'

'There will be times when we will need you to accompany Clara,' Mrs Winton added. 'She likes to walk in the park occasionally, weather permitting. We trust you will make yourself available to walk with her?'

'Oh yes, madam. I enjoy the outdoors,' Kate replied with enthusiasm. 'I was brought up in the country. I'm used to walking from Micklewell to Stoke on market days, that's five miles or more.'

Clara stifled a giggle and Mrs Winton gave her a sharp look.

'Very well then, I'm sure you will soon get used to our way of doing things. As long as you pay good attention to the children's needs and familiarize yourself with my daily routines, then we shall have no cause for complaint. There are certain times of the day, of course, when I receive visitors and am not to be disturbed, but that will all be explained in due course. Welcome to our home, Kate.'

'Mrs Bowden will explain the rules of the house,' Mr Winton added. 'Punctuality and high standards, Kate! If you can deliver those then we shall get along very well.'

Mrs Winton's tone was firm but kindly and Kate was grateful for it, but the unwelcome stare and sharp manner of Mr Winton made her uneasy. She didn't trust a man whose mouth seemed to be in a constant fixed smile whilst making his expectations clear. She hoped she wouldn't have much occasion to be in his company, she would avoid him at all costs.

# CHAPTER THREE

*October 1912*

'Well, thank God, you've arrived is all I can say,' Eliza whispered to Kate as they followed the children upstairs. Clara went straight to her room, closing the door immediately and giving a clear signal that she wanted privacy. Philip, on the other hand, turned to the twins and said, 'Now, you two rascals. You behave yourselves for your new nursemaid or you'll have me to answer to.' He looked across at Kate and held her gaze until she felt her cheeks glowing and was relieved when Eliza said they should get on with the business of baths and bed.

Eliza showed Kate the bedtime routines and where everything was in the bedrooms that the children might need. She gathered the laundry together and explained how to check shoes for cleaning and clothing for any missing buttons or minor repairs. Kate hoped she'd be able to remember it all.

She looked around for the twins who were very quiet. Eliza pointed to one of the beds. They were hiding underneath it saying that they wanted to play hide and seek before bedtime.

Eliza said, 'I'll leave you to it then,' and left.

*Now what?* Kate thought.

Mrs Winton had said that she would come upstairs to kiss the children goodnight and that made Kate feel nervous. She wanted everything to go well. Eventually with the promise of a longer game of hide and seek tomorrow and an extra biscuit at elevenses, the twins came out of hiding and accompanied her to the bathroom.

Thomas was a more amiable child, thankfully. He was slow but he eventually got on with the business of night-time preparations. Simon and Sophie, however, needed telling several times to wash properly and not just flick the flannel over their faces. Kate had the feeling that those two were going to be a bit of a handful. Now they were asking to be read a bedtime story but couldn't seem to agree on which one.

'*Goldilocks*,' said Sophie. 'I like the bears.'

'Not that one. It's my turn to choose and I want *Little Red Riding Hood*,' Simon insisted.

'*Goldilocks*.'

'*Red Riding Hood*.'

'*Goldilocks*.'

'*Red Riding Hood*.'

'What's all this noise?' a voice said. 'Why aren't you in bed yet? Your father is trying to read some important papers in his room and mustn't be disturbed.'

It was Mrs Winton standing in the doorway.

At the mention of their father, the twins immediately stopped. Kate's heart jumped. She thought quickly. 'How about I tell you one instead?' she asked. They nodded their agreement. She began the story she knew so well: *The Town Mouse and the Country Mouse*. Their delight was evident on their faces and Kate could see that even Thomas, who had already settled to his own choice of book, was listening to her tale. Mrs Winton stayed and listened too and then kissed the children goodnight.

Once the other side of the door she congratulated Kate on the way she had dealt with the situation.

'That was well handled,' she said. 'They're both such determined characters, neither one of them wants to give in. But then all my children are strong-willed, Kate, as you will find out, I'm sure. It has always been important to me that they should develop their own personalities and find their own way in the world. Education is not just book learning. Having said that, you will please let me know if any of them display any rudeness. Bad manners will not be tolerated.'

Kate was feeling pleased with herself when she joined Mrs B and Eliza for their evening meal. She'd managed to avert that little crisis quite successfully, she thought. The conversation over their dinner was relaxed and good humoured and Kate felt at ease. After they'd washed the dishes, Mrs B sat back in her favourite chair and folded her arms in her lap.

'Now, Kate,' she said, 'we must go over your duties. You will be up and about before six and help Eliza to prepare the breakfast room, which in winter means setting a fire. Ten minutes for your own breakfast. Then wake the children at seven, washing and dressing, breakfast, then to the nursery. Take no nonsense from those twins, they will lead you a merry dance, or try to anyway. At eleven thirty precisely you are to take them to the mistress who will hear them recite their numbers and their nursery rhymes and she will expect a full report of how you have occupied them.'

Her speech, delivered almost in one breath, left little doubt in Kate's mind that the housekeeper had a firm hold on the helm of Woodland House. Expectations were high, but Kate felt that she would be safe under the guidance of Mrs B and, as for Eliza, well Kate liked her already.

* * *

Kate had to take in a lot about the household routines in those first weeks. From six in the morning until eight at night it was one endless list of things to do. If she wasn't looking after the children in the nursery, she was washing, ironing, folding and tidying. If she had a moment to herself then

21

Mrs B would soon find something else to occupy her in the kitchen.

She didn't mind all the household chores — she'd had plenty of practice in her own home — but the time she liked the best was that spent with the three youngest Wintons, even if they sometimes tested her patience. She reported to Mrs Winton every morning and could always tell by the expression on Eliza's face whether the mistress was in an amiable mood or not. Kate would wait outside Mrs Winton's dressing room until Eliza emerged after attending to the mistress's needs. As they passed each other on the landing, Eliza would send her a silent message. Eyebrows furrowed and lips pursed indicated 'watch out!'. Eyebrows lifted and a brief nod of the head, told her that she was safe to go in. Eliza always said that she could tell how things were going to be by the way the mistress reacted to her hair-brushing and toiletries. If Mrs Winton spoke to her or smiled then all was well. If she remained silent throughout, then the whole household needed to creep around her all day.

After receiving her instructions, Kate could then turn her attentions to the children. Most mornings she could be found sitting with the twins on the highly patterned rug in the centre of the room, playing with the doll's house or the knight's castle or piecing together the alphabet blocks. Young Thomas would be with his tutor and the twins would be clamouring for her attention.

The nursery was a bright and airy room with high ceilings. On a fine day, the autumn sun filtered through the curtains, casting a criss-cross of windowpanes across the polished floor. The twins delighted in showing her all their toys and for the most part enjoyed one another's company.

Two weeks after her arrival, however, Kate was struggling to keep the twins both occupied and happy. Simon had his toy soldiers lined up in battle formation and Sophie wanted to play marbles.

'But you've been playing wars all morning,' Sophie protested. 'Put them away right now!'

Simon ignored her and went on righting the injured and replacing the fallen.

Sophie retaliated by taking the whole bag of marbles and tipped them onto the figures, obliterating one army entirely.

'There,' she said. 'The red soldiers have won. Now we can play marbles.'

Simon's answer to that was to throw as many of the marbles as he could lay his hands on into the far corners of the room. Kate could feel a storm coming. She was so preoccupied with trying to keep the peace between the two of them that she didn't hear the nursery door open. Nor did she see Philip put his hands to his lips and encourage Thomas to keep their arrival a secret.

'Perhaps we can play with both the marbles and the soldiers,' Kate suggested. 'I have an idea. Simon. You set up the two armies again and Sophie, you collect up the marbles and I will show you both a new game.'

The two children looked at each other, a mixture of puzzlement and irritation on their faces. But they did as Kate asked. She then helped them divide the marbles evenly between them. She took one red soldier and one blue and hid them in her closed fists. Stretching out her arms, she asked them to pick one hand each.

'You're red then, Sophie, and you're blue, Simon.'

She showed them they could aim and flick the marbles and try to knock each other's soldiers down.

The children let out a cheer each time they were successful.

'Can I play?' Thomas asked.

'And me,' said Philip, his sudden appearance beside her making Kate jump.

They spent the next half hour taking turns and when Kate decided it was time for them to tidy up and wash hands for lunch, they did so with the promise that they could play the new game again tomorrow.

'You have a way with them, Kate, that their last nursemaid didn't have,' Philip said.

'How long have you been watching?' Kate asked.

'Long enough to see how you dealt with their little dispute. Very clever of you,' he replied.

Kate smiled in acknowledgement of his praise. She was beginning to like Philip Winton and feel comfortable in his company. He was open and friendly with her and didn't treat her like a servant at all. Something she was both pleased and surprised about. She had yet to get any real response from his sister, Clara, as she seemed to be more absorbed in her own daily activities and spent little time with Kate, apart from their daily walks, when there was more walking than talking done. Kate was curious about Clara, but she suspected that Clara never gave Kate a passing thought. They might be close in age but their experiences of life were so different. Kate was a servant and her purpose was to accompany Clara and that was the sum total of their relationship to one another. Their walks were mostly conducted in silence or with Clara listing all the social engagements she was invited to in the coming weeks.

Kate was surprised, then, when Clara entered the nursery one day and said, 'Follow me, Kate. I need some help with something, urgently.' After glancing at the twins who were happily playing a game of skittles while young Thomas was curled up in a chair with a book, Kate followed Clara to her room. Clara walked straight over to the window.

'Good,' she said, 'they're still there.'

She turned to Kate. 'Come here, quickly, before she goes.'

Kate stood beside Clara who pointed out a young woman and her mother on the opposite side of the street. They were engaged in conversation with an elderly couple.

'Look closely at the young woman,' Clara said. 'What do you think of her attire . . . her clothes?'

'She looks lovely,' Kate replied.

'Be more specific,' Clara insisted.

'Well . . .' Kate paused, she wasn't sure what Miss Clara wanted her to say.

'Her suit, her hat, come on, Kate. I need to know.'

'I've never seen clothes like that before,' Kate said. 'The black-and-white stripes certainly stand out.'

'And . . . what else?' Clara prompted her.

'That scoop at the front of her straight skirt and the buttons, it's . . . it's well, it's most unusual. Her hat certainly sets it all off and what's that round her neck?'

'A feather boa. They're the height of fashion,' Clara explained.

Kate could hear some sounds coming from the nursery and looked towards the door.

'Mother is taking me shopping for a new outfit. I'm going to look for something just like that,' she said. 'We've been invited for dinner at the Carnforths'. Edward Carnforth's a friend of Philip's. They're at school together. No doubt you'll meet him at some point.'

The noise from the nursery was getting louder.

'You'd better go and sort that out,' Clara said. 'Thank you, Kate.'

Kate bobbed and turned to go. She wasn't sure why Miss Clara wanted her opinion, she didn't know much about fashion but she hoped she'd said the right things.

\* \* \*

Kate was learning more about the family as time went on. What to do and what not to do. When to respond and when to keep quiet. Time seemed to fly by, yet every night before she went to sleep she wondered what was happening in her own family home. Those thoughts didn't last for long though, as exhaustion overtook her and she fell asleep.

Kate's Sundays were a welcome change from the rest of the week and the chance for a moment's rest. After church and the serving of Sunday lunch, she had some free time. When the family were not in need of their services and Mrs B was taking a nap, Kate and Eliza would often spend time together. One Sunday, Kate accepted Eliza's invitation to take a walk. As they passed in front of the other elegant Georgian houses in Ford Street, Eliza told Kate about those who lived inside. Her descriptions were full of doctors and businessmen, people of wealth and distinction, a world that they could only ever glimpse at and imagine. Eliza was a creative storyteller and Kate was amused by her portraits of women gossiping over their bone china teacups, their fulsome figures swelling with too much cake. As she talked, Kate could imagine the beady, rat-like eyes of their husbands calculating the cost of the new drapes and the expensive gowns for their daughters.

When they reached a house with white pillars framing the front door and tall chimneys, Eliza stopped and gave out her most florid description so far. With a flourish of her hand and the clear confidence of a stage performer she announced, 'We stand before the town residence of Lord Grabbit. A member of parliament and a well-respected gentleman here-abouts, he's a businessman and the owner of dozens of shops across the county. A man of property, he's the landlord of so many houses round here that he could spend a night in a different one each day of the month, and he probably does. Grabbit by name, Grabbit by nature,' Eliza said, nudging her with her elbow. 'Know what I mean?'

The two of them stifled their giggles. Kate was so glad that she had found someone like Eliza. She might have ended up in a house with a sour-faced misery for a kitchen maid but Eliza was fun and, when Kate felt homesick, she made life away from Micklewell bearable.

'But do you really know any of the people who live in these houses?' Kate asked. 'Other servants, I mean, not the ladies and gentlemen, of course.'

Eliza blushed and giggled.

'Why Eliza Brown, you do. Which house, this one?'

The nameplate indicated that this was 'The Laurels'. The tidy and formally planted front garden was surrounded by spiked metal fencing and at the side of the building steps led down the side towards the back of the house. It was up those steps that a young man wearing a dark jacket and a beaming smile came running, taking two at a time.

'Morning, Eliza. Who's this you've brought with you?' the young man asked.

'This is Kate, our new nursemaid. Kate, this is Tommy. All you need to know about him, Kate, is to only trust him as far as you could throw him and make sure he keeps his hands in his pockets.'

'Don't you believe a word of it.' Tommy beamed. He offered his hand. 'How do you do, Kate? A pleasure to meet you, I'm sure.'

Kate shook his hand and replied, 'Pleased to meet you, too,' and together they walked to the park.

The streets and pavements were quite busy for a Sunday afternoon with families out and about together. The three of them moved to one side as two young boys came bowling their hoops along, much to the consternation of their parents.

'George, Charles. You were told not to play with your hoops in the street,' their father said. The reprimand brought them into line.

Kate was getting used to the new sights and sounds of the town, although the closeness of so many houses and people felt claustrophobic sometimes and she missed the wide-open spaces of the countryside. She had to become more aware of vehicles and be especially careful when crossing the street. The new automobiles frightened her with their loud engines and tooting horns. But today she could relax. For a few hours she only had to worry about herself and not three young children.

The three of them chatted as they walked. Tommy was quite the entertainer too, with his tales of life in the 'Grabbit' household. His employer was actually called Mr Greaves, it turned out, and he had made his money from a chain of butcher's shops which his father had set up and he had added to and established across the county of Hampshire. Mr Greaves' story was of a working man who had made good for himself and his family. They treated Tommy well apparently and, when he turned twenty-one, there was promise of his becoming head butler and taking over from old Richards.

The current butler and his cook and housekeeper wife were both due for retirement.

Tommy stopped beside the pond and handed Eliza and Kate some bread pieces that he had in his pocket.

'Here you are, ladies, let's give the ducks a Sunday treat, shall we? Best fatten 'em up now so they'll be nice and plump for the Christmas table.'

'You'll not take one, will you, Tommy?' asked Kate. 'People don't eat them round here, do they? Why even the poorest in Micklewell would never take the ducks from the village pond.'

Eliza and Tommy looked at each other and tried, unsuccessfully, to stifle their giggles.

'You're so easy to bait, Kate,' Eliza laughed. 'Take all he says with a pinch. Like I said, don't trust him as far as . . .'

'I'll throw you if you don't watch it,' Tommy said reaching out to grab her.

Eliza dodged away from him and stood behind Kate. 'Now, Thomas White, mind your manners and remember you are in a public place.'

'You wait 'til I get you in private then.' Tommy smiled. 'Not so long now.'

Kate wondered what he meant by that. Was Eliza keeping secrets? Did they have plans?

They had enjoyed each other's company but the wind was beginning to find its way through Kate's coat and she suggested they should keep moving. Tommy explained that he had to be home before three, as there were special preparations in the house for a family gathering tomorrow. They said goodbye to each other and walked back to their own separate houses.

As soon as Tommy was out of sight, Kate asked the question that had been burning her tongue. 'What did Tommy mean when he said not so long now?'

'He's asked me to marry him, Kate. I was going to tell you. That's the trouble with Tommy, no sense of occasion.'

Kate's expression changed; she was shocked to hear that she might be losing Eliza so soon.

'But don't worry, it won't be for a good while, more's the pity. The sooner we can get married the better.'

Kate was sure she detected a ripple of worry lines appear on Eliza's forehead.

'I thought you were happy at Woodland House. Aren't you happy?' Kate asked.

'Oh yes,' Eliza hesitated. 'It's just that . . . well a girl wants to get married, doesn't she?'

Eliza's pensiveness was only fleeting, however, and she quickly returned to her usual light-hearted self.

'Don't look so worried, Kate. It will be a while yet. As I said, Old Richards is not exactly on his last legs yet. I'll probably be an old maid before it all happens.' She laughed.

There was something strange about Eliza's mood. Kate suspected that Eliza wasn't telling her everything. Sooner or later the time would come when her new friend would move on. She decided not to dwell on such thoughts. Sometimes there was little to be done but accept that things never stay the same.

When they entered the kitchen, Mrs B was rolling out pastry.

'Ah good, just in time,' she said. 'I've prepared tomorrow's lunch and this is the apple pie for their pudding. All you have to do is heat up the beef casserole and then you can serve the pie with some custard. I think I can trust you to do that, Eliza, can't I? I'll be back in time to serve the dinner, but the two of you will have to manage afternoon tea. Now, make sure you measure the tea carefully. You know what the master's like, too strong and he says money is being wasted by adding extra water and throwing tea leaves away, too weak and he says that we get enough housekeeping money and we're trying to cut corners.'

'I think we'll manage just fine, Mrs B. You relax and enjoy your day off. Going somewhere nice?' Eliza asked.

'To visit my sister in Monkton,' Mrs B replied. 'She's been laid up with bronchitis, poor thing. I'm taking her some of my beef tea, that'll set her right.'

'You deserve some time off,' said Kate. 'A pity your sister's not well enough to enjoy it with you. We'll be fine here.'

'Well you'd better be. Make sure you follow my instructions to the letter. I'll have no time to pick up the pieces once I'm back. It will be full on preparations for Christmas come next week.'

Kate didn't even want to think about Christmas. It would be the first one spent away from her family. She was going to miss the gathering of the holly and the glow of candlelight in Micklewell church, the carol singing around the village and the making of biscuits on Christmas Eve. Christmas at Woodland House would, no doubt, be a grand affair but she would be thinking of them all gathering firewood in Micklewell woods while she laid fires in another family's hearth.

# CHAPTER FOUR

*December 1912*

Kate took a deep breath and counted to twenty. Persuading those twins to get washed and dressed in their Christmas finery was proving a struggle. She'd been up before dawn to help in the kitchen and now the children were not being helpful. Mrs Winton had been quite specific about the timing of the entire day and had emphasized that the children must be ready for family breakfast by half past eight.

'Ouch, you're hurting,' Sophie squealed as Kate struggled to untangle the night-time scramble that wound her unruly curls around the brush.

'All done now,' Kate said and neatly distracted Sophie with choosing a ribbon. The red silk slipped through Kate's fingers and fell to the floor. She fought to make it stay in place, but it finally succumbed to her deft fingers.

'There,' Kate said, 'now don't you look beautiful?'

Sophie twisted and turned in front of the mirror and a smile crept across her face.

*One down, one to go*, thought Kate and turned to find Simon.

'Where's . . . ?' Kate began and then noticed the tip of a sock peeking out from under the bed.

'Thomas,' Kate said. 'What did you say about present opening time in this house? Always after breakfast, wasn't it?'

Thomas looked up briefly from his book. 'Yes, always,' he replied.

'So, the quicker we are all dressed then the quicker we can all have breakfast and get to the presents. I bet you're looking forward to opening them?'

Kate looked away, giving Simon time to emerge from his hiding place.

He appeared at her side, with his bow tie in his hands.

'Can't do it,' he said offering it to her.

'I agree, they're awkward things to tie, aren't they? Here, let me help you,' she said taking it gently from him.

'So, are we all ready now?' Kate asked, looking directly at Thomas who was lost in the pages of *King Arthur*.

When he didn't reply, she stood right beside him and repeated her question.

'Last page,' he replied, not taking his eyes off his book.

Kate hoped they wouldn't be late. She would then get the blame for 'not being mindful of the importance of time', as Mr Winton put it.

At her insistence they should hurry, the twins hurtled out of the nursery door and collided with their older sister, treading on her new silk slippers and making her gasp and frown with disapproval.

'Now look what you've done, you little monsters,' she complained. 'I'll never get those marks off.'

'I'm so sorry, Miss Clara. I'm sure I can do something to mend the damage. If you remove them after breakfast and give them to me, I'll have them good as new, ready for this evening's party. You won't need them until then, will you?' Kate asked.

'No, she won't,' another voice answered. It was Philip emerging from his room, looking smart in his morning suit. 'We're going for a carriage ride and a walk in the country after luncheon and she will need her outdoor shoes for that. Such delicate frippery as those slippers would spoil in the muddy lanes, am I not right, Kate?'

Kate nodded. 'Oh yes, Mr Philip, indeed. They'd get well and truly spoiled.'

'And we can't have that can we, Clara?' He winked at Kate, who let the corners of her mouth release the inkling of a smile back.

Clara drew her skirts up and flounced down the stairs.

'Come on now,' Philip said to his siblings, 'we're late enough. Pa will be livid and Ma will need to send for the smelling salts if her perfect plans are spoiled. You know how she is.'

Kate whipped the book out of Thomas's hands as he walked past her. He threw her a puzzled look that said, What's all the fuss about? He then joined the others, all in his own good time. Kate liked Thomas and Philip very much, particularly Philip.

By the time she returned to the kitchen, luncheon preparations were well underway. The turkey, which had been all trussed up and sitting goose-pimply without its feather coat before breakfast, had now been placed in the oven.

The long kitchen table was weighed down with the principle ingredients of what Mrs B called a 'proper Christmas dinner'. Orange carrots still attached to their green fringes, creamy white parsnips in a neat row, earthy potatoes and a bowl overflowing with green knobbly sprouts.

'What are those?' Kate asked pointing at a bundle of long, spear-shaped things lying amongst the vegetables.

'That's asparagus,' Mrs B answered, thrusting a knife into her hands. 'A thing you're never likely to taste at the price they are at this time of year! Now stop asking questions and let's get on. It's all hands to the pump, if we're to sit down by one o'clock. Now get yourself over to that sink and peel those potatoes, thin peelings mind, we don't want to be left with marbles to roast now, do we?'

And so, the clattering chaos of Christmas morning began. Orders were thrown in all directions to: 'Chop that parsley, slice those onions, stir the bread sauce, something's burning! Check that dripping, not too hot mind! Fetch a saucepan, no not that one, get a bigger one. Kettle's boiling, top the steamer. Don't put that there. Saints preserve us!'

This last cry was emitted as Mrs B dropped the burning handle of a pan, spilling the milky contents over the top of the stove and collapsed into her favourite chair, flapping her apron at her apple red face. Mrs B was in a fluster, the potatoes weren't boiling quickly enough and the turkey was browning too quickly. Mrs B shouted instructions that Eliza should get it out of the oven and place it on the side. The oven range steamed and throbbed with the demands of the feast. As fast as the two girls worked, it wasn't fast enough and someone had put the gravy browning back in the wrong place and it couldn't be found!

Kate brought Mrs B a glass of water and a cold compress for her hand and took over fanning her face with a tea towel. She wondered how the job of nursemaid had miraculously expanded to incorporate kitchen assistant, administer of first aid and general fetcher and carrier. As Eliza cleared up the spilt milk, Kate remembered that she still had to retrieve Clara's shoes to remove the stains. She was relieved that the family present opening would take a while and she could concentrate on helping Mrs B and Eliza. They still had the task of serving the dinner ahead of them. By the time she got to eat her own Christmas dinner she'd be ready for bed!

Despite the early mishaps, Mrs B regained her composure and orchestrated the serving of all three courses to perfection. When the figgy pudding had been flamed and eaten and the coffee served, Kate was instructed to fetch the children's coats and the family prepared for their carriage ride. There was high excitement amongst the younger children and she was having trouble getting them to calm down. The twins were fighting over whose muffler was whose and Thomas said he couldn't possibly leave without his notebook to record what they saw. Philip was trying to explain that the carriage would be too bumpy to write and draw and the volume of noise was increasing. Mr Winton appeared at the top of the staircase and stunned them all into silence with just one word: 'Stop!'.

Kate and the children waited while he descended the staircase. Kate felt like she was amongst a group of scared rabbits, faced with a hungry fox. When Mr Winton reached the bottom he simply walked in measured strides to the silent group. His voice might have been quiet but his stare and the low, determined tone of his voice made Kate fearful of what he could be capable of if he ever lost his temper. His controlled anger was enough to make the children obey and they each finished dressing in silence.

Mrs Winton joined them looking a little flustered and Eliza helped her into her fur-edged cape and gloves. As the family moved across the hall, Kate saw Mr Winton take his wife firmly by the arm and say something in a sharp, low voice that she couldn't quite hear.

A sprinkling of snow blew into the hall when the Winton family finally departed for their ride. Kate shivered and went to help Eliza clear the table, relieved that no further mishaps had occurred.

'Phew, glad that circus is over, for a few hours at least. We have a bit of breathing space while they're out,' Eliza said. 'Come on, let's get to it.'

The room was still warm from the huge log fire that they had lit earlier and fed with more fuel throughout the meal. The silver baubles on the Christmas tree sparkled in the flickering firelight and beneath the tree, the unwrapped presents lay abandoned. Kate thought for a moment of her own family and what they would be doing now. A sliver of pale light peeked between the heavy, velvet drapes and shone upon the silver salver in the centre of the damask covered table. A few scattered crumbs betrayed the speed with which Mrs B's mince pies had disappeared into the sweet-toothed mouths of the Winton children.

'Just look at this lot.' Eliza sighed. 'Looks like I'm in for another bad case of dish pan hands. Mrs B makes me have the water so hot! It might leave a sparkle on the crystal but it ruins my lily-white hands. I'll just have to wear the best kid gloves to cover them, won't I, dearest?' she added, flipping both her wrists towards Kate. They both laughed. Eliza then turned her attentions to the bottle of unfinished wine on the table. Picking it up, she held it towards Kate. 'Here, ever tasted claret? Take a swig,' she said.

Kate shook her head, she'd never tasted wine before. 'I don't think . . .'

'Just a little taste. It's Christmas after all,' Eliza said. 'They won't miss it.'

She swilled out two glasses from the jug of water and poured a little out for each of them. 'Cheers,' she said, clinking her glass against Kate's a little too enthusiastically. Kate was holding her glass by the stem. It all happened in a breath. The stem broke and the glass bowl parted company from it, spilling the red wine over the carpet. Kate watched as the stain spread across the pale green carpet, soaking into the pile. She knew what red stains could do and immediately panicked. As she darted through the door towards the kitchen, she ran straight into Master Philip.

'Where's the fire?' he said, stepping back.

'Oh, Master Philip, I thought you'd all . . .' Kate said loudly enough so that Eliza could hear.

'Bad headache,' Philip said holding his hand to his temple and pulling a face. 'Came on very quickly, as soon as I heard Aunt Mildred was going to be coming with us, in fact. A constant earbashing only makes a person's head ache more, don't you agree?'

Eliza appeared at Kate's side and asked if she could get him anything. An attempt to stop him seeing the mess.

'No, thank you. I'm just looking for my pocket hand-kerchief,' Philip said. 'It must have fallen out of my jacket. You know how Mother hates things hanging around.'

He walked past both girls and into the dining room where the damage was in full view. Kate immediately started to apologize over and over until Philip held up a hand and said, 'Enough Kate! I can see that an accident has occurred

36

and will, of course, explain to Mother how it was entirely my fault. I knocked it off the table whilst getting a glass of water for my headache.'

'But Master Philip ... .' Kate interrupted.

'Now don't argue. Please let me deal with it. You do enough for us, Kate. Let me do this small thing for you,' he replied. 'I assume you have the right materials to clean this up, Eliza?'

Eliza nodded. 'Yes. I'll do my best but there may be a permanent mark,' she explained as she left Kate to pick up the broken glass.

'Thank you, Master Philip,' Kate said. 'I'm so sorry for causing such a disaster and on Christmas day too!'

'Just think of it as my little present to you.' Philip smiled. 'I need to make sure you stay with us, Kate. You're ten times better than the last nursemaid we had. I've seen how good you are with the twins and Thomas. I mean to persuade my parents to let you go with us in the New Year.'

'Go with you? Why, where are you going?' Kate asked.

'It's still a secret but Pa has got himself a new position. He's to be manager of a new bank in London. Not a word to anyone though. Pa wants to bask in his own glory. No doubt Mrs B will have apoplexy but she'll come around to the idea.'

Kate turned away from him in an effort to hide her reaction to this news. Her feelings always showed on her face. She had only just got used to being here in Andover, in Woodland House, and now they were moving to London! London was the city and she wasn't ready for that! London was even further away from Micklewell and her family!

'Don't look so worried, Kate,' Philip said. 'It's not going to happen right away. These things take time. You'll get used to the idea. Have you ever been to London?'

She hadn't but she'd heard stories about the crowded streets, the pickpockets and the drunks lying in the gutters. She wasn't sure she wanted to go, even if not going with them to London meant finding another job.

'I'd best get on with the clearing up,' she said.

Between them she and Eliza managed to get rid of the stain and the broken glass without alerting Mrs B.

'But we'll have to tell her,' Kate said. 'If we don't then Mrs Winton will instruct her to replace the broken wine glass and Mrs B will say "what broken wine glass?" and then we'll be in trouble!'

'All right, leave it to me. We'll tell her how it was Master Philip, like he said, so we're in the clear,' Eliza replied. Kate was only too happy to let Eliza do the explaining.

As Eliza relayed the details of the accident to Mrs B, Kate found herself wondering what the future had in store for all of them. Philip hadn't mentioned anything about Eliza coming to London but this talk of a move was sure to disrupt her plans for the future. She wouldn't leave her Tommy, would she? What would her own dear parents say and how would she tell her sister, Dot? This was turning into a Christmas to remember in more ways than one.

# CHAPTER FIVE

*January 1913*

It was several weeks into the new year when things began to move in a new direction. It was evening and Eliza had persuaded Kate to go and turn the gas lights out in the study. Mr Winton had retired some time ago, she said. Mrs B had nodded off in her chair in the kitchen and Eliza had taken her shoes off to warm her feet by the last glimmers of the fading fire in the kitchen range.

'Oh, go on, Kate, please. You've still got your shoes on and you didn't have all the fireplaces to clean and lay for the morning. My feet are killing me. I'll help you with the children's washing this week if you do.'

Kate sighed and got up. She closed the kitchen door quietly and made her way into the dark hallway. Kate had rarely entered the study and only with Eliza. It was Mr Winton's private room. The house was quiet except for the ticking of the grandfather clock. It chimed eleven as she opened the study door. The pungent smell of gas and cigar smoke in the closed room escaped into the hallway. Kate left the door open so that fresher air could enter.

The flickering of the gas lights moved across the rows of books making their dark spines with gold-edged bindings ripple. Kate moved slowly and carefully, taking time to look more closely at the dark wood bookcases that lined the walls. She had only ever stood briefly in this room while Eliza dealt with the lights and checked the fireguard. No time to really look, only to glimpse. The number of books astounded her. No one would know if she just pulled one down and looked at it. She so missed the time to read and escape into a world of words. At school she had been the best reader in her class and she had 'gobbled up books' as fast as her teacher, Miss Clarence, could give them to her.

She opened the first bookcase and squinted at the titles. There were books on history, politics and travel, books on the world of science and nature, books about explorers and inventors, artists and great leaders. Her fingers strolled across the leather bindings until she spotted a copy of *The Mill on the Floss* by George Eliot. She had heard Miss Clarence talk of the writer who disguised herself as a man in order to be more readily accepted by her readers and was intrigued. Such courage and determination! So clever to find a way to become what she wanted to be and not be dictated to by the opinions of others.

She opened the book and began to read. She turned the pages carefully trying not to disturb the silence of the room. It felt almost like the stillness of an empty church. When she got to the part about the river Floss she couldn't help but lift her voice and make the words sing, tracing the image so clearly in her mind that she could hear the water flow across the page.

'"How lovely the little river is",' she read aloud, '"with its dark changing wavelets! It seems to me like a living companion while I wander along the bank, and listen to its low, placid voice, as to the voice of one who is deaf and loving. I remember those large dipping willows. I remember the stone bridge".'

She held the book close to her chest and closed her eyes, bringing her own village to mind with its watercress stream flowing beside the road. She sighed.

'That passage makes you sad, Kate. I'm sure Miss Eliot would not wish to upset you.'

She dropped the book and turned to see Master Philip standing beside the fireplace. He must have been sitting in the winged armchair and escaped her notice. Across the dimness of the room she could not see if he was angry or amused, but his voice told her all she needed to know. It was a gentle prompt. He waited for her to speak and when she did not but remained fixed to the spot, he walked across the expanse of floor.

He stooped to pick up the volume and handed it to her, their eyes met briefly and Kate felt a flicker of pleasure. Philip had a way of looking at her that made her feel different somehow.

'I'm sure Pa would not miss this. It's Mother who's the novel reader and she will have read this as soon as she bought it. She has plenty more to choose from.'

'You know the book?' she asked.

'I make it my business to know what is different in the world,' he replied, 'and she is a most interesting woman, as are you, Kate. I've not met a nursemaid with such curiosity for learning before and this house has seen a few female servants come and go, believe me.'

'I'm sorry, sir. I had no business touching the books,' Kate apologized. 'I've come to turn the lights out for the night but if you're still up then I will wait.'

'I've no desire to keep a hardworking maid from her bed. You turn out the lights. It's time I went upstairs anyway. Goodnight, Kate. Don't stay awake reading for too long and take my advice, let Eliza extinguish the lamps in future, it's her job. You stick to the nursery. It might have been my father here this evening instead of me. You're lucky he had a glass too many at the Hargraves' party this evening.'

Kate listened to Philip's warning and understood. Her delight with the book showed on her face. She meant to read it whenever she could grab a minute to herself. She felt a lightness inside. Philip had spoken with her, they had been alone together. He'd shown an interest in her. She was confused by it all and mostly by her own feelings. There was no doubting he was both an attractive and likeable person. But she must be careful, for she was a servant and had no place in expecting anything other than to serve. She wondered if he could guess the effect that their brief exchange had upon her. She must try not to blush in his presence for that would surely betray her secret.

The book lay in the box beneath Kate's bed for a good many days before she had the time and energy to retrieve it. Mrs Winton had taken the children out to visit her elderly mother for afternoon tea. Kate and Eliza had finished all their duties so Mrs B said they could have an hour or two to themselves.

'Best make yourself scarce and keep out of the master's way,' she warned.

Kate said that she was going to rest on her bed for a while and Eliza went to wash through a pair of stockings and hang them to dry.

Kate was so lost in her book that she forgot the time and, when she realized that Eliza hadn't joined her, she began to wonder what had kept her. It wasn't like Eliza to miss the opportunity for a rest and a gossip. Kate left the book on her bed and began to go downstairs when she heard some unusual sounds coming from the lower floor. They were muffled sounds as if someone was trying to say something with a hand over their mouth.

Kate stood still and listened. There was definitely someone there. She held her breath. What if they'd heard her? She didn't know whether she should leave or stay. There were whispers. Then she heard the master's voice: 'Stay still, damn you.'

She waited. She crept to the base of the servants' stairs and peaked around the corner. The master's back was towards her. He had Eliza pinned up against the wall with his hand on her breast. Kate didn't know what to do. She hesitated and then Eliza looked directly at Kate. She could see the panic in

Eliza's face. Kate did the only thing she could think of and returned on tiptoe to the top of the stairs. She deliberately slammed the door and walked heavily downwards, making quite sure that she could be heard. When she reached the bottom of the stairs she saw the master enter one of the bedrooms and Eliza disappearing down the corridor as fast as she could go. Kate had witnessed something she was not meant to see. She felt sickened. Mr Winton, owner of Winton Banking, respected member of society, a rich man and her employer, was a man who could not be trusted.

When Kate entered the kitchen, Eliza turned and mouthed 'thank you' to her. Kate took it as a sign that Eliza didn't want to talk about it and decided to wait until they were alone together.

Later that evening, Kate asked Eliza if Mr Winton had tried anything like that before.

'Yes,' she whispered, turning towards Kate. 'I dread the mistress leaving the house.'

'Oh, Eliza, what can you do?'

'Nothing. I can do nothing. I have to hope that he doesn't catch me on my own in one of the bedrooms. If he tried to . . . what would I do? That could ruin everything for Tommy and me.' She began to sob, her shoulders shaking and her breath coming in short gasps.

Kate held her close until the sobs lessened and her body relaxed.

'Have you told Tommy?'

'What good would that do except to make me feel dirty?' Eliza said. 'He knows that I'm ready to marry and that I'm impatient to be with him. He's a kind one is Tommy but if I told him what was going on and he could do nothing about it, then it would drive him crazy. I just have to hope that we can marry soon. At least he's not tried it on you.'

Kate held her friend's hand and they both wept together for their powerlessness.

# CHAPTER SIX

*March 1913*

Kate was passing the master's study one morning after breakfast, when she heard him raise his voice and say, 'I've told
you before, Dorothea, that you are to consult me before
making any new purchases. How do you explain this bill
from Wilkinson's drapers? I don't recall authorizing such an
extortionate amount.'

Mrs Winton's reply was not clear but Kate caught the
words: 'chaise longue' and 'threadbare'.

'If I wanted the chaise longue recovered, I would have
told you to see that it was done,' he replied getting angrier.

'Did you not notice that it had been recovered when you
sat on it?' Mrs Winton asked. 'It needed doing badly, James.'

'I'm a busy man. I cannot be expected to notice such
things,' Mr Winton replied.

'Precisely, James. Which is why I didn't see fit to bother
you,' Mrs Winton said with more strength and clarity in her
voice.

Kate had never witnessed an exchange of this kind between
her employers before and felt conscious of the fact that she
wasn't meant to either. She watched the slightly open door,

shifting uncomfortably from foot to foot but was intrigued to hear Mrs Winton standing up for herself. When she heard the sound of a chair scraping across the floor, she decided it was time to move. She didn't want to be caught eavesdropping.

Later that day, Clara asked Kate to take a turn around the park with her. The walks that the two young women had taken together earlier in the year were brisk and brief due to the cold weather, but now the daffodils were peeping through and the air was milder, Clara's pace was more leisurely and she engaged Kate more in conversation. Her initial coldness was beginning to melt. She was kinder to Kate and Kate was beginning to relax and be easier in her company.

'Do you ever wonder, Kate, what life might be like if we could do as we pleased, more like men?' Clara asked. 'I sometimes feel like a caged bird. At least since you arrived, I have had a little more freedom.'

'If you don't mind me saying, Miss Clara, I think young ladies of your station feel it more than us country girls. I was able to work amongst the men in the fields along with the women. We don't lead such a divided life in the countryside as you do here in the town.'

'Do you still think of yourself as a country girl, Kate? Do you miss the country?'

'I miss some things about it, my family of course and the bubbling of the stream through our village. At this time of year, the blackthorn will be out. A splash of white that looks like the snows have returned,' Kate replied. 'And I miss the soft green grass to walk on, these pavements are so hard on the feet. But I don't miss the mud in winter. If you don't mind me saying, those shoes of yours would be soon ruined on the rough lanes of Micklewell.'

'But I could wear boots, could I not?' Clara said.

'Pardon me for saying, miss, but boots would look very strange with your fine clothes,' Kate said.

'Yes, I suppose so.' Clara smiled. 'Imagine what Mother's society friends would think of that!'

They both laughed at the thought.

It wasn't long after Kate's observance of the disagreement between the Wintons and the walk with Clara, that they were all told the news that Mr Winton would be away for prolonged periods of time for business reasons.

'So, he's setting up a new bank, in the city and leaving the mistress to manage here on her own!' Eliza said.

'She's not on her own, is she?' Mrs B said. 'She's got us and she's always managed perfectly well when he's been away before. She's used to his comings and goings by now. I dare say there'll be a few changes coming, you wait and see.'

'A blessing for all of us, I say,' Eliza whispered and then asked Mrs B, 'How long will he be away?'

'How should I know?' Mrs B replied. 'But be prepared. I expect we'll be packing this house up and moving to London with him before too long.'

As it turned out, Mrs Winton said that they would not be moving immediately on account of Master Philip's studies. He had one more term with his tutor before he could take the entrance exam for university. That would be the right time to move, she said, not before.

Late one afternoon, Eliza and Kate were folding the linen, when the jangling of the sitting-room bell sent Eliza scuttling upstairs. The mistress wanted an afternoon tea to be prepared for that Friday when she would be receiving a particularly important group of friends.

'She says she knows she can rely upon you to prepare something special,' Eliza told Mrs B on her return.

'Oh, she does, does she?' Mrs B replied. 'Well it's a good job I've got plenty of flour and eggs in then, isn't it?'

On the appointed day, Mrs B prepared an exceptionally good spread, as expected. Eliza, wearing a clean white apron, picked up the tray of scones and jam and the Victoria sponge cake and asked if there would be any left over for them.

'Just you get on with the job, young lady, and stop your cheek,' Mrs B said. 'And make sure you get straight back here for the tea tray. You know how the mistress insists on the tea being hot.' She turned to Kate. 'And you get upstairs and keep those children quiet. Here, take them these biscuits in case you need to use some bribery.'

Eliza winked at Kate and whispered, 'I saw her put three scones away in the pantry. I'll give you the report on the gossip, later.' Eliza was alert to all the topics of conversation on these occasions. She was adept at listening to all the chatter whilst serving the ladies their tea. She always had something to tell Kate about what Mrs Winton and her friends discussed during their afternoon visits and today was no exception.

When all the guests had gone and the children were in bed, Eliza was keen to tell all about what went on between the sips and the cake. They had hardly sat down to their evening meal when she said, 'You'll never guess who was taking tea with the mistress today, Kate? There were the usual ones, like Mrs Wickham, but there were some ladies I had never seen before and they were talking about women getting the vote. Called themselves suffragettes, or something. Seems like they were encouraging the mistress to join some sort of club. Mrs Wickham said that it was the duty of all of them to join the cause.'

Mrs B tutted but passed no comment. She didn't usually join in with such conversations but neither did she stop Eliza from repeating what she'd heard.

'Do you think the mistress will join?' Kate asked.

'How should I know?' Eliza replied. 'From what I can gather, though, it sounds as if she might. She's agreed to go to some meeting.'

'What about the master, what's he going to say about the matter?'

'Well he's not here, is he? The mistress may be married to him but she's got a will of her own, hasn't she? And what else has she got to do? He's gone off and left her here to take charge of the house and if she can do that she can surely make up her mind who to vote for. Good luck to her, I say!'

Kate had to agree.

'What's it all going to mean for the likes of you and me, then?' Kate asked Eliza. 'Or is it just rich ladies who are going to get the vote?' The whole idea of women striving to be free to have the same freedom to choose as men, fascinated her.

'Will you two just get on with eating?' Mrs B said. 'We've a deal to do before bedtime. Whatever happens with the Votes for Women you can be sure there'll still be washing-up to do. Talking of washing, you better make sure everything's in order with the clean laundry. I'll be the only one here with you two off home for Mothering Sunday.'

\* \* \*

It was with much excitement and a light heart that Kate returned to Micklewell for Mothering Sunday, at primrose time. Her first trip home since taking up her job at Woodland House. A whole weekend, such joy! The pony and trap she had taken from Hatch station dropped her at the top of Green Lane. The edges of the lane unfolded before her like a welcome carpet. The stream ambled along with her and she thought of her old school friend, Elsie. They were now both in service and hadn't seen one another for some time. Elsie had not moved so far away, to Hambleton, a bigger village with shops, and many more big houses to soak up the services of girls such as them. They had promised to write to each other but so far they hadn't.

Kate listened to the prattling of the brook and was reminded of their prattling as children. Her and Dot and Elsie and Mary White with their skirts rolled up and tucked into their knickers as they paddled in the water searching for crayfish. 'Tom Chuggs' they called them, she couldn't remember why, it had always been that way.

Passing Wellhouse Farm, she looked to see if the Soldier on the Wall was still there. He was! Still standing to attention in his black bearskin, larger than life! She wondered how many years the paint would last. If she could come back twenty years from now, would his white stripes on his trousers and his bandoleer still shine out in the dark on a moonlit night?

She made her way down the village street towards number two, Mead Cottages. The narrow alleyway between number one and the outhouses was the same. As she passed by Mrs Geary's window she could hear the lively chatter of her and her sisters inside. No doubt the kettle would be on and the biscuit tin rattling in tune to their gossiping chorus. Mrs Geary was a dear but if you wanted anything kept quiet, you didn't tell her a word.

She clicked open the low gate that separated the Geary's house from theirs and before she could lay her hand on the latch, the door was flung wide and Dot threw her arms around her sister.

'Kate, Kate, oh Kate! I'm so happy to see you. We have chicks, six of them and I found an injured baby rabbit. Pa says I can keep it so long as he doesn't have to feed it and that I mustn't weep over the dead ones he brings home, 'cos he's not going to stop shooting them, we need the meat. But I don't mind eating them still, just not this little one. Do come and look,' she cried grabbing Kate's hand and pulling her in the direction of a small, wooden hutch against the shed wall.

'Let your sister get in the door before you start on at her,' her father called from inside the kitchen. His large form followed his voice and filled the doorway. His sleeves were rolled up revealing his muscled arms and broad hands in which he held a bread knife.

'Kate, what a breath of fresh air you are. You look well,' he said. 'You're just in time for some bread and cheese. Your mother's upstairs changing the sheets for you. She's been working herself to the bone knowing you were staying the night.'

Just as she was about to pick up her bag and follow him inside, two small hands grabbed the side of her father's trousers and a face full of curiosity peeked around to observe her from a safe distance.

'Why, our little Henry, how you've grown,' she said to her youngest brother. 'You do remember me, don't you? It's your sister, Kate.'

The bedroom window opened and Kate's mother looked out.

'Kate, our very own Kate! I thought I heard voices. I'm coming right down,' she called. 'Get her inside and pour her a cup of tea, Jim. She must be gasping.'

Dot followed Kate inside, carrying her bag and keeping her excitement in check. Henry ran to his mother as soon as she appeared and she picked him up, carrying him to Kate and holding them both in her arms at once.

'It's so good to see you,' her mother said. 'Are they treating you well?'

'Look at her, Ada, does she look like they're starving her and flogging her to death?' Jim joked.

'Now, I've something for you, Henry.' Kate smiled. She went to her bag and bent to retrieve the small gift. Noticing Dot's expectant gaze, she added, 'And you too, Dot. It's only something small but I hope you'll like it.'

Kate held out a colourful ball to Henry and gave her sister an embroidered handkerchief with a D on it. Henry immediately started rolling the ball and Dot pressed the handkerchief to her cheek.

'It smells of you, Kate,' she said.

'Just make sure you don't lose it or use it to wipe your shoes, like all the others,' Ada chided.

'I'll keep it for best,' Dot replied giving her mother a look that said 'so there!'.

They all laughed and the old, relaxed atmosphere between them returned. Kate told of most of her experiences over the months, except one which worried her and she didn't want that worry to show on her face so she put it to the back of her mind. They delighted in her tales of life in the 'big, posh town house' as Dot called it.

When they all fell silent for a while, Kate asked after her brother, Fred.

'He's well enough,' Ada said. 'He's been staying with your Aunt Ena over in Greywell. They work him hard at the chalk pits. He won't finish today until six and then he's like a

50

walking snowman, covered in chalk dust. He'd have to clean up and by then the light would be gone. A pity he won't be here to see you, but I told him the walk from Greywell in the dark was too far. Next time perhaps?'

They spent the rest of the day catching up on all the local news, who had married, who'd died, who'd given birth and who'd newly arrived. The population of Micklewell didn't alter much, some went away to work, like Kate and, occasionally, others moved in. Old man Addison had died out hunting with hounds and Addison Farm was now occupied by the Potter family. The time drifted by in a pleasant wave of accounts of comings and goings.

As the afternoon shadows crept over the back yard and the fire was banked up to warm them through the evening chill, Kate eventually plucked up the courage to tell them all of the Winton family's move to London, knowing what their reaction would be.

'London?' they all exclaimed in unison but for different reasons.

'How exciting,' Dot said.

'Andover is far enough, Kate, but London! Will we ever see you?' her mother asked, her face losing its colour.

Her father's reaction was as she expected. 'As if she has any say in the matter,' he said. 'If she's to keep her job then she must go with them, Ada. She'll still write to us, won't you, Kate?'

'Of course, I will,' Kate replied.

Her mother remained silent on the matter for the remainder of the evening while Dot did a good job of changing the subject with her talk of all the local news, who was courting and who was tying the knot, who had a new job and who was moving away.

The old feelings of being at home, really at home, over-whelmed her as she thought about missing her family and missing Eliza. She understood why Eliza could not come to London with them, but at the same time she was concerned about how life with the Winton family would be without her.

# CHAPTER SEVEN

*June 1913*

While Mr Winton pursued his business dealings in London, Mrs Winton continued with her usual routines and maintained her social engagements and as time passed she began to rather enjoy the personal freedoms that her husband's absence gave her. She made several decisions without consulting him, including the ordering of new drapes for the sitting room, despite their planned move. She just couldn't bear their dowdiness any longer, she said, and it was she who had to suffer the indignity of inviting ladies into a less than perfect room.

She had also decided upon other changes that she had been contemplating for a while and, since James had been in London, she had enjoyed the luxury of time to think. She rang the bell. When Eliza appeared at the door she dispatched her to fetch Kate.

'I have decided that I will walk with you and Clara today, Kate,' Mrs Winton announced. 'Let me know in good time when you will be leaving for the park so that I may prepare myself. And by the way, how are you getting on with *The Mill on the Floss*? It's one of my favourite books.'

Kate's face turned pink.

'It's all right. Philip told me of your love of reading. I'm pleased to hear it, Kate. It's good to know that a young woman interested in literature is looking after my children. They seem very happy that you are here and if they're happy, I am too. Please let me know when you would like to borrow another book. As you have discovered, I have plenty of them.'

Kate bobbed and smiled. The appointment of this young woman was the right decision, Mrs Winton thought to herself. She had a spark about her and seemed to have more than the usual level of intelligence expected of a maid. George Eliot was not the average reading matter for a servant. She detected an expression of puzzlement on Kate's face. It was unusual for Mrs Winton to 'take the air', it was true, but she'd decided she was going to do more to keep her own body and mind in good order instead of attending to her family's needs all the time.

So, walk they did and it was a beautiful afternoon. The flower beds in the park were a picture and the bright sunlight showed them in their truest colours. The vibrant reds and yellows of the stately lupins saluted the women as they entered the park. There were many people strolling along the pathways, some nodded and smiled, some men lifted their hats, others were deeply engaged in conversation.

Nursemaids pushing prams congregated near the pond area and pointed out the antics of the ducks, tails bobbing, heads down. One over-adventurous child was being rescued by the collar of his jacket, his toy boats a little too far to reach. His loud objections, heard all over the park, appeared to be more to do with the lost boat than his dripping wet clothes.

'Time to move on, I think,' said Mrs Winton, not attempting to cover her intolerance of other people's wailing children.

As they entered the shrubbery, two older women came towards them. As they came closer, Mrs Winton recognized them.

'Mrs Wickham, Mrs Trimbrell, how delightful to meet you,' she said.

'Likewise,' replied Mrs Wickham. 'We don't often see you out and about, Dorothea. Perhaps you have more time on your hands since James's departure for London?'

'We heard of James's new venture, many congratulations. You'll be joining him soon, of course,' Mrs Trimbrell added.

'Yes, just as soon as we can. Will you both be coming to tea at Mrs Hargraves' next Friday?'

'No, we must decline,' Mrs Wickham said. 'We have other commitments, in Shawford. We go to join with the Winchester Society to meet the march from Land's End to London. We need to show our support. If women like Emily Davison are prepared to sacrifice themselves for the cause then it's the least we can do.'

'She threw herself under the king's horse, you know,' Mrs Trimbrell added. 'I presume you've seen the papers?'

'What march?' Clara asked, her interest suddenly piqued.

'Why the suffragette march, of course,' Mrs Trimbrell replied.

'Why exactly are they marching?' asked Clara.

'My dear, your mother needs to educate you on such things,' Mrs Wickham said looking pointedly in Mrs Winton's direction.

Mrs Winton's face flushed. She had been caught off guard by the ladies' forthright opinions.

'We'll talk about it later. Come along, Clara, or we'll be late for tea,' Mrs Winton said turning away. 'Good afternoon, ladies.'

Clara was in a bad mood all the way home having received no answer to her questions except that it needn't concern her at the moment. Mrs Winton walked rather more quickly on the way home and kept urging Kate to hurry the children along. Was she being too cautious about joining the suffragettes? Was Mrs Wickham, right? Clara was growing up in a society that might well be different for women like her. She should be prepared for it. There had always been some sort of unspoken rule in most houses that what the man decided was law, but times were changing.

She'd been invited to the Winchester Society meetings on a number of occasions but had found excuses. Yes, she thought it was important that women should hold responsible positions in society and obtaining the vote was an important step in establishing women's rights but . . . and there were buts, the chief one being what James would say, how it would affect his position.

Mrs Winton debated with herself for several days after that chance meeting in the park, struggling with the arguments for and against. It was a letter that decided her. Four days after her encounter with Mrs Wickham and Mrs Trimbrell, a large envelope was delivered to Woodland House addressed to Mrs Dorothea Winton. She rarely received post herself, except letters from her sister and her aunt. She sat in the study and read its contents. The two items in the envelope were accompanied by a note from Mrs Wickham encouraging her to read and 'decide for herself what was the right thing to do'. It encouraged her to bring her daughter and her maid too. 'For this is a fight that affects all women, regardless of class, and they are the next generation. We are doing this for the women of the future as well as today.'

She read the pamphlet first. It was written by a Lord Curzon and entitled *Fifteen Good Reasons Against the Grant of Female Suffrage*. A document that referred to 'women's proper sphere and highest duty which is maternity' and suggested that suffrage would lead to 'divisions which will break up the harmony of the home'.

Dorothea Winton's anger began to rise. It was fine for men such as Lord Curzon to talk of women's duties and breaking the harmony of the home, but they did not have to suffer the pain of childbirth, sometimes to be followed by the pain of losing that child. Nor did they think twice about putting their own success before the needs of their wives and children. Her own husband was not with her and yet she had survived his absence. She had coped perfectly well without him breathing down her neck to sanction and double check her every decision in life.

She turned to the second document entitled *Fifteen Valid Arguments for the Grant of Female Suffrage* in which Lady Laura Ridding had discounted all Lord Curzon's arguments in a very clever poem exposing his arguments for what they were, opinionated and one-sided. It ended with the lines: 'No valid argument will win of all the great fifteen. They will have vanished into dust as if they'd never been'.

Mrs Winton decided then and there. Mrs Wickham was right. She would attend the Winchester Society's reception for the suffragettes and she would take Clara and Kate with her.

# CHAPTER EIGHT

*July 1913*

The hall was buzzing. Kate had never seen so many women in one place. Not even at the Christmas Bazaar in Micklewell village hall. Purple, white and green rippled across the room. Kate thought she was walking across a Hampshire heath.

The invitation to attend the meeting with Mrs Winton had come as a complete surprise. The mistress had become more relaxed somehow, since the master's departure and she and Clara seemed closer to each other, there were less disagreements. Perhaps that was why she had been asked to come, or perhaps Clara had asked if Kate could come too? Whatever the reason, Kate was pleased to be there. This was an experience that she would never have had in Micklewell.

Eliza had commented that Kate shouldn't get above herself 'hobnobbing with the gentry', but Mrs B said it was an honour to be included and that Kate should be on her best behaviour.

The three stood just inside and Mrs Winton scanned the room as if she was looking for someone. 'It's very crowded,' she said. 'I wasn't expecting quite so many.'

Kate watched as a fulsome figure wearing a bold sash walked towards them. Her purposeful stride making the ostrich plumes on her hat bounce to her rhythm. 'My dears, welcome. Isn't it wonderful to see so many of us?' she said. 'Now there's a table over there where you can choose from a sash like mine, or a ribbon. Our seamstresses have all been busy sewing.'

She sailed swiftly on checking the attire of all in her path. It was not a familiar sight to see her mistress take orders from someone else, but she led the way and Kate and Clara followed. Armed with the less conspicuous ribbons, they pinned them to their chests and joined the crowd.

Within a few minutes the ostrich plumes made their way onto the platform at one end of the hall and there was an announcement that there was news of the march. They would be arriving at the outskirts of the village very soon.

'We have banners against the wall over there.' Mrs Ostrich Feathers beamed. 'Volunteers needed, please, to carry them.'

Clara, clearly seduced by the excitement, made a step forward and was barred by her mother's arm.

'Well, well, Dorothea Winton, what a surprise?' a voice called from behind them.

Mrs Winton turned. 'Mrs Barnes, Amelia, how lovely to see you,' she replied. Kate couldn't help but notice that Mrs Winton was anything but pleased to see the face with the inquisitive eyes and a slightly lopsided mouth.

'And who have we here?' the woman quizzed, peering out from under her ribboned hat.

'This is my daughter Clara, and Kate, the twins' nursemaid,' Mrs Winton replied.

'Unusual to bring one's maid to such events,' Amelia Barnes commented.

'I didn't think the suffragettes discriminated,' Dorothea Winton replied.

'No, we don't,' a voice behind Mrs Barnes intervened. 'And you should know that, Amelia.'

Mrs Wickham emerged from the crowd and Amelia Barnes scuttled off.

'Although perhaps with some people we should?' Mrs Wickham whispered into Dorothea's ear but not so quietly that Kate and Clara couldn't hear. Mrs Winton smiled.

'I'm so pleased you came and that you brought these two young ladies, too, Dorothea. It's so important that we engage the next generation in our fight.'

'I'm happy to be here,' Mrs Winton replied. 'As long as you don't expect me to get involved in some of the more militant activities. I do support what you're all doing and I will do what I can, but I must draw the line somewhere. You do understand, don't you?'

'I quite understand,' Mrs Wickham said. 'Any news from London? Have you heard from James at all?'

They all moved towards the door where the excitement of raised voices indicated that the march was approaching.

\* \* \*

'And what happened then?' Eliza asked as Kate was relaying the story of the day's expedition.

'We all went out to greet the women who'd marched from Eastleigh. They'd walked all the way from Land's End, some of them. It's taken them over a month,' Kate said.

'Shouldn't fancy darning their stockings,' Eliza joked, 'nor washing them neither. Phew! You say there was tea laid on for them. Plenty of cake was there?'

'There was cake, yes,' Kate said slightly impatiently, 'but that wasn't the thing I remember most about the day. You should have been there, Eliza. The speeches . . . so many women all of one mind and hardly a man in sight!'

'Not my idea of a good time,' Eliza said.

'Oh, Eliza! The things that those women said. Things that I'd never thought about before. There's been women trying to get the law changed for forty years and men have stood in their way. Parliament has refused to listen. It was so, so . . . inspiring. Yes, that's the word. Women pay taxes, so women are entitled to vote, they said. Parliament decides upon things of vital interest to women so women must be able to express their opinions through the ballot box.'

'Such as what?' Eliza asked.

'Such as education, housing and employment,' Kate replied. 'I believe in what they're saying, Eliza. Meetings and petitions are not enough, it's time for action!'

'Hark at you!' Eliza said. 'Sounds like they've got a new recruit. Just you be careful what you get yourself into, mind. I bet some of those women's husbands don't have a notion of what they're up to. Mr Winton surely wouldn't approve if he knew, but then he's not here, is he?'

Kate looked at Eliza. She was so much happier now Mr Winton was away. She and Tommy would soon be together.

'No, probably just as well. But then she's not the only woman who will have to face that challenge, is she? There were plenty there that the mistress seemed to know. There was one, though, who made the mistress agitated. A woman called Mrs Barnes, the mistress seemed troubled by her. Why's that?'

'Ha! She's the local busybody, likes to poke her nose into everyone else's business, got a vicious tongue. Used to come around here for tea, until her husband was passed over for a promotion at the master's bank. She never forgave the master and therefore the mistress too. She's best avoided that one!'

Kate hoped that the woman wouldn't make trouble for Mrs Winton. She could sometimes be demanding, but she was a good mistress. Eliza had told her stories of how cruel some employers could be. She was learning more about the world every day and her place in it. Life in Micklewell had been so sheltered. She knew nothing of how society worked, what more she could accomplish, what more there was to experience and learn. Coming to Andover had taught her a great deal. The country mouse was learning how to be a town mouse. She had seen a glimpse of what women could strive for and wanted to be part of it. She put her hand in her pocket and held the ribbon. She wanted to wear the purple, white and green. She wanted to become a suffragette.

Her first opportunity to do something about that desire was when she managed to talk to Philip for the first time in weeks. She was in the garden, taking in the twins' washing, when she saw Philip strolling beside the flower beds. She tried not to look in his direction but she felt his eyes upon her.

She was folding the last of the clothes, inhaling their sweet smell of sunshine and placing them in the basket, when she realized he was standing right beside her.

'A beautiful day, Kate,' he said.

She stuttered the reply out, trying not to appear flustered by his presence. 'Yes, Master Philip. A good drying day.' It had been several weeks since she'd seen him and she smiled at him, trying to gauge if he was as pleased to see her as she him.

'Are we not past the stage of such formalities, Kate? Call me Philip, please.'

'Oh, I couldn't, not in front of anyone else anyway,' she said, blushing.

'Well, to me then at least,' he replied returning her smile. 'You know, everyone is so pleased that you came to work here, Kate. The whole atmosphere in the house has changed. The twins are less argumentative with each other and Mother is impressed with your desire to read and learn. As for Clara, she says that she thinks of you more as a friend than a maid. You really are different, Kate, quite remarkable in fact.'

Kate felt embarrassed by his compliments but pleased at the same time. She bent down to lift the basket and he stooped to help her. Their eyes met and they stood locked in each other's gaze until she broke the spell.

'I really should get this washing back inside. Eliza will be out here looking for me,' she said.

'Always so busy.' Philip sighed. 'I wonder that you find any time to read at all. Have you finished *The Mill on the Floss*? I can recommend *Silas Marner* too. I'm sure there's a copy in the house somewhere. Shall I ask Mother for you?'

'Ask her what?'

It was Clara's voice. Kate hadn't noticed her approaching them across the grass.

'I was just telling Kate how Mother would be happy to lend her another book,' Philip said.

'Oh, yes, of course. She's quite the reader, is Kate, amongst other things,' Clara replied casting a knowing look in Kate's direction. Was it obvious that Kate was attracted to Philip? Was he attracted to her?

'In fact, she's a most unusual young woman altogether,' Clara continued. 'She's going to join the suffragettes. Has she told you about the meeting?'

'What meeting?' Philip said.

'Mother took the two of us to a meeting at the Winchester Society. There was a march and banners and there were so many women, all calling for the vote.'

'Does Father know?' Philip asked.

'Does Father need to know? He'll only object,' Clara said, becoming more animated. 'You know, Philip. I don't want to spend the rest of my life at tea parties being weighed up by old dowagers as suitable wives for their sons or nephews. I want to do what you're doing, take the university entrance exam. I want to be like those women who are standing up for their rights. I believe that their cause is a just one. Women should have the vote.'

Kate felt uncomfortable being on the edge of this discussion and began shifting her feet. Clara's voice was becoming more insistent. She started to move away when Philip clearly sensed her discomfort and said, 'No need to get heated about it. I agree with you, Clara. I won't say anything to Father. I think you should talk to Mother. She went to the meeting too, she must have some sympathy for the idea of a woman contributing more to society.'

Kate took the pause in the conversation as her opportunity to leave. 'Excuse me, Miss Clara, Master Philip, I think I should be getting on with my work.'

'Of course,' Philip said. 'We mustn't keep you. Clara and I will continue this debate alone.'

'No wait, Kate, stay. You're just as involved in this as I am. You'd like to know more about the suffragettes too, wouldn't you?'

'Yes but . . .'

'Well then. I have a plan. Will you help us, Philip? Will you come to the next meeting with us?'

'I thought it was all women?' Philip said.

'No, there are some men that support us as well. There was one who spoke at the meeting, a Mr Kennedy, he came all the way from London just to show that there are men who agree with what we're trying to do, not only for us privileged women but for working women as well.'

'Us? You are suffragettes already, then, are you?' Philip teased.

'I can't call myself one until I've done something positive to help,' Clara replied. 'You know I won't be allowed out unless I'm chaperoned. We could say we're going to an event at the Meeting Rooms. I believe there's a talk in the Guildhall on the same evening as the suffragette meeting, about the origins of the Twinings company or some such.'

'Not one of my major interests but all right then,' Philip said.

'And Kate must come too,' Clara added.

'Of course, she must,' Philip agreed.

So, she was to be invited out by Clara, and Philip would be there too! She couldn't quite believe what was happening. What would Eliza make of it, she wondered? Probably best not to tell her the whole story, in case she blabbed to Mrs B who would be all ifs and buts. Enough to say she was required to accompany Miss Clara for the evening. Her mind was busy working out how this had all occurred while she said a flustered thank you and took her basket of washing back to the kitchen.

# CHAPTER NINE

*July 1913*

'Excuse me, sorry, thank you, excuse me.' Clara apologized to everyone as the three of them moved along the line of seated people.

'Why do intelligent women sit at the edges and leave a gap in the middle?' Philip asked his sister.

'Sssh,' Clara responded, her glare in Philip's direction signifying her embarrassment.

'Probably in case they need to dash for the ladies' room,' Philip whispered to Kate, who blushed and suppressed a giggle.

Kate was full of anticipation. The Assembly Rooms had a raised platform at one end with a long, wooden table around which were seated four women and one man. The walls were painted green and there was wooden panelling with a dado rail painted in a darker shade. The windows, high up, let in a strange yellowish light from the outside streetlamp. All the chairs were now occupied and, swivelling her neck, Kate could see that people were even standing at the back. The room hushed as the first speaker was introduced and stood up. Lily Faith was a jeweller and stationer in the town.

'My father recognized my organizational abilities,' she began, 'my head for figures and my nose for making a profit. He never for one minute thought of me as second best or compensation for the son he never had.'

She spoke from experience about what women had to offer. Kate hung on every word.

'And finally, to the MP for Ludlow in Shropshire, who is quoted as saying, "How is a poor little man to get on with a couple of women wearing enormous hats in front of him?" I say, do not worry Mr Hunt. If you and others so small of stature, fear they won't be seen or heard in the House, I am happy to remove my hat!' And with that she did, bowing to her audience with a dramatic flourish.

The roar of approval and the applause echoed around the hall. When the room finally returned to order, Kate sat stunned, gazing at the woman on the platform. Such energy, such determination and such complete confidence that she was in the right and was prepared to fight to have that conviction recognized! It wasn't until the next speaker was being introduced, that she realized her hand was touching Philip's hand. She moved her hand swiftly away and tried not to look in his direction but, out of the corner of her eye, she detected his broad and knowing smile.

A gentle buzz of conversation rippled around them as people started to move out of the hall. Kate, Clara and Philip joined the flow of people all talking of the speakers and of how successful the meeting had been. Just as they reached the door, two women were handing out leaflets and urging people to take notice. 'Please, read the leaflet. We must all do what we can to support the Women's Franchise Bill. Please write to your MP, the newspapers, anyone who is thinking of joining us but who hasn't yet. We have many supporters in the House but we need more if this bill is to be passed.'

As they walked home, Clara talked excitedly about how things were changing for their generation of women and that the idea of going to such a meeting would've been unthinkable a few years ago. Kate wondered what her own mother would think if she could see her now, attending meetings and rubbing shoulders with the gentry.

'What did you think of the meeting, Kate?' Philip asked.

'So many people. How does a person get the confidence to stand up and speak like that in front of such a crowd?'

'Weren't they wonderful?' Clara interrupted. 'All the speakers were so passionate about women's rights. I wonder what the leaflet says?'

'Too dark to read it now,' Philip replied, 'even by the streetlamp. Probably inciting you all to rebellion. If it does, just make sure you don't get yourselves into trouble,' he warned. 'I'm not coming to bail you out of jail.'

'Jail!'

Kate suddenly felt out of her depth.

'Oh yes,' Clara said. 'Some women have been arrested over this issue of Votes for Women and took a jail sentence rather than pay a fine.'

'But I couldn't . . .' Kate stood still, petrified at the thought.

'Don't worry,' Philip reassured her. 'We wouldn't let you languish in jail having your toes nibbled by the rats.'

He made little nibbling motions with his fingers in front of her face and Clara burst out laughing. Kate was getting used to his sense of humour and allowed herself a nervous smile. Any sort of trouble could cost her her job and then where would she be?

As they approached the house, Kate went to enter by the side gate but Philip said that she should come with them through the front door.

'Oh, I couldn't . . .' Kate began.

'It's late and that side of the house is dark. We don't want you falling and breaking anything, do we, Clara?'

'No, indeed, she's needed to run out to the post for me tomorrow,' replied Clara, 'for I intend to get my letter off to our MP as soon as the ink is dry.'

Philip held the door open for them and then stepped inside. Kate turned to close it. She couldn't forget her position and knew it was always the servants' job to secure the house for the night. As Philip leaned forward to take over the job from her, she froze. Was it her imagination or did Philip let his hand linger on hers just that little bit longer as they both shut the door together?

Clara called,' Good night,' as she handed Kate her coat and moved towards the stairs. She gave a backward glance at the two of them left standing together and said to Philip with a slight smile, 'Now, don't keep Kate talking too long, will you? She has things to attend to before bed, I'm sure.'

Philip nodded at her and they exchanged glances. He waited until his sister was on the staircase and then turned to Kate and asked her once again if she'd enjoyed the evening.

'Oh yes,' she replied. 'I've never been to such a thing in my entire life. In Micklewell they don't have such meetings. The only time there's a deal of people together in one place is in church and then the vicar is telling us what we must think and do, not encouraging us to question and think for ourselves. That lady with the speech about the hat, the way she had everyone's attention! There was no chance of me drifting off, like I sometimes do during the sermon.'

Philip laughed. 'You have a way of putting things, Kate, that is refreshingly candid.'

Kate looked at him with a puzzled expression.

'You tell things exactly as they are,' he explained. 'You're truthful . . . straightforward, uncomplicated. I like that.'

Kate smiled. She liked the fact that he liked her. 'Good night, sir,' she said.

'Good night, Kate, and I hope Clara invites you to more of her suffragette meetings. I've a feeling that they need people like you to join them. I can see that you have a lot to offer.'

'Thank you,' Kate replied.

As she made her way up to the servants' quarters, his words went around and around in her head. 'A lot to offer,' he'd said. She let out a deep sigh at the thought of what that might be.

\* \* \*

'Oh, come on Kate. I thought you were serious about all this,' Clara insisted to Kate a few days later, as she sought her out in the nursery.

The twins were laying out the train track and were fighting over who should have the red engine.

'Now why don't we settle this by doing eeny, meeny, miney, moe ?' Kate suggested.

Sophie won and that settled it much to Kate's relief for if Simon had won there would have been tantrums and tears.

'You have so much patience, Kate. I couldn't be bothered with all those hysterics,' Clara said. 'What would we do without you?'

'Such things are important for children,' Kate said. 'They are only just finding their way in the world. The same went on in my house back in Micklewell. Standing up for yourself is important.'

'My point precisely,' Clara emphasized. 'I couldn't have expressed it better myself. We must be listened to, Kate. We need to take a stand!'

'But . . .'

'The idea is that we set fire to postboxes on the same day across the country. That way the government will take more notice, know that we mean business,' Clara said.

'I don't know, what if . . . ?'

'If the women who started the campaign thought only of the consequences do you think we would have made any progress at all? Do you want to be a suffragette or not?'

Kate nodded.

'Good,' Clara said. 'Now go and post this for me quickly so that it makes the last post and gets to our MP for who knows when we'll get the call, it might go up in flames tomorrow.'

# CHAPTER TEN

*September 1913*

An unusually warm September throbbed through the house and Kate took every opportunity to escape the airless confines of the nursery. She longed to be strolling beside the river in Micklewell or walking the shady towpath next to the Basingstoke Canal. The remembered joy of removing her shoes and socks and dangling her legs in the cooling waters made her ache inside. A visit to the park was a poor substitute for such delights, but it would have to do. She needed to get outside and do more than stroll round the garden.

The twins were only too happy to agree to her suggestion and, despite the heat, bowled along, eager to feel the freedom and wide-open space of the park. Thomas was less keen but, when Kate suggested bringing his magnifying glass and collecting box, he agreed it could be an interesting venture. Sophie and Simon rushed through the park gates and shouted to Kate and Thomas to hurry up. They were carrying their model boats and were impatient to begin floating them. Thomas dawdled with his nose in a classification book.

'Come along, Master Thomas, we must catch up with the twins or we'll end up dragging them out of the pond.'

Thomas had stopped and was bent over looking through his magnifying glass, his book tucked under his arm.

'Look, come and look, quickly before it flies off. It's a fine specimen of Lucanidae, a stag beetle.'

Kate was stuck between the older child and the two adventurers who were likely to get themselves into trouble. She knew neither of them would be distracted from their main purpose, but it would be easier to get Thomas to move than ask the twins to wait.

'Fascinating, Master Thomas,' she said. 'Now I know that in the plants around the edge of the pond there are dragonflies to be found. Let us get there before Sophie and Simon disturb them.'

Thomas rushed off. He didn't need more encouragement.

'Cleverly done,' a voice said from behind her.

She turned to see a stranger smiling at her. He removed his hat and released a tumble of dark hair which curled over his collar and around his ears. He had a broad mouth and was clean-shaven. He was a good-looking young man and Kate felt herself blushing at his comment. There was a dimple in his chin and his eyes were wide and blue and fixed upon hers. Kate didn't know what to say. So instead she looked quickly away to check on the children who were all happily engaged in their separate pleasures.

'My apologies, Kate. It is Kate isn't it? How rude of me. Let me introduce myself. I'm Carnforth, Edward Carnforth, a friend of Philip Winton's.'

Kate wondered how he knew her name.

Kate's tongue stuck to the roof of her mouth which was dry and unresponsive. She tried to speak but nothing came.

'I'm sorry, I've startled you,' Carnforth said. 'Come, let us go and sit on the bench where you can watch over the children and I will explain myself.'

Kate followed as he led the way to a place where the children were in full view. He waited until she sat first and then took his place at a suitable distance, at the other end of the bench.

'I recognized the children. Young Thomas doesn't change much, looks as serious as ever. Philip has told me all about you, Kate, how good you are at your job and how Clara depends upon you,' Carnforth said. 'You're more than a maid to her, I understand. She counts you amongst her friends.'

Kate finally found her voice. 'I don't know what . . .' she began.

'What business it is of mine? Quite so! Impertinent of me, I can only apologize again,' Carnforth said. 'I'm in town on business and I'm arranging to pay a visit to Mrs Winton and family so I thought it polite to just say hello. Philip tells me that Clara is getting you involved in all sorts of activities that may get the two of you into some trouble.'

Kate looked at him. 'Trouble?' she asked.

'Yes, this suffragette business. He says he'd feel happier if you two young women had someone to call upon, other than his parents, should you need assistance, without drawing too much attention to yourselves, you understand?'

He handed Kate a gilt-edged card. She read the black print: *Mr Edward Carnforth, importer of fine goods, Carnforth and Sons, London, Southampton and Andover.*

'Thank you, Mr Carnforth,' Kate replied,' but I can't think when I might need it.'

'Well, we'll see what the future brings, shall we? Philip asked after you when I saw him and . . .'

'Which was when, sir?' Kate asked.

'Just a few days ago actually, I was in Cambridge conducting some business for my father and we had lunch together. He seems to be settling in well. Finding his way around and so on.'

'How is Master Philip?' Kate asked.

'He's well and I'm sure he wouldn't want you to refer to him as Master Philip anymore, he's out of his short trousers now.' Carnforth grinned.

Kate blushed and looked away to where the children were playing.

Carnforth called out to them, 'Simon, Sophie, Thomas, look who's here, you rascals.'

Sophie and Simon came running and threw themselves around Carnforth, holding onto his legs and pleading, 'Chase, chase, hide and seek, piggyback, please.'

Thomas dawdled up and shoved his specimen jar in Carnforth's face. 'Name the species, Edward,' he said, adding that his collection was ready to be viewed whenever Edward would like to see it.

'Now, now children, that's enough. I must get the children back for their lunch, Mr Carnforth,' she said standing up. 'Thank you for taking the time to speak with me and the children. Please give my best regards to Master Philip when you see him again. Now, I must wish you a good day.'

Carnforth stood, straightened his morning coat and replaced his hat. 'Good day, Kate. We shall meet again very soon,' he said pursing his lips and then smiling broadly.

Kate pocketed the card, gathered up the children, who were protesting, and marched them home to Woodland House.

She thought about the encounter all the way back home and tried to make sense of it. She couldn't quite understand why such a man would feel the need to make her acquaintance. All that talk of wishing to help if she was in trouble! She couldn't dwell on it though, for as soon as they returned she was greeted by Mrs Winton with a list of demands which included getting the children's lunch. Mrs B and Eliza were making last-minute preparations for the unexpected arrival of a guest for dinner and were therefore far too busy to talk.

Mrs Winton had eaten an early lunch and intended to take an afternoon nap, as she was expected to entertain that evening. The children must be instructed to read or draw or entertain themselves with some quiet activity that would not disturb their mother's repose. Kate served their lunch and then sat with them to ensure that peace and calm prevailed. She busied herself with sewing duties, ever mindful of Mrs B's caution about 'idle hands' and 'the devil's work'. She had been instructed to embroider the twins' full names on their handkerchiefs so that they didn't argue over whose had been lost and whose had been used to clean their shoes. A simple S was no longer acceptable as it gave too much room for arguments.

Kate hadn't been sewing for long when Clara opened the door and stood looking at her. She had her scheming face on. A half smile with a puckered frown. Instead of coming in, Clara beckoned to Kate and she followed Clara out of the room. Clara closed the nursery door quietly and whispered, 'They'll be all right for a while. I need to talk to you. Come with me to my room.'

Kate had been in Clara's room before and she always wished that she could show her sister, Dot, the beauty of the decorations and furnishings, which Clara had been allowed to choose for herself. The walls were painted pale pink with a raised white panel design and picture rail. The bed had silky light-green drapes with a delicate floral design and the same material was used to cover a pretty little tub chair. There was a large mirror on the wall in a cream frame, adorned with hand-painted flowers in pinks and greens. The huge wardrobe in the corner, also painted in the same style, stretched from floor to ceiling and held, Kate knew, many expensive dresses.

Clara closed the door and ushered Kate to the bed where they sat side by side.

'The children told me you met Carnforth in the park,' Clara said.

'Yes, he tells me he's—'

'A friend of Philip's, yes. When he's in town, he's invited to all the important social gatherings. He's in high demand,' Clara said.

Kate could see that she was not the only one to appreciate Edward Carnforth's extremely good looks. Clara seemed flustered and shifted about. She bit her upper lip and her eyebrows raised a little as she let out a sigh. She reached over and took Kate's hand.

'I want you to do something for me, Kate,' she said. 'I believe I can trust you. Can I trust you?'

'Of course, you know I will always do what I can to help you in any way, Miss Clara,' Kate replied. 'What is it?'

Clara put Kate's hand gently down and turned to look directly at her.

'Edward Carnforth and I have been writing to each other for some time, without my mother's knowledge I should add,' Clara said. 'Philip has been my go-between, bless him. He'd get into such trouble if our parents ever found out. Edward and I have known one another since childhood. He could be annoying sometimes when we were young, but we're both adults now and he's, well what can I say, different. He's much more . . .'

'Engaging?' Kate suggested.

'You could say that,' Clara said with a smile. We've met a few times at various social events. He's in Andover on business and is coming to dinner this evening.'

'Oh, so he's the reason that Mrs B is in such a tizzy?' Kate said.

'Yes, and he'll be here at five but will only stay for two hours at the most, and then he'll be expected to leave and return to his hotel.'

'So exactly what do you want me to do, Miss Clara?' Kate asked.

'I want you to unlock the side gate at six thirty so that he can meet me in secret. When he leaves, I shall say I need to take a turn around the garden and he will be waiting behind the summer house. We can be together, completely alone, for the first time.'

'Without a chaperone? But what if you're seen?'

'If women can fight for the vote then they can make decisions about who they want to meet and when, can't they?' Clara insisted.

Kate didn't know how to answer that, but what she did know was that if her part in this deception was discovered then what could she say? Clara's request put her in a very difficult position.

'Well, Kate, will you do it?' Clara asked, her eyes pleading and her hands clenching.

Kate agreed, although she was more than a little worried about the whole thing.

'Oh, thank you, thank you, Kate,' Clara said springing to her feet. 'Give us some time together and then lock up again. We must be very discreet. Now, help me choose what to wear for dinner. I want to look my best.'

Kate could only suppose that Clara knew the risk she was taking. A young woman's reputation would soon be sullied if word got out of her unchaperoned liaisons with a young man, but Kate would not be the one to betray their secret. What puzzled her was the need for them to meet in such a way. Why didn't he just propose marriage to her and then all would be well? There was no one she could ask about this puzzle, except perhaps Philip. She would have to wait until his next visit home.

# CHAPTER ELEVEN

*September 1913*

When dinner was over and before the children needed their bedtime story, Kate did as Clara had asked and opened the side gate. She carried out the night-time routines with half an ear to the front door. From the children's bedrooms, she heard voices calling good night and tried to hurry the story along so that she could check on whether Clara's plan had worked.

No such luck! When she tried to shorten the crucial descriptions of Goldilocks visiting each chair, bed and porridge bowl either Sophie or Simon insisted she say it properly.

By the time she got down to the kitchen, Eliza and Mrs B were in full flow complaining about the amount of washing-up. Their backs were turned and there was so much clattering of pans going on that Kate was able to open the back door very quietly, without being noticed, and creep outside. Coming back in might not be the same story, she suspected.

Kate's eyes took a while to adjust to the darkness. The night air was cool and she shivered. She waited and then heard Clara's voice. She moved silently along the stone path until she realized that they must be behind the pergola.

She daren't go any closer for fear of being noticed. She felt embarrassed about eavesdropping but she needed to know that everything was kept within the bounds of propriety, for Miss Clara's sake. Not that Mr Carnforth seemed to be the sort who would take advantage, at least she hoped not.

Clara's voice carried through the night air. 'Oh Edward. How will I ever be the woman I want to be? It's all right for young men, they are given so much more freedom to make their own choices in life. For us women, our lives are mapped out for us. Piano playing, needlepoint and polite conversation. I want so much more than finishing school and a good marriage.'

'So, marriage isn't part of your plan?' Carnforth asked.

'I didn't mean that. Of course, I want to marry, eventually. I meant it's not the only thing I want and I don't want my husband to be chosen for me.'

'Is that the suffragette in you talking?'

'I thought you were in support of women's suffrage?'

'I am,' Carnforth replied. 'I just don't want you to get involved in something that you might regret. I don't want anything to get in the way of us being together.'

'Neither do I, Edward.'

The voices suddenly stopped and Kate didn't know what to do. Had they moved? Where were they?

The gas light from the street came on, casting shadows across the garden and her question was answered. Carnforth was holding Clara in an embrace, but she pulled away at the appearance of the light and, although Kate didn't hear what passed between them, their hasty separation told her that they were fearful of being seen. Carnforth turned and went through the gate and Clara returned indoors. Kate locked the gate and placed the key in her apron pocket.

As she entered the kitchen she was asked by Mrs B where she'd been, and she said she'd been looking for a toy that Simon had thrown out of the nursery window and was desperate to have back. It was only a little white lie. Simon was in the habit of doing such things at a whim, just not that particular evening.

'And did you find it?' Mrs B asked.

'No, it was too dark,' Kate replied.

'Mmmph!' Mrs B grunted. 'Well, get over here now and help put this crockery away if you want to eat this side of midnight.'

\* \* \*

When Kate wasn't with the children, her time seemed to be taken up with many trips to the postbox and much talk of Clara wanting to be like Philip and further her education. She spoke of her wish to apply for a place at King's College, London.

'But I know what Father will say,' she complained. 'He'll say what's the point in paying for a university education just to walk down the aisle and bear children!'

Kate listened to Clara waver between wanting to go to university and learn more about women's position in society and her attraction to Edward Carnforth.

'But can't you have both?' Kate asked. 'There are suffragettes who are married. Or is Mr Carnforth not a supporter of Votes for Women?'

'Yes, he is . . . but, oh Kate, if only life were that simple.' Clara sighed. 'I'm caught in a Gordian knot and I can't see any way out.'

'I don't know who or what Gordian is, but I know when knots need untying, the only way out is to work your way carefully through it. Hurrying only makes it worse. Either that or take a pair of scissors to it. Dot's hair got in such a tangle with a briar once; I just had to cut it out.'

'There are some things that cannot be mended, Kate. Mother and Father have been making plans for my future,' Clara said.

'I thought you wanted to go to London. I thought you had plans to—'

'I do, I did, but my parents have other ideas,' Clara began. 'Father wishes me to meet one of his business partners,

Mr Arthur Makepiece. I am told he would make a very good match for me.'

'Oh,' replied Kate,' I see.' This was the first she'd heard of it and she could see why Clara was so distracted. Such a match would be the end of her and Mr Carnforth.

Kate could do nothing to lift Clara's mood. Days went by when Clara didn't come to the nursery at all. She had little appetite for walks and conversation but fell into routine occupations with little joy. Clara would take her lessons in the morning and read, write, play piano or sew in the afternoons. She seemed to retreat into herself. Kate gave up hope that their previous relationship would ever return and then, one day, Clara arrived in the nursery waving a newspaper.

'Listen to this,' she said reading out loud in a dramatic tone.

'"A serious outbreak of fire was discovered at Alston Manor, an unoccupied house in Basingstoke, in the early hours of Sunday morning. The fire brigade succeeded in saving the house from complete destruction, though damage to the extent of about £400 or £500 was done. Suffragette literature was found in the vicinity." And there's more.' She continued reading. '"A woman has been arrested for breaking the glass cabinets in the Jewel House at the Tower of London—"'

'What's arrested?' asked Sophie.

'Taken to prison, locked up,' Thomas replied. 'Actually, she was already in a prison, that's what the Tower is, I've read about it.'

'There have been fires in post offices and banks,' Clara continued.

'Not in Daddy's bank?' Sophie asked.

'No, not in Daddy's bank,' Clara replied.

'When's Daddy coming home?' asked Simon.

'Soon,' Clara said, 'but not too soon, I hope,' she whispered to Kate. 'We have things to do.'

Clara was so animated that Kate wondered what she had in mind, for this sudden return to her old self was to be welcomed but somehow Kate felt that she was about to be bowled along by a force that was running out of control. Clara was planning something. It was only a matter of time before she disclosed her intentions. Kate just hoped she wasn't intending anything that might get them both into serious trouble.

* * *

Kate's answer came a few days later when Clara came to the nursery door and beckoned for her to follow. Kate saw that the twins were playing happily in their opposite corners of the room and Thomas was carefully copying a drawing from one of his books on insects, so she followed Clara to her room.

'Shut the door, Kate,' Clara said. 'First of all, I don't think I thanked you properly for helping me to meet with Edward. It was so good to really talk to him about important things, not just the quality of the cake and the changes in the weather. Now, I know that you are as keen to show you support the suffragette cause as I am, so I am going to explain my plan to you and I'm sure you'll want to be a part of it.'

Kate wouldn't have used the word sure. She wondered what Clara had to say.

'I've read you the reports on the campaign of action. Deeds not words are the important thing. We need to show our willingness to act, Kate. So, I have decided that we will set fire to a post box.'

'Which one?' Kate asked trying not to show her alarm.

'Does it matter which post box? The one just down the road, of course, the one you use to post our letters.'

'But isn't that rather close to home?' Kate said. 'Won't we be recognized?'

'We'll go at a time of day when there are less people taking the air. Just around teatime. We can take a roundabout route from the park and wait until we can't see anyone we know in the immediate vicinity.'

'Oh, Miss Clara. You've written to the local MP. Shouldn't you wait for a reply?' Kate suggested.

'Wait, wait. All I do is wait! Deeds not words, Kate. Well, are you with me or not? If you're not then . . . then . . .'

Kate waited. Then what?

'Then there's no hope for any of us. We might as well stop now, give up. Accept that we are lesser beings than men. Is that what you think we should accept, Kate? We're either suffragettes or we're not.'

Kate thought about what might happen if Mr and Mrs Winton found out, if someone recognized them and told on them. But then she recalled the rousing speeches that she had heard at the meetings. She thought about what might be possible if women were able to influence decision-making at the highest levels of government. For one brief moment she thought about her own ambitions to become a teacher which would never come to fruition unless young women like her were better educated. The future might be different for her children or even for her own sister, Dot, if change could happen.

'All right,' Kate agreed.

# CHAPTER TWELVE

*September 1913*

Kate and Clara walked up and down the street a few times until Clara decided that there were enough people to witness the protest. Kate still felt extremely nervous about the whole thing and it must have shown on her face for Clara said, 'We must have the courage of our convictions, Kate. Be brave. There's no point in doing the deed without making a public point about why it's being done.'

Kate hoped that they would not be recognized by any-one and reported to Mrs Winton, for although Dorothea Winton was a supporter, she did not approve of the more violent forms of protest.

'Do you have the methylated spirits?' Clara asked.

Kate lifted the cloth off her basket and removed a small bottle of the purple liquid and gave it to Clara.

'And the matches?'

Kate nodded.

Clara took the bottle, removed the cap and began pour-ing the contents into the opening of the post box. Kate stared at the lurid flow, as the bottle emptied. There were several people on both sides of the road, couples out for a Sunday afternoon stroll and one or two automobiles were cruising past. Clara lit the match, threw it and they stepped back.

A child shouted from one of the vehicles, 'Look, Mummy, a bonfire.'

Two or three men rushed towards the flames as Clara and Kate unfurled their banner and yelled, 'Votes for women' at the top of their voices.

'Stand back,' one of the men called out, frightened for their safety, Kate thought. But as the group neared them, she saw that their concern was not for her and Clara but for the other passers-by.

Two women stopped and looked on. The more elderly of the two held a handkerchief to cover her nose and mouth.

'My goodness, Gwendoline, whatever is going on?' she asked her companion.

'It's a protest, Votes for Women, Aunt,' the younger woman replied.

'What do you think you're doing?' a bearded and bespectacled gentleman bellowed at them.

'Destroying public property, that's what,' a younger man with too much pomade in his hair said, pointing his gloved hand at them.

'They should be arrested,' said a third looking about him for any passing policemen.

'You should be ashamed of yourselves,' the spectacled man added, raising his walking stick.

'So, you'd beat a woman standing up for her rights, would you?' Clara retaliated.

'Stop,' the elderly woman suddenly called out.

Kate wasn't sure if the woman was talking to them or to the men. The woman held on to her companion's arm and raised her own stick. 'This is abominable behaviour,' the woman said addressing the group of men. 'It's precisely your kind that these two young women are protesting about. If the men in the Houses of Parliament had listened to reason then women such as these would not have to resort to unreasonable behaviour.'

Kate was astounded at the woman's outburst in support of their actions, but she was becoming more uncomfortable and when she saw more people approaching, her nerve broke.

'I think we should go now, Miss Clara,' she said. 'We've done what was necessary. Let's go before . . .'

By now the flames had subsided but the smoke hung in the air along with a noxious smell.

'Perhaps you're right,' Clara said, rolling up their banner and placing it in the basket.

'I believe that's Mrs Hargraves coming this way. We don't want to be seen by her. She'll make it her business to inform Mother. We've achieved what we set out to do. The old lady was quite a surprise, wasn't she? Good for her.'

* * *

'Phew,' Eliza said as Kate entered the kitchen. 'Smells like you've been turning a spit over a roasting fire. What have you been up to?'

'Sssh,' Kate hissed indicating the sleeping form of Mrs B in her favourite chair. 'Come upstairs and I'll tell you.'

'Well let's hear it,' Eliza said, unable to contain her curiosity. 'Judging by your red cheeks I'd say you've been up to something.'

'Promise you won't tell a soul, for if you do I'll be out on my ear,' Kate said.

Kate related most of the story of the morning's escapades but stopped short of telling how many people had seen them, especially she didn't mention Mrs Hargraves.

'Oh my God, Kate! You be careful. Those women who get caught end up in . . .'

'I know,' Kate replied. 'I just couldn't ignore what's happening all around me. If we don't do something, then the men will always have the upper hand. Why do you think so many of them get away with things? Get away with using us women for—'

'All right, Kate, I see what you're saying. I don't need to be reminded of that.'

'No, I'm sorry. I'm sorry, Eliza. Please forgive me. Let's talk about something else. Any news of a position for you at "The Laurels" with Tommy?'

'No, but he says it will be soon. The cook and her husband are both getting too old to stand for long hours. They'll be retiring to the countryside where they have family to look after them.'

Kate smiled and said Eliza would make a very good cook. She'd learned a lot about running a kitchen from Mrs B.

'Talking of which, it's time for me to wake her, the tea should be prepared by now. You know what the mistress is like if it's late,' Eliza said bustling out of the bedroom.

\* \* \*

Every day since the letterbox burning, Kate had been expecting to be summoned to Mrs Winton to explain herself. She had been prepared for the reprimand. Clara had drilled her in what they must agree to say.

'Just remember. Like true suffragettes we're stronger when we stand together.'

It came as a complete surprise then, that nothing was said. Clara insisted they should relax and forget about it as she believed that Mrs Hargraves might not have recognized her.

'She's as blind as a bat, you know, too vain to wear glasses in public!'

When the mistress announced, a week later, that the master was coming home in three days' time to deal with family matters, the whole house went into spasms of industrious preparations. Silver was polished, floors were washed, bed linen was aired and sprinkled with rose water, special menus were agreed, orders placed and the kitchen became a constant production line of cakes, puddings and sweetmeats to satisfy the master's sweet tooth.

The clatter of children's feet running up and down the stairs added to the atmosphere of anticipation. The need to gather everything together to show their father on his arrival sent the children into a bustle of activity. Questions and demands were hurled at Kate. 'Where's my picture of Mamma in her green dress? We can't find our new colouring pencils. My new shoes want cleaning.' Even Thomas, usually so measured in his responses, became excited about showing his father his new microscope and collection of pinned butterflies. The twins collected arms full of their drawings, none of which could be thrown away, and had practised their cup and ball skills to perform.

As soon as the initial excitement of Mr Winton's arrival was over, Kate was shocked to receive a summons to the study almost straight away. There was hardly time for the family to greet him properly before the children were packed off back to the nursery and Eliza told her that they had finished their tea and she was to report to the master immediately. Clara was already in the room when Kate opened the study door.

There was no greeting from the master and Clara avoided looking at her, her head bowed. Hanging loosely from her hand was a handkerchief which had clearly been needed, for Clara's cheeks were wet with tears. Mr Winton's expression was severe. He told Kate to stand beside Clara and proceeded to wave a paper in front of them.

'I've already read the contents of this letter to my daughter,' he said, in a sharp, clipped tone. 'Now I shall tell you that you are a very lucky, young woman, that both my wife and my daughter have pleaded for my mercy with regard to your punishment and I have listened. If I had my way I would be sending you packing, but they have said that your services are invaluable to them, so I have decided you will be allowed to stay. I don't believe that either of you could have acted in such an irresponsible way if you hadn't had your heads turned and filled with such nonsense as you have been subjected to by these misguided women.'

Kate felt every word stab into her as Mr Winton's anger surged through him. His attempts not to lose complete control made his lips tighten and his face redden as he spat the accusations at them. What would happen to her and Clara? What would their punishment be?

Kate noticed Clara's head lift and she feared she was about to try to defend what they had done, but Clara simply looked at Kate with a sadness that made her shudder. If Clara was despairing then what chance had she?

'My decision about what is to be done with you both in the long term must wait. You will both be told what my intentions are when I am ready. I will write to Mrs Hargraves and thank her for her concern but tell her she need no longer concern herself over your reputations. In the meantime, you will both keep away from these women and put this ridiculous idea of suffrage out of your minds. Your mother and I agree—'

'But Mother believes—' Clara began.

'We will not discuss what your mother believes, Clara. That is a matter between your mother and myself. What this will do to your reputation and the proposed arrangement with . . .' At this point Mr Winton gained control of his anger and stopped short although Kate knew what he was referring to.

'Kate, you may leave us,' Mr Winton said.

As she closed the door, Kate could hear Clara's voice continuing to try to reason with her father, but Mr Winton had the last and most powerful word.

'Enough!' he shouted, and Clara emerged from the room to run upstairs. Kate stared at the open study door and wondered what Mr Winton would do. She worried for Clara, but she worried more for herself.

# CHAPTER THIRTEEN

*October 1913*

The house was quieter without Clara. She'd been sent to finish her education at the Lawnside School for Young Ladies in Great Malvern. Kate didn't get to say much more than a secretly snatched goodbye, as the two young women had been instructed to spend no further time in one another's company before her departure. The whole arrangement was speedily attended to. Clara was to spend a few days with an aunt in Tewkesbury and from there she would travel to the college.

How quickly things could change! Master Philip had tried to reassure her, when he came home from Cambridge for a short while, that it would soon all blow over and be forgotten. Kate wasn't so sure.

The post box had been cleaned up and there was no trace of what had happened that day, but, whenever Kate walked by it with the three children, she felt that the fire had left an invisible scar inside her. She couldn't suppress a sense of regret. But what was she regretting? That she had ever got involved in the protest in the first place, that she had lost Clara, or that she had even come to Woodland House at all? She might have talked to Eliza about her feelings, but

Eliza could only think about herself right now and what was happening in her own life. Eliza's wedding date had finally been set for December. It was all planned; Eliza had given her notice but would stay to help prepare for the family move. Mrs B and Kate were to go with the family to London, but a new kitchen maid and a butler would be employed for the new London house. The move was set for early November.

Kate was pleased for her but would miss Eliza terribly. It would be like starting all over again, but there was nothing she could do about it. Things could never stay the same. Mr and Mrs Tommy White would take up their new positions as Head Butler and Cook at 'The Laurels', Dorchester Road. Kate would be alone. No Eliza to joke with, no Clara and no Philip to . . . to what? Whatever did she think was going to come of any of it? They were far above her and far away from her. She must concentrate on doing her job.

* * *

The packing and preparing was interminable. Every way Mrs B, Eliza and Kate tried to suggest organizing things, Mrs Winton disagreed. One day she instructed them to pack the best china and the next she said they must unpack it again for she couldn't possibly serve dinner to her sister and family on the second-best dinner service. They were coming to take the children to stay with them temporarily so that all the staff could concentrate on the removal arrangements. Kate spent a good deal of time telling the children that the days would soon pass and they would all be together again in London 'in the wink of an eye'. Thomas, now approaching eight years old and very grown up, was very matter of fact about it all, and said he was looking forward to it for he would be going to one of the best schools in London, Dulwich College, and Father had said there would be a science laboratory with microscopes and petri dishes. The twins weren't so sure.

They were to be separated for the first time. Simon was to join his brother but Sophie would be attending James

89

Allen's Girls' School, a short distance away. They, like Kate, had little choice in any of these matters and were obliged to do as their parents bid them.

The whole performance was gradually ended and the move took place in early November. Thankfully it was a dry day and not too cold. As Kate lifted her bags into the hansom cab that was to take her and Mrs B to the station, she looked back at the house. The windows looked back at her with the sadness of a child abandoned. What waited for her in the city was a mystery to her, for the closest she had ever come to the capital was through the descriptions given by Clara and Philip, and through photographs glimpsed in the papers. When she would see her family in Micklewell again, she had no idea. She had expected to be able to go back home to say her farewells but Mrs Winton had said she couldn't possibly spare her and there would be time enough once they had settled.

Kate tried not to think about such things and set her mind on what awaited her, but it kept drifting back to Eliza's laughter and Clara's determined frown. She knew that she would probably never see Eliza again. As for Clara, she wondered how long the master and mistress would keep her in isolation in Gloucestershire and if their plans to marry her off to some wealthy curmudgeon had only been delayed, not dismantled. These were questions that could only be answered in the fullness of time. She must have patience and fortitude. She found that recently the former was somewhat harder to achieve for she had been given a taste of what life could become, even for women in service such as her and she so wanted for change to come sooner rather than later. She could feel her pulse quicken at the thought that she was living and working in such times. Surely in London there would be opportunities. She hoped Miss Clara would be allowed to return, and that they could explore those opportunities together. She could never enter the sector of society that Clara belonged to, but they could both, in their own separate ways, ensure that they would not give up their right to strive for a better future.

PART TWO

# CHAPTER FOURTEEN

*November 1913*

As the train click clacked on through the Hampshire countryside and towards the city, Kate wondered what her new
life would be like. She had never travelled any further than
Andover and she had certainly never expected to be journey-
ing on a train towards the capital.

'It's not the city proper, you know,' Mrs B had informed
her. 'If you think we're going to be seeing Buckingham
Palace and the Changing of the Guard, you'd better think
again. Besides which we're not likely to see much holed up
inside the new place, there'll be too much to do. And you can
forget going home any time soon, young lady. We'll be busy
getting everything straight, the way the mistress likes it. She's
decided already that we shan't be doing any entertaining this
Christmas. Wants to keep it just a small family event this
year she says, to make it easier on me. I have my suspicions
there's other reasons, though, like moving house and coping
with a wayward daughter and a demanding husband is all too
much for her. She's arranged for Miss Clara to stay with her
aunt down in Gloucestershire and Master Philip is going to
the Carnforth's apparently.'

Kate knew she could always rely upon Mrs B to be forth-right. She was never one for over-egging the pudding. She was disappointed to hear that both Philip and Clara would not be coming home for Christmas but there was little she could do about it. She was here, travelling to London and life was going to be very different from now on.

Kate took a long look as the fields and farms flicked before her eyes, a kaleidoscope of greens and yellows and browns. The undulating ground, veined with tracks and roads, connecting the hamlets and villages together. Her heart took a sudden tumble as she realized the chasm that was opening up between her and all that she was familiar with, her homeland diminishing into the distance until it became a tiny spot on her memory. How would she ever find her way back? She closed her eyes for a moment to picture Micklewell. Her birth-place lay some distance from the train track but as they passed Hook station, she took herself on a mental journey. She could almost see the white signpost on the outskirts of the village indicating Nately Scures and Up Nately, the row of thatched cottages on the banks of the stream and the smithy where the furnace was glowing. She smiled as she imagined the Taylor sisters out tending their garden and old Nethersole mending his bicycle. She shivered at the thought of the adder catcher, Brusher Mills, outside the Queen's Head Inn with his bag of wriggling cargo, his guarantee of payment for clearing the grounds around Micklewell House.

The train gave a jolt and she opened her eyes. They had left the wide-open spaces behind. There were a great many more houses, carts, cabs, motorcars and people.

'Oh my goodness, Mrs B, what is that?' Kate said.

'That, my dear, I believe, is an omnibus. I've heard about them but never seen one,' Mrs B replied.

'But there are people on the top and below. How many people can it carry, do you think?' Kate asked.

'I have no idea, Kate. You must ask Mrs Winton when we're all settled or, better still, Master Thomas. No doubt he knows all about them, how they work and all.'

The train was slowing and the platform swept into view.

'Oh my, we're here,' Mrs B exclaimed and immediately jumped up.

'But the sign says Clapham Junction,' Kate said.

'Yes, don't you remember, Mrs Winton said that we must change here and take the Forest Hill train?' Mrs B snapped, struggling with her bags. 'Don't you listen to anything I say?'

The two women hurried out of the train and stood on the platform bewildered by the movement of people and the signs. Kate had no idea which direction they should go in. Unfamiliar sounds and smells surrounded them. Smoke billowed from waiting trains and brakes squealed.

'Mind yer backs,' a barrow boy shouted, as he struggled by with a cart loaded with bags and boxes. They moved quickly to one side only to be in the path of another stream of people descending a staircase. Kate noticed Mrs B's colour turning from pink to purple, and the little beads of sweat forming on her forehead. Her hat had slipped over one eye and the other held a startled expression as if she couldn't quite believe where she was.

Kate offered to carry one of Mrs B's bags along with her own and approached a man in uniform to ask where they might catch the Forest Hill train. The man pointed them down the staircase towards a tunnel which took them under the track to platform three, where Kate helped Mrs B to a bench to sit and regain her composure. A large gantry indicated that their train would be leaving in ten minutes.

'Not long to wait,' Kate said.

'I just hope someone on the staff has thought to get in some provisions,' complained Mrs B. 'I'll be good for nothing when we get there. No good expecting me to cook without having a cup of tea. Good thing I thought to pack a couple of slices of me best fruit cake,' she said.

Kate was starving hungry. It seemed an age since breakfast but, with any luck they would be there soon, and be able to put their feet under their new kitchen table. She wondered what the other servants would be like, but felt that no one would ever replace Eliza in her affections. She wondered what Eliza was doing now, at this very moment and if she was missing her too?

'Come on then, Dolly daydream,' Mrs B said. 'Train's pulling in, let's get aboard.'

As they stepped out from Forest Hill railway station, Kate felt insignificant. People brushed past her, intent on their own path and no one looked her in the eye. Finally, she managed to catch someone's attention and asked which way for Dartmouth Road. Mrs Winton had said it was walking distance, and that therefore they would not need to take a cab but, by the time they arrived, Mrs B was on her last legs. Vanburgh House was much larger and grander than the house they had left behind in Andover, but Kate was too tired and Mrs B too cranky for them to do more than just relieve their aching arms of their baggage and thankfully accept the offer of a reviving cup of tea. Kate was pleased to find that her new roommate and serving companion was a smiling sort of girl, with round cheeks and even rounder waistline, who was happy to show them the essential rooms of the house while the kettle boiled.

'Elders and betters first,' said Mrs B. 'I don't know how much longer I could have waited,' and she disappeared outside the back door as fast as her weary legs could carry her.

Kate watched as the newly appointed girl, Mary, busied herself about the kitchen, boiling the kettle and setting out the tea things. She couldn't help but think how different she was to the Mary she had gone to school with back in Micklewell, she was as broad as Mary White was tall and quite a contrast to her old friend. She had a similar kindly look to Eliza, though, and that made Kate feel more at ease. Perhaps she and Mary would become friends too? She hoped so, for she was beginning to feel homesick and lost. She felt like a small person in a big place that was far outside her experience and understanding. At least she had Mrs B, though. For all her gripes and groans, Mrs B had a kind heart and her presence gave Kate a little reassurance that she was not completely without a familiar face to rely upon. There were many other girls in service who would be far from home and alone. At least she knew the Winton family and Mrs B.

# CHAPTER FIFTEEN

*March 1914*

Forest Hill was a pleasant enough place to be. The streets were wide and, when Kate was out on errands or with the children, she was fascinated by the people, the elegant fashions and the number of motor cars. Andover had been a busy place to her, coming as she did from a small village in the heart of the Hampshire countryside, but to be on the outskirts of the capital city broadened Kate's horizons and altered her perceptions of the world. Who'd have thought that a little Hampshire girl would be living in London of all places?

Life soon settled into a pattern. Her main duties had changed a little in that she spent a good deal of her time going back and forth to the children's schools. The walk took about fifteen minutes and they did it every school day morning, unless the weather was so bad that the children would've been drenched before they got there. On those mornings they were permitted to take a cab, but she was told to take the best and biggest umbrella and wear her galoshes for the walk back.

Dulwich College was the far side of the gardens surrounding the Horniman Museum. She encouraged the children to play tag or follow-the-leader on the way to make Thomas hurry along. If Thomas was in one of his silent, uncooperative moods she'd introduce I Spy, for he was always more interested in mental than physical games.

The grounds were an absolute joy to walk through and, once the children were safely delivered, Kate delighted in taking her time on the return journey, ambling along and enjoying her freedom. She walked the children as briskly as possible down the main avenue going towards the school but on her way home, weather permitting, she wandered beside the water gardens, the wishing seat and the putting green. The tall trees reminded her of her Hampshire home and, when they were in bud in the spring, she stood beneath them looking through the woven scramble of their branches to the sky. At those moments she felt as if she could float away. She cherished her time in the gardens and took great pleasure in exploring different areas as the year progressed.

One morning, Kate took a path she had never taken before. In one corner of the outer reaches of the garden, she noticed a group of trees showered in white. She recognized the clusters hanging beneath the branches. Before she even got close to them, she could smell the familiar perfume. One of her favourite tasks at this time of year in Micklewell was to pick the lacy capped flowers of the elder tree with her mother and sister and make the thick cordial that filled the air with the scent of summer. Before she could stop her hand from reaching, she'd picked one of the clusters and brought it to her nose. She inhaled deeply.

'Oy, you're not supposed to pick the flowers. Can't you read?' a young man called, indicating one of the many signs about the gardens.

Kate dropped the bloom instantly. 'I'm sorry, I didn't think,' she stuttered.

'No, you didn't,' the young man said.

He wore a navy flannel shirt and peaked cap, which made him look official, although his boots were muddy, and he had a wheelbarrow with him with a fork and spade poking out of it. His jacket was flung over the side of the barrow and he stood with both arms folded across his broad chest. Kate noticed the sleeves of his shirt were folded up and his lower arms looked firm and strong and covered in dark hair. When a smile cracked across his face, Kate felt relieved. It altered his appearance completely. It was quite a handsome face, Kate thought, wide-set eyes and heavy brows with a strong chin, peppered with stubble and a bold moustache. His hair, hidden mostly beneath the cap, was very dark and curled around his ears.

When he saw Kate's blushes he laughed. 'Don't worry, I won't tell on you,' he said.

He came towards her and swept up the elderflower cluster in his hands. 'Mmm, I can tell why you felt tempted,' he said. 'Such a wonderful perfume. Nature's is always best,' he added, cupping the cluster in his hands and holding it to his face.

'Reminds me of home,' Kate replied, emboldened by his friendliness.

'Which is where?' he asked.

'A long way from here, in the country, I was born in Hampshire,' Kate said.

'And what brings you to the city?' he asked.

'I'm a nursemaid. I work for a family. We moved here in the autumn,' Kate replied.

She didn't know if she should be talking to this stranger in such a personal way but she didn't feel at all threatened by him. He put her at ease and it was a change to talk to somebody outside the household, someone who appeared to want to talk to her.

She was aware of the morning disappearing faster than she wanted it to and asked him if he knew the time.

'Just come from my tea break,' he said, 'so it'll be about quarter to ten. I start work at six thirty every morning.'

'Oh, my goodness, I must go! I've got errands to run before I go back,' she said. 'It was nice to meet you.'

'Likewise, Miss . . .'

'Truscott, Kate Truscott,' she replied.

'Well, Kate, I'm here most mornings, except on a Sunday. That's my day off,' he said. 'The name's Archie, Archie Mabbs. I hope to see you again.'

'Yes, yes . . .' Kate called back to him as she walked away. She turned her head so that he couldn't see her cheeks reddening and her lips curving into a self-conscious smile.

Kate did see him on many occasions after that day. She learned that he'd been a gardener at the museum since he'd left school. They got on really well and either exchanged a brief good morning chat or talked for longer, depending on her duties for the day. He was learning a lot about trees and plants and growing things, and he'd a great deal of respect for Mr Fellows, the head gardener. Archie explained that his ambition was to become the head gardener too one day and Kate told him that if he continued to study and learn and work hard then there was no reason why that couldn't happen.

She confided in him, explained how much she missed Eliza and Clara and how, although Mary was pleasant enough, she didn't have the same spark that Eliza had and she was not as funny, they didn't laugh as much together and she missed that. She told him of her interest in the suffragette movement and how she was sorry that her contact with the organization had come to a halt since she'd moved to Forest Hill.

He was intrigued with the idea of Votes for Women but didn't understand why it was causing women to throw themselves under horses, break windows and get themselves arrested.

'Sometimes trying to change things by shouting loudly just isn't enough,' Kate said. 'There are times when action must be taken, wouldn't you agree?'

'Depends,' Archie replied, 'on who's doing the acting and what the consequences are. Is it worth going to prison for?'

Kate decided she wouldn't argue the case with Archie just now, as they had only known one another a short time, but it was a topic only shelved not forgotten.

She found in Archie a new friend and they soon became comfortable in one another's company in their snatched morning moments together. He wasn't Philip but he was a likeable man.

As the summer months moved on, Kate found she was less homesick but she still missed the fun and laughter that Miss Clara and Master Philip had brought to the old house. She willed the time to pass quickly, looking forward to when they would once more share good times together.

Kate hadn't discovered much about when she would see Miss Clara again. The only news she had was when she saw Master Philip briefly on a rushed visit at the end of the college term. The meeting had left Kate concerned for Clara's well-being. Philip had told her of his sister's unhappy state, and how her letters were full of an eagerness to be free of what she described as 'complete torture to the body and the soul'. The young women at the academy were obnoxious in the extreme, she'd written, they talked of nothing but coming out balls and eligible young men. Apparently, the young men were either 'chinless wonders' or 'dowry-seeking opportunists'.

The description made Kate and Philip laugh. She so enjoyed his company and she was beginning to feel that she wanted to be more than a friend to Philip. She suspected that there might be similar feelings for him too; his gaze lingered on her face whenever they saw each other. When their eyes met or their bodies accidentally touched, she tingled in a way that she couldn't control.

She wanted to keep him talking and said she was sad to hear that Clara was so unhappy. She asked Philip if she might write to her but he explained that there would be little point as Clara was about to embark on a tour of Europe with her aunt.

'They will be moving from one city to another,' he said. 'Aunt Beatrice can be a bit if a tartar sometimes but at least Clara will be seeing some of the world. A step up from being stuck inside that stuffy finishing school. Appropriate name, don't you think? It would certainly finish me off.'

'What about you?' Kate asked. 'Will you be going on your travels too?'

'Unfortunately not,' Philip replied. 'I have important exams coming up and I will be tied to my desk with a pen in my hand. Once they're over, though, Carnforth and I plan to go to Scotland for the stag hunting. The season opens on July 1st.'

'Stag hunting! I'm not sure I could . . .' Kate began.

'No, I'm not sure I want to shoot them either but the stalking is a wonderful experience apparently. At least that's what Carnforth tells me.'

'So you'll both be away all summer?' Kate asked, a tinge of sadness in her voice.

'We'll both be back in August,' Philip replied. Kate was relieved to hear that and allowed herself to hope that, once Clara and Philip returned, things might return to how they were in Andover. But was this just a childish wish? Life moved forward; that was the nature of things. Miss Clara and Master Philip's lives were so far removed from her own life of service that things were bound to be different between them. They were all turning into different people and she wanted to stop the changes that separation and new experiences were making, hold up the passage of time and apply a brake to their growing apart. Whenever wishful thoughts of turning back the clock crept into her head, she reprimanded herself.

'Grow up, Kate and accept what must be,' she said to herself. 'Remember the rhyme . . . If wishes were horses then beggars would ride.'

# CHAPTER SIXTEEN

*June 1914*

Kate was due some time off and when she told Archie, he insisted that she should come to tea and meet his mother.

'I've told her all about you,' he said. 'She'd like to meet you. Will you come?'

Kate was taken aback by this sudden invitation. She had thought that they might go somewhere else together, explore a different part of the city. Perhaps even take an omnibus ride if it wasn't too expensive.

'Of course, if you think it's too soon. You know, if you think I'm being too forward, expecting too much,' he began.

'No, no, it's just that . . .'

'What then?'

She didn't know how he would take it, but she would say it anyway.

'Well, I'd hoped we might go somewhere. I've not seen anything of London except the inside of Vanburgh House, the shops hereabouts and these gardens,' Kate replied.

'All right, but can I tell my mother that you'll come and meet her soon?'

'Yes,' replied Kate, 'tell her, soon.'

That Sunday, at one o'clock, Archie arrived to escort her for their afternoon out. She appeared dressed in her best white-starched blouse and dark-grey skirt. Around her shoulders, she wore a warm shawl in case it got cold later on, hand-crocheted by her mother, and she had polished her one good pair of lace-up shoes. Mrs Bowden had said that she really couldn't step out without a hat and had lent Kate her own 'Sunday best', with a wide brim and two large blue flowers attached to a blue and green hat band. Kate felt like a real lady as she approached Archie, who was waiting on the pavement a suitable distance away. Kate thought he looked quite the gentleman in his clean white shirt, waistcoat and jacket.

'My but don't you look a picture.' He beamed. 'Now, I hope you've worn comfy shoes because we've got a bit of a walk ahead of us.'

Kate nodded and smiled to herself. So, they were going on an adventure.

'We're about to see one of the—'

'No, don't tell me,' Kate interrupted. 'I like surprises, the good sort anyway.'

They walked on through the familiar route of Horniman's Gardens and right by the museum itself. So that wasn't it! She would like to see inside one day but she wasn't disappointed, for to be going somewhere entirely new was much more exciting.

On a Sunday afternoon there were many people in the park, families out spending time together, children playing happily, bowling hoops and skipping. When they passed through the gates at the far end Kate felt a tingling in her fingertips and a buzzing in her head. Where were they going? Archie took hold of her arm and tucked it through his.

'Just in case anyone should bump into you or you should step off the pavement in front of one of those motor cars. We couldn't have that, could we? It would spoil our day,' he said, winking.

After walking along the edge of another park they reached a high point and an elegant mansion.

'That's Westwood House,' Archie explained. 'Wouldn't it be grand to be Head Gardener there? Not long now and we'll be on the downward slope,' he said as Kate paused for a rest.

It was just a few minutes later when they entered another parkland and in the distance Kate could see what looked like a glasshouse. She held her breath for a moment, stood still and stared. It was so vast that she couldn't believe a structure of such size could be made almost totally of glass. All that she could manage to say was, 'Oh, oh my.'

'Isn't it something? I knew you'd like it,' Archie said squeezing her hand.

'Oh Archie, I've never seen anything quite like it,' she whispered.' It's like a glass church rising up to the sky. To the glory of . . . of . . .'

'Of God?'

'No, it's not like a church at all. I feel as if it was made for worship but not of God. It's like a monument to the achievements of man, as if whoever made it was seeking to do something that had never been done before.'

'Well, there's certainly nothing else like it that I've ever seen,' Archie said. 'It was Prince Albert's idea, so I'm told. Though I don't think he even lifted a pencil to draw it, let alone a shovel to dig the footings.'

They laughed a good deal about the sight of the prince in work boots and an ermine cloak. There was no doubt about it, Kate enjoyed Archie's company and for a while, when she was with him, she forgot about Philip. Archie was a good man, but meeting his mother, well that might give him ideas. She didn't feel ready. Kate asked if they could sit for a while, and Archie found them a bench where they could rest and admire the building. He explained that it was called the Crystal Palace and it was built for the Great Exhibition.

'Did you go?' Kate asked.

'I wasn't even born, Kate, and neither were you. It was 1851. Even if we had been alive then, that wasn't for the likes of you and me. Only the richest could afford the entry fee.'

She had so much to learn. There was so much out there in the world to discover. They strolled around the park for some time until the evening air began to cool and Kate wrapped her shawl more tightly around herself. They agreed that it was time to leave as the walk back would see the best of the daylight out. When they reached Westwood Hill again the evening was getting cooler. Kate was shivering despite the climb and Archie removed his jacket to put around her shoulders. As he lifted it over her head, he drew her to him and kissed her briefly but sweetly on the lips. Apart from pecks on the cheek in the playground as a girl, Kate had never been kissed. She raised her hand and touched her own lips with her fingertips as if to hold the feeling there a little longer.

'I'm sorry, I shouldn't have,' began Archie. 'It's just you're so lovely,'

Kate did for a moment wish it was Philip who had given her that kiss, but she brushed the thought away, placed one finger over his lips and then returned the kiss. She could feel a turning in the pit of her stomach like the falling sensation on a swing. Sometimes just one day could change many things. Today had been full of surprises, of the good sort, she decided. She would wait and see what the following days would bring.

# CHAPTER SEVENTEEN

*August 1914*

The twins almost collided with Kate as she was passing the sitting-room door with a basket full of freshly laundered clothes. They danced around her calling out, 'Hoorah! Hoorah! Hoorah, hoorah, hoorah!' She placed the basket on the floor and stood waiting for them to calm down.

'What's got you two so excited?' Kate asked.

Mrs Winton appeared behind them with Thomas and said, 'Quiet children, do stop shouting. You are making my head ache. Your brother is pleased too but do you see him making such a fuss?' The twins looked suitably chastened but continued to make little nodding and smiling gestures to each other. Mrs Winton turned to Kate. 'Philip and Clara are coming home. Their rooms need to be aired and made ready. Would you tell Mrs Bowden please, Kate?'

Kate felt a thud in her chest. She tried to control her breathing and not let her face betray her joy. She had missed both Philip and Clara so much. Hearing of Philip's return particularly made her light-headed. She could feel his breath on her face and hear the unmistakeable tenderness in his voice when he spoke to her. How would their first meeting

106

be? She could expect too much but she couldn't stop herself from dreaming.

'We can play hide and seek and Grandmother's Footsteps. So much more fun with all of us!' Simon said.

'Ooo, yes, Clara's so good at hiding,' Sophie added.

'And Philip can help me with my Latin,' Thomas joined in. 'If I'm to be a scientist or a doctor, Latin's important, you know.'

Kate smiled at the simplicity of the children's desires. Hers were so much more complicated. She wanted to share her own excitement with someone too but who could she tell? Perhaps, in time, she would be able to confide in Clara. Their friendship had developed through their shared interest in the suffragette movement but would Clara understand the love she felt for her brother? Or would she dismiss Kate's feelings as a completely impossible situation that could never be reconciled with their social differences? And what of Philip? Were his feelings for her as strong? Would he dare to go against his parent's expectations? The spiralling circle of questions made her head throb.

Her only option was to deal with these things one at a time. She would try to gain some impressions of how Clara might have been changed by her recent experiences. She might come home a different Clara to the one who left. She hoped she would be able to see Clara in private, although given all the hullabaloo around their imminent arrival, she thought it unlikely. She had been instructed to assist Mary in the making up of the bedroom that was to be Clara's. As well as airing the room, there should be freshly laundered sheets. The rugs were to be beaten and fresh flowers needed to be picked from the garden.

'Roses, Kate, the pink and yellow ones will look well in that room and they smell so beautiful,' Mrs Winton instructed.

Kate was just adding the finishing touches and plumping up the cushions on the window seat when she saw a carriage pull up outside. She hardly recognized the young woman who got out. She was wearing a neat hat with a huge green, white and blue band around it finished with a bow on the side. Her hair was swept up neatly inside it. A shawl collar edged her pale green dress with pin tucks on the sleeves and, as the coachman took her hand, Kate could see she wore delicate, white gloves. So, this was what finishing school was meant to achieve, Kate thought. She wondered how Clara felt about being sent away and if she was relieved to be home? She must have so much to tell about her travels in Europe.

She didn't have to wait long for as soon as Clara had entered the house and been greeted by her parents, she heard the clatter of feet down the stairs and cries of, 'Clara, Clara, you're home, come and play with us, come and play. I have a new doll's house.' Sophie's voice rang out along the landing.

'And I have the best set of soldiers,' added Simon.

'Where's Thomas?' Clara asked.

'Thomas will be somewhere with his nose in a book,' Mrs Winton said. 'Don't expect an enthusiastic welcome from him. He's a studious boy, my dear. He doesn't see the need for such outbursts of emotion. He'll seek you out soon enough, no doubt, Clara, when he has some piece of new information to impart.'

Clara was swept up the stairs in a tide of pulling, pushing and talking and, when Kate greeted her at the door of the nursery, it was as if she had never been away. Her hat removed and her hair already slightly dishevelled, she beamed at Kate and said, 'I've so missed that smiling face. Oh, Kate, it's good to be back. I can't tell you what a prison I've been in for the past few months. It feels like years. Even the Europe tour didn't lift my spirits much. I just exchanged one gaoler for another. Aunt Beatrice is such a puritan. She's stuck in the past. Paris and Venice would have been so much more fun if you'd been there with me.'

'It's good to see you, Miss Clara, I'm so pleased you're back,' Kate replied.

'Now, you must tell me everything,' Clara said, taking Kate's hands. 'We have a good hour or two before dinner and I want to know all that's happened since I've been away.'

They talked and talked while the twins constantly complained that Clara wasn't paying attention. When the interruptions got too loud, Clara and Kate took a moment to admire their new playthings and then got back to the business of catching up with each other's news.

Clara was intrigued to hear about Archie, and Kate was equally intrigued to hear about how Carnforth's letters had been smuggled in to the school.

'Where there's a will there's a way,' Clara said. 'You'd be amazed how inventive and adept at deception young ladies are,' she giggled.

'And what of Mr Arthur Makepiece?' Kate asked. 'Is he no longer after your hand in marriage?'

'I sincerely hope not!' Clara said screwing up her nose in distaste. 'No doubt he heard about the post box thing and decided that I was not suitable material to make polite conversation around a dinner table. Father hasn't mentioned any more about him, thank goodness, and I am certainly not going to raise the subject.'

'So when will Philip be here?' Kate asked.

'Tomorrow and there's to be a dinner, a welcome home dinner party for friends and associates of the Winton family no less,' Clara explained, 'and guess who's coming because he's a friend of Philip's?'

Kate didn't need to guess, she could tell by Clara's expression that it was Edward Carnforth.

Kate was told that she would be needed to serve at table. So, she wouldn't get to meet Master Philip until he was seated round the table with all the other guests. She was disappointed. No, she was more than disappointed, she realized, she was upset. She had tried to persuade herself that she could be happy with Archie and she did like him a lot, he was good company but she couldn't stop thinking about Philip. She didn't want their first meeting for a long while to be in front of so many others, with her as the servant and he as the man whom she could never be equal to. But there was nothing to be done. She was busy in the kitchens and getting the children ready for bed, and he was in his rooms, dressing and preparing for an evening of entertaining, eating and drinking.

Kate served all the guests with their main course but paid special attention to Philip, making sure he had enough of everything he wanted and retrieving more roast potatoes from the kitchen at his request. He thanked her and said to make sure to tell Mrs Bowden that she had not lost her touch.

'Well, we had all better make the most of the splendid food and hospitality here this evening,' one of the older guests with greying hair announced with a seriousness that hushed the room.

'The way tensions are mounting in Europe, we could well find ourselves in all-out war before the end of the year. We've already sent troops into France. And don't expect it to be over quickly. This assassination of the Archduke Ferdinand has sparked quite a conflict. We must expect there to be many casualties and if our enlisted men don't prove enough to defeat the enemy then other means will have to be found.'

'What are you saying, Charles?' a man with a huge moustache and red, veined cheeks said. 'Are you suggesting that things might get so bad that we need to recruit more men?'

'The German army is a formidable force,' the grey-haired gentleman replied.' We must fight might with might. The German aggressors must be stopped.'

'Hear, hear. Well said,' added another guest.

Kate returned to the kitchen upset by what she had heard. She relayed the information to Mrs Bowden and Mary.

'Well we knew it was coming,' said Mrs B. 'The papers have been full of it for weeks. Things were bound to get worse. We can't stand by and let those Germans invade other countries. It will be us next! But war comes at a price and it's paid by the men who fight it, not the men who declare it. My brother served in the Boer War. He came home a changed man. He's no longer in the army thankfully, but it did for his confidence and he lost his cheeriness forever, poor soul.'

'My brother says that he'll go and fight if they need him,' Mary said. 'He's not in the army though and I can't imagine him with a gun in his hand. He's more likely to shoot himself in the foot, he's that clumsy.'

'I can't imagine being asked to kill a man,' Kate said. 'Don't know if I could do it.'

'If you're a soldier and you're called to fight, then you must,' Mrs B said. 'Either that or be killed yourself. A good thing the Winton family are not army people, for we'd be waving our goodbyes to Master Philip and God knows what would happen to him then!'

Kate didn't want to think about that at all. Her thoughts turned to brighter things. She had the opportunity during the dinner to observe Clara and Carnforth. Although they were not sitting next to each other, there was plenty of eye contact and the exchanging of discreet smiles. Carnforth had done his best to impress Mrs Winton and engage her in conversation. She noted that the mistress laughed several times during the course of the evening. Perhaps Clara would get her heart's desire after all?

\* \* \*

Kate was sufficiently concerned about the thought of a war that she mentioned it to Archie the next time she saw him. Now Philip had returned, she felt strange about continuing to see Archie but she couldn't let him down. Archie didn't reply immediately but looked thoughtful. Kate prompted him.

'Well, what do you think about it all, about civilians being encouraged to enlist?' she asked him.

'Kate, my brother's in the army and he's been posted to France. What he said in his last letter sounds serious,' Archie replied. 'There just aren't enough of our soldiers. We have to stop these Germans. Before we know it, they'll be invading our shores. I'm going to be with my brother. I'm joining up.'

'But the war's in France. We have the English Channel between us and them,' Kate replied. 'You don't need to go, Archie. No one says you have to go.'

111

'No one says I have to, no, but I want to. Look about you, Kate, you must have seen the posters on the shop windows, in the streets? Our country needs us. I'm not going to be one of those left behind. It's the national duty of every able-bodied man. I'm fit and strong and I can learn how to be a soldier just like my brother. Besides, I won't be going on my own. There are several of us going from my street; we're pals, known each other since school days.'

'It's not a good reason to go to war, just because your pals are,' Kate argued.

'I don't expect you to understand. My mother doesn't understand either.'

'Well she won't be delighted to have two sons in uniform carrying guns, will she?'

Kate recognized a wild determination in his eyes. His lips were tight set and his hands were placed firmly on his knees. He would not be moved. She couldn't keep her anger and disappointment down.

'Isn't fighting best left to those who are trained to do it?' Kate said.

'We will be trained,' Archie replied. 'I'm fit and able and ready. I want to go, Kate, and there's nothing you can do to persuade me otherwise. I'm not going to be one of the ones left behind. I'm no coward. It's my chance to prove myself.'

'Prove yourself to who? Not me,' Kate said. 'What if you don't come back? What if . . .'

'Don't you think I've considered that? I'm not a fool. I know what I'm letting myself in for, but the alternative is worse, Kate. Would you have me wave goodbye to my pals and not be there by their sides? We'll look out for each other.' He reached across and took her hands.

Kate wasn't sure he did know what he was letting himself in for, but she knew what it would mean for her, waiting and not knowing. She could feel the tears welling up inside her. She had only just found Archie and now he was leaving her. God knows when he would be back or if he would be back at all!

She let him hold her hands for a while longer, her mind racing through everything that had happened since she had left Micklewell. She was good at her job, she was capable of taking on new challenges and she had survived the departure of Eliza. She had found herself accepted by Clara and Philip despite being a servant in their parents' house. Oh God, Philip! What of him? Would he want to go to war too? If Archie was going to join up then surely Philip would too. The tears trickled down her cheeks.

Archie pulled out a clean handkerchief and gave it to her.

'It will be all right, Kate, you'll see. I'll be back home before you know it. And we'll write to each other. It can't last forever, can it?'

Forever was a place that she didn't dare think about at that moment. Even tomorrow, next week, next year was lost in a mist of unrecognizable shapes and shadows. The future was a place that kept eluding her. She wasn't even sure of where she wanted that place to be or who she wanted it to be with. All she knew was that she couldn't hold on to those who were beyond her reach.

# CHAPTER EIGHTEEN

*September 1914*

The letter she received from her mother that Friday morning troubled her, so much so that she was fearful of opening it. Kate had written a few weeks before and had asked about everyone's health, about Dot and how she was managing with the household chores, about the baby, Henry, who was no longer a baby, but a toddler now, and about her brother, Fred. She scanned the letter looking for her brother's name. Fred was just the right age now to enlist. At twenty years old his head would be full of the same foolhardy ideas as Archie. There it was in her mother's shaky handwriting! She could feel the fear in the shape of her letters; touch the tear stains on the page. She saw her mother sitting at the kitchen table trying to work out how to put her worries into words. In the end there had been just the three stark words: *Fred's joined up.*

Kate sat on the edge of her bed with the letter in her lap. So, it was beginning, the world she had become accustomed to was changing again. Mary came into the room and flopped down on her bed.

'I've got to get these shoes off,' she complained. 'I've been on my feet all day, they're killing me.'

114

Once she had removed them she sat wriggling her toes and revived a little, gradually taking in Kate's expression.

'Bad news?' she asked.

'My brother's enlisted. He'll be going to France once he's completed his training,' Kate replied.

'Him and thousands of others,' Mary said. 'That's Lord Kitchener's idea. Mrs B says she thinks that Master Philip will be joining them as well before too long.'

Kate couldn't bear the idea of yet another of the people she cared about getting swept along in this insanity. For that was what it was. Men giving themselves up to be shot. She couldn't forget Mrs Bowden's words about her brother and how his experiences of war altered him, disturbed his state of mind as well as injuring his body. She couldn't bear the thought of Fred, Archie and Philip placing themselves so readily in harm's way. She determined to try to speak to Philip. He wasn't due to return to Cambridge until October and had been working at the London County and Westminster Bank at his father's suggestion to 'get some experience of the real world'. He was often late home. Their movements about the house rarely coincided but she needed to find out about his intentions, whether he was going to volunteer and join the flow of young men leaving for France. Clara would be the one to ask.

Since returning from Malvern, Clara had involved herself in getting to know as many influential women as possible. According to Mrs B, the mistress had given her instructions not to make luncheon for Clara because most days she was meeting with some of the most important women in the area, some of them with titles. She had joined various women's groups. Many of them were suffragettes who continued to campaign for women's rights, but at the same time were determined to do what they could to support the war effort. Kate had seen very little of her as she was busy accepting invitations from a number of wealthy women involved in fundraising. Her social circle moved her far out of Kate's reach, but Kate wanted to know what Clara was involved in and if there was any way she could help. She missed her talks with Clara and the involvement with the suffragettes. The country was at war and she had to accept it, but if men like Archie and Fred could join up and risk their lives, then there must be something she could do to help the war effort too. She also needed to know about Philip. Kate had a plan.

'Mary,' Kate said, 'would it be all right if I take Miss Clara's tea into the breakfast room tomorrow morning? There's something I need to ask her.'

Mary didn't even lift her head off the pillow. 'Anything that means I have less to do is all right with me.' She yawned. Kate was grateful for her tiredness and therefore lack of curiosity.

Clara was surprised to see Kate appear with the tea tray at half past eight the following morning.

'How lovely to see you, Kate,' she said smiling, 'but what's wrong with Mary? Not ill, I hope?'

'No, Miss Clara, I asked to bring your tea,' Kate replied. She placed the tea tray down carefully on the bedside table and stood waiting for Clara to take her eyes off the book she was reading and give her full attention.

Kate's silent still pose must have made Clara aware that something was troubling her for she said, 'I'm sorry I haven't had much time for our chats lately, but I've been busy here, there and everywhere. You might have heard of Lady Randolph Churchill?'

Kate shook her head.

'Well, she's persuaded me to get involved with the American Women's War Relief Fund. They're raising funds to support the war effort. The idea is to set up knitting factories to supply warm clothing to the soldiers at the front. We should be able to pay women wages to work there. There are also plans for a hospital.'

'What about the suffragettes? What will happen to Votes for Women?' Kate asked.

'This is important for the suffragette movement, Kate, our chance to show that we women are as strong as men.

We may not be on the front line, but we can still get things done. There's more to war than holding a weapon in your hands. I feel privileged to be involved in this, to be doing something to help and, of course, it's completely acceptable to my parents. Lady Randolph Churchill's personal invitation, you understand. Father didn't dare object. She might be an old lady but there's nothing wrong with her powers of persuasiveness. Just leave him to me, she said. I don't know how she got him to agree, something to do with her social contacts and suitable suitors for young women who show their capabilities through their actions, I believe.'

'What about Master Philip?' Kate asked. 'Will he continue his studies?'

'He's told me that he and Carnforth will enlist. They need men who can be officers. He's heard from the university. They are writing to all their students to encourage them to sign up. They are both to go to a training camp in Surrey very soon,' Clara explained. 'They seem quite excited about it, but going to war is no small thing, is it, Kate? I just hope they know what they're doing. I will be worried for them, as you no doubt are for your brother too?'

Kate nodded but could say nothing. There was a hollow feeling inside her as if someone had pulled all the strength and resilience out of her. She needed to get home and see her family. She needed to be close to them again. Everything was slipping away and she had no one to hold on to.

# CHAPTER NINETEEN

*October 1914*

Kate nearly dropped the milk pan she was warming , when the knocking started. She went to the bolted door and stood, listening. There were voices and sniggers from the other side. Whoever was out there was making a lot of noise and threatened to wake the whole household. When the banging got louder and the voices more insistent, she waited for a pause in the din.

'Who's there? Stop your banging, you're making enough noise to wake the dead,' Kate said, a note of stern irritation in her voice.

'Open the door, Kate,' came the reply.

Kate's heart missed a beat as she recognized Philip's voice.

'Is that you, Master Philip?' she asked.

'Indeed, it is,' came the reply. 'Open up, Kate, I'm locked out.'

Kate drew back the bolt and stepped back as Philip tumbled through the door. She could see that he was intoxicated. If she'd been in any doubt, the strong smell of whisky confirmed it.

Kate was caught off balance by his presence in the kitchen and didn't know quite what to say to him. She realized that his present state meant he couldn't possibly have shown himself at the front door and she couldn't help but smile to herself that this had given her the opportunity to see him at last.

'You need a cup of tea and I will make one in just a moment,' Kate said. 'I need to take this to Miss Sophie. Now please keep quiet, everyone's asleep.'

By the time Kate got back to the kitchen, Philip was slumped across the table with his head on his arms.

Kate bolted the door. 'My goodness, Master Philip, where have you been? Whatever can you be thinking of, coming home in this state?'

'In answer to your first question,' Philip said, pronouncing each word carefully. 'I've been drinking with Carnforth. He holds his drink better than me. He gave me a leg up so I could climb over the wall. And as to what I'm thinking, well, if a man's going to go to war, then he's entitled to a little drink, I believe.' Philip pushed his chair back and tried to stand. 'He needs to see a little of life, don't you agree?'

Kate caught hold of his shoulders and tried to stop him from falling. Philip turned towards her and whispered, 'Thank you, Kate. You've always been understanding . . . special . . . different. If things had been different for us, then I . . .'

'You're not making any sense, Master Philip,' Kate said trying to hold him up.

'Then actions must speak louder than words,' Philip replied, pulling her to him.

The kiss was long and deep, not like the kiss with Archie. Kate's reaction should've been to pull away, this was her employer's son after all! But she liked it too much. She kissed him back. He kissed her neck and held her gently.

'You're so lovely, Kate,' he whispered. 'I've been wanting to do this for so long, to touch you, to hold you.'

Kate's eyes shifted to the door. Would someone see them?

'Don't worry, Kate. We won't be found. Please stay with me for a while. I don't know when I'll see you again.'

He took hold of her hand and led her quietly into the study, making sure that his shoes didn't scrape across the floor. He pulled her down beside him on the chaise and placed his hands gently on her shoulders, leaning her back. She couldn't stop the feeling that her body was in control and her body wanted him. His mouth was on her mouth and his hands were on her breasts. No one had told her about the tingling, the rush, the sensation of heat and longing. She was overwhelmed and didn't want it to stop. He whispered tenderly to her. She was sinking under waves of pleasure and wanted what he wanted, felt what he felt.

He fumbled with her underclothes and she helped him. The darkness of the room closed in around them and she cried out, partly in pleasure and partly in pain.

'I'm hurting you,' he said. 'I don't want to hurt you, I just want . . .'

She put her finger over his lips and guided him inside her again.

'I'll be careful, Kate,' he reassured her.

When it was over, they lay in each other's arms. His head was on her chest and she kissed his forehead and ran her fingers through his hair. He was breathing deeply. She shifted a little under his weight and he stirred. He pulled himself away from her and stood up, buttoning his trousers. She straightened her clothes and, although she couldn't see his face clearly, she sensed that he was looking at her.

'We should go to bed,' he finally said.

He didn't reach for her hand or touch her again. He started towards the door and she followed.

'No, it's best we don't go up the stairs together,' he said. 'Wait until I've had time to get to my room. There are more reasons for you to be about the house at night than me, Kate. We must be careful. You agree?'

'Yes,' she said, hoping that this would not be the only time they lay together.

\* \* \*

120

Kate woke early from a deep sleep. She ached between her legs and lay for a moment or two reliving what had happened the night before. Part of her was elated that Philip had finally declared what she had hoped was true and the other part was an irritating voice of caution that told her this just could not be. How many servant girls ended up being married to the men who employed them? None.

She thought of Eliza and Mr Winton's treatment of her. At least he'd not taken advantage of Kate in the same way. She suspected that the master's time alone in London, before the family had arrived, was her saviour there. He'd had plenty of time to arrange such secret encounters outside the family home. She believed Philip to be as unlike his father as a dove was to an eagle. She turned to face the wall, with her hands between her knees. What now? How would Philip be with her when they met face to face once more? What of Archie? She should be honest with him but she also needed to be honest with herself. She liked Archie a lot but not in the same way as Philip. Going over and over it all wasn't helping her to decide between them. Must she decide? She could end up losing both of them. It was making her head spin. The world was turning upside down and she was helping shake its foundations even further. There was no one she could talk to about her fears for the future. What had happened between her and Philip could lose her this job if Mr and Mrs Winton found out. She might fall pregnant. Philip might abandon her. These questions had no answers and continuing to dwell on them was not helping. She would just have to keep her worries to herself and get on with her work.

The daily tasks kept her busy enough. Philip did not appear during the morning or, if he did, she didn't see him. When the evening came around again, she met Miss Clara in the hallway and enquired as to how her fundraising was progressing.

'So much to do!' Clara sighed. 'Didn't even get a chance to say goodbye to Philip. He left it rather late to catch his train. He should be in Kingston-upon-Thames by now, officer training for the Sussex Regiment. I never thought it of him. My brother an officer! Proud of him though. We all are, aren't we?' Clara said.

Kate nodded but could not smile or agree with Clara. She was hurting too much inside. He was gone and he might never want to be with her again. She could be carrying his child. Could she trust him to stick by her whatever happened? She didn't know.

# CHAPTER TWENTY

*January 1915*

They had all been gone from home three months now. It was an empty and dismal Christmas, no one had the heart for any celebrations. The new year had begun with little will for wishing anyone happiness. She stood with two rag dolls in her hand gazing out of Sophie's bedroom window. The children were having their afternoon visit with their mother and Kate was meant to be tidying, but although her body was in the room, her mind was elsewhere. She traced the path of a raindrop down the window pane and then another and another. If the weather was as bad in France as it was in England then they would be having a cold and miserable time.

What was it like across the Channel? Was it much the same as England? It wasn't so far away after all. There would be towns and villages, fields and rivers, farms and woodlands. There might even be a village just like Micklewell, with its stream flowing down the main street and sticklebacks weaving in and out of the watercress beds.

Whatever must it be like to be in a foreign land, where the people spoke another language, to walk into a strange place and look for the enemy at every turn, to have a rifle put in your hands and told to shoot at someone? Philip was such a gentle person. She could feel that lingering sense of touch, his hands moving across her body, reading her responses, finding her, holding her. She couldn't see him leading a battalion of men, ordering them to fire, aiming at someone's heart.

Perhaps it was easier for Fred given that he had been taught how to fire a gun by their father. The two of them would go out hunting rabbits or pheasant, or sometimes they would take a shot at pigeons closer to home. She couldn't picture Philip doing the same thing. Archie was skilful with a shovel and a rake, and was strong and hardworking, but faced with killing a man, could he do it? She didn't want to think about what they would see and be expected to do. She was grateful that her father, at forty-four, was considered too old.

She came away from the window, placed the dolls on the pillow and sat down on the bed. She reached into her skirt pocket and brought out the letter from Fred she'd received before he went to France. She unfolded it carefully. The paper was getting fragile and beginning to fall apart along the creases.

*Dear Kate,*

*Well here I am about to get on a transport for Southampton Docks. Next time I write I will be in France. The training was hard but me and the boys are all looking forward to it. We're defending our country and doing our bit. I don't have much time to write more as I have to get my kit bag together and leave soon. I'll be home before you know it and we can eat pheasant stew and have a glass of ale or two.*

*Your loving brother,*
*Fred.*

Kate hoped that he was right and that they could all get back normal. Everyone around her was on edge. Everyone had someone in their family who'd gone to fight. Mrs B had a nephew in the navy. Mary's cousin was serving in the Army

Transport Corps. Mr Winton was always scanning the newspaper reports and Mrs Winton had joined Clara in raising funds to support the war effort. There was nothing else on people's minds.

Mr Winton saw it as his responsibility to keep the staff informed of what was going on in the war effort though, whether they wanted to hear it or not. As Kate finished her tidying tasks for the day she heard the bell that summoned them to the evening report from the master.

She hurried downstairs and arrived at the sitting-room door at the same time as Mary and Mrs B. Mrs B knocked on the door.

'Come!' Mr Winton called.

They trooped in, one behind the other and stood in a straight line, facing the master who remained seated. Mr Winton cleared his throat, folded his newspaper meticulously and placed it on the side table.

'Now,' he said, pursing his lips and smoothing his moustache. 'The current situation is complicated, but I have simplified it in order that you may understand.'

Mary shifted uncomfortably. She'd told Kate that when the master was holding forth, she thought he was going to question her afterwards to make sure she'd listened. He never had yet but there was always a possibility that he might, so Kate attended to everything he said.

'There have been battles between the Turks who are on the side of the Germans and the Russians who support us. The Russians, I am pleased to say, are winning the fight and pushing the Turks back.'

Kate tried to take in the information and listen patiently but was hoping to hear of the British army, not the Russians and the Turks. They were rooted to the spot though and unable to escape or interrupt. The master's voice droned on but he eventually turned his attentions to news closer to home and Kate renewed her efforts to show interest.

'There have been Zeppelin raids in the east of England. Now, I expect you're wondering what a Zeppelin is. A

Zeppelin is an air ship, like a gigantic, cigar-shaped balloon. It's made out of a steel framework and filled with hydrogen . . .'

Some of the more technical details were lost on them and Kate was pleased when the lecture finally stopped and they were dismissed. Mrs B huffed a sigh of relief. She left it until they were outside the door, though, and out of the master's earshot.

The routines in Vanburgh House remained much the same. Mr and Mrs Winton believed that being occupied was a good thing. Kate and Clara did not see much of each other but, when they did, they avoided talking about Philip and Carnforth and the news from the front. It was better not to think too much about what might be happening to them for that was a recipe for sleepless nights and constant worrying.

One afternoon, Kate heard some news about the progress of the war that interested her far more than Russians and zeppelins. She was helping Mary serve the afternoon tea and Mr Winton was reading aloud to Clara and the mistress about the latest battles.

'This report from Sir John French mentions Philip's regiment,' he announced. 'The headline reads "Brilliant Fighting". That's my boy! The Sussex Regiment took back territory the Germans had control over. Says here there was "Great Gallantry in Two Fierce Battles", Bethune and Givenchy.'

'I thought Philip was in Ypres,' Clara said, pronouncing it "eep".

'He was when he wrote his last letter,' Mr Winton replied, 'but remember that once a battle has been won they move on. Got to keep the Germans on the run!'

'I do hope the next letter brings good news. It's such torture waiting,' Mrs Winton said.

'Don't expect this war to be over anytime soon,' Mr Winton replied. 'There'll be more casualties and no let up until we've reclaimed France and stopped the threat to our own country. Quite right too!'

Kate felt the heat of suppressed anger rise up through her neck and into her cheeks. It was all right for wealthy men, such as Mr Winton, to talk about what was right, passing comment from the safety of their own homes. What of those who had no choice?

She noticed the deep concern on Mrs Winton's face and was annoyed at how Mr Winton could be so insensitive. He was talking as if his son was just another number, an anonymous face.

Kate and Mary returned to the kitchen. Kate could barely speak.

'Master Philip is so brave,' Mary said.

Kate didn't reply. The thought of Philip lying injured somewhere, or worse, was too painful. Please God let him come home safe.

Back in the kitchen, they found Mrs B slumped in her favourite chair. They crept around whilst making their own tea, fearful of waking her, for she was a demon if disturbed during her nap. Kate was grateful for the time to calm herself and the sight of Mrs B fast asleep with her mouth open, oblivious to everything, lifted her spirits and made her smile. After a particularly loud intake of breath, she came to.

'Humph!' she groaned, looking in the direction of the kitchen table where the two girls were sitting.

'I was just . . .' Mrs B began.

'We know,' Kate said.

'. . . closing your eyes for a few moments,' Kate and Mary chorused, giggling at each other. Even Mrs B couldn't resist a smile.

'Oh, you two!' She grinned. 'You wait until you're my age. You'll be glad of forty winks now and again. Now what's happened to that butcher's boy? I need the steak and kidney for tonight's pie and should have started it by now!'

As if he'd been waiting outside for mention of his name, the door opened and in came Sam with his striped apron and his bundle all wrapped up in paper and tied with string. He plonked it down on the scrubbed table and said, 'There y'are, Mrs B. Sorry it's late but the bike had a puncture and I had to push it most of the way. Thank the Lord you're my last today!'

'Don't put it there,' Mrs B snapped. 'I just scrubbed that table. Fetch a dish, Mary. There'll be blood everywhere.'

'Not as much blood as is being spilt over there in France, though,' Sam said. 'And on top of being shot at there's a new danger for our boys now — gas!' Sam was always eager to impart any news that he had received about the war. Sometimes in more detail than Kate actually wanted to hear.

'Mustard gas. It burns your throat and lungs if it's inhaled and even if you're lucky enough to be issued with a gas mask, it soaks into your skin and leaves huge blisters.'

'That's enough, Sam,' Mrs B said. 'We don't want to hear anymore.'

Kate felt sickened by what Sam had described. Her thoughts turned immediately to Philip and Archie and her brother. Please God let them not have to suffer such pain.

'Those poor boys being sent out there to their deaths.' Mary sighed. 'As if bullets weren't bad enough, now they're being gassed.'

'There's huge casualties on both sides,' Sam continued, ignoring Mrs B's request.

'The badly wounded are now being sent back home, too many for the doctors and nurses to deal with out there.'

'I wish I could do something more to help,' Mary said.

'What will they do when there's no more young men volunteering?' Kate asked.

'I don't know,' Mrs B said. 'Let's not think about that.'

But Kate couldn't stop thinking about what was happening across the Channel. She was carrying out her daily tasks but all the while her mind was occupied with thoughts of Philip, Fred and Archie.

# CHAPTER TWENTY-ONE

*March 1915*

Kate was on her own in the kitchen. It was mild for March so she had the door slightly open. She'd taken the children to school and put the washing to soak. She sat down to read Fred's letter again, kissed it and then folded it neatly and placed it back in its envelope. She put it gently in her pocket and took out her sewing basket. The children's clothes always needed repairing or adjusting.

Mrs B and Mary had gone to the market, so it was quiet as she settled into the rhythm of her sewing, needle in, needle out, the threads criss-crossing, the cotton pulled tight. Sewing was something they used to do together, she and her mother. If she had been at home now, would she tell her mother about Philip? She thought not; her mother would tell her not to be foolish, filling her head with hopes and wishes, instead of facing up to the realities of life.

There had been no letter yet from Archie. He'd said he would write as soon as he could but there was nothing. Perhaps he was one of the wounded that Sam had been telling them about? She hoped not. She tried to push the thought out of her mind. Philip hadn't promised to write but she still hoped that he would somehow get a message to her that he was all right, through Clara perhaps? Was she wrong to encourage Archie? He'd gone off with a happy heart and, whatever the future held for them, she couldn't let him go to war knowing that she was having doubts. Perhaps she should go to visit his mother and see if she'd heard anything? But what would she say? I'm the girl who Archie wanted you to meet? Her head was all of a muddle.

She carried the mended clothes back up to the children's bedrooms and as she was putting them away, she thought about Eliza and wondered how she was getting on, how married life was for her. She was sure that Tommy would be serving out in France; he wasn't the sort to be left behind. Being without him would make Eliza sad but the thing about Eliza was that, however sad she was, she always found something uplifting and amusing to say. She could almost hear her saying, 'Looks like you've lost a pound and found a penny. Cheer up girl, it's scones for tea!'

She closed the bedroom door and walked across the landing and downstairs. As she straightened the cloth on the hall table, she inhaled the smell of lavender from the potpourri. The beautiful fragrance reminded her of the fields of home. As she entered the kitchen, a gabble of voices told her that Mrs B and Mary had arrived back with the shopping. Mrs B was all of a twitter and Mary was trying to calm her down.

'Now, Mrs B, don't take on so. I'm sure the mistress will understand. She's helping out herself after all and so's Miss Clara.'

'Whatever's the matter?' Kate asked.

'Oh, Kate, you'll never guess what's happened now? Mary is leaving us. She's decided she wants to do something to help with this war. Get me some water, will you, Kate? I need to sit down. As if we haven't got enough problems without you deserting us!' She glowered at Mary. 'And she hasn't told the mistress yet,' sighed Mrs B as she handed over her shopping basket to Kate.

'What on earth do you think you can do? You're just a slip of a girl. You're not a nurse, are you?'

'No, but I can do factory work, like my sister,' Mary said. 'She's signing up to work in a munitions factory and I intend to join her. The pay is good enough too, she's told me.'

'Well good luck with telling the master and the mistress. They're not going to be happy, leaving them in the lurch,' Mrs Bowden continued.

Kate suspected that it was Mrs B who felt left in the lurch. Unless they could find someone else to fill Mary's place, the work would be doubled for the two of them. She wondered how they would be able to maintain things as the Wintons would like.

* * *

Kate's fears proved to be unfounded for a replacement maid was quickly found. She was sorry to see Mary go but life was so upside down anyway that the arrival of a new kitchen maid seemed a small disruption. Mrs B didn't share Kate's opinion.

'We'll be back to square one,' Mrs B grumbled. 'It takes a time to train a new maid and I don't have the patience I used to have. I just hope she's not a butterfingers, that's all. Before Mary and Eliza, we had a girl who dropped everything she touched, she couldn't seem to get the scales right when she was weighing out the cake ingredients and she couldn't follow instructions for toffee . . .'

At that point Kate switched off. She'd heard it all before but once Mrs B was on a roll, woe betide anyone who interrupted her.

When the new maid arrived, it turned out that she was very young but a fast learner. Ida was tidy and precise and had what Kate's mother called an old head on young shoulders. She had a small, round face with big round eyes and a turned-up nose that looked like a button. She scurried about the kitchen and had an uncanny knack of pre-empting what

131

Mrs B was about to ask for. She was already on the way to the pantry before Mrs B had time to shout her next command. Even Mrs B had to agree that she was a very good find.

Kate and Ida were easy with one another's company and Kate was relieved that she had settled into the routines of the household. Ida was shaping up to become a good friend too; she was cheerful and kindly and enjoyed sharing stories of home with Kate. They both had younger sisters whose liveliness they missed, and older brothers serving in France.

'Do you miss your family?' Kate asked Ida one afternoon, a few days after Ida's arrival. They were changing the bed linen, paying particular attention to folding the corners correctly. 'When I first arrived in London, I felt homesick for my family and I missed the countryside, but I suppose you were born here and your family aren't far away. You'll be able to see them more often than me.'

'I haven't had time to miss them yet, there's been a lot to learn,' Ida replied. 'I'm very pleased to have got this job. We needed the money badly. With Dad and my brother in France and there being three little ones at home, Mum was finding it hard to make ends meet. And they treat us well, don't they, the master and mistress? My cousin Daisy, she warned me against going into service. She told me some dreadful tales about girls being mistreated and not given enough to eat. You're better off down the factory, she said. But I like to cook, see, and Mrs Bowden, well she's got to be one of the best to learn from, don't you think?'

'Oh yes, she's a good sort is Mrs B. She might bark a bit sometimes when she feels things are not going right, but her heart's in the right place,' Kate replied. 'Talking of Mrs B, I smell baking. That cake should be out of the oven by now and it's time for tea.'

The clatter of cups and saucers was accompanied by general chatter about the changeable weather and the problems of drying the bed linen.

Ida poured the tea and Mrs Bowden smiled as she passed Kate a slice of fruit cake.

'Our Ida made this mixture, her first attempt, all on her own. She's going to make a very good cook,' Mrs B said.

Kate took a bite and agreed. Ida could never replace Eliza in Kate's affections but she was a good sort and Kate felt she could rely upon her. So, there was at least this one thing that was going right for Kate at the moment. She couldn't allow herself to hope for more.

# CHAPTER TWENTY-TWO

*August 1915*

It was Sunday afternoon and Kate waited outside Vanburgh
House on the pavement. Archie was home on leave and his
letter had told her to be ready and waiting for him at two
thirty p.m. She found it difficult to stand still and kept shifting her weight and glancing up the road. She felt both conspicuous and nervous. How would he look? How would it
be between them?

He might not come. His leave might have been cancelled
or the dates changed. She decided that if he didn't come,
then she would just go for a walk in Horniman's Gardens by
herself. The sun was beating down and she was pleased that
Ida had reminded her to wear a hat. She'd treated herself to a
straw boater and sewed her own blue, green and white ribbon
around the crown. She recalled the final words of his letter:

> *Remember our visit to the Crystal Palace, Kate? It's what's
> kept me going the past few months, the picture of you in your
> Sunday best. Happy times.*
> *Your Archie*

Her Archie? Was he hers? It was true she liked to be with him and the visit to Crystal Palace was something she would always remember, but was it because she had been with him or her excitement at seeing the palace? She wasn't sure. She would know when she saw him, she hoped, for she was aware that continuing to see Archie would send him signals that she wanted the relationship to go further. Something made her hang on to her thoughts of Philip, though. Was it a forlorn hope that he could return her love?

She looked up and saw Archie coming along the road wearing his uniform, the buttons on his tunic glinting in the sun and his peaked cap sitting proud upon his head. She noticed he had a slight limp but that he stepped out with determination and pride. He attracted the attention of passers-by who called out their greetings to him, a man who was fighting for his country.

How surprised she was, then, when he tried to greet her. The words wouldn't come.

'K-k-k-Kate,' he stuttered. 'H-how . . . a-are y-y-y . . .'

'I'm well, thank you. How lovely to see you, Archie,' she said, kissing him on the cheek. 'Shall we go to the gardens?'

'Y-yes, let's,' he replied.

He didn't talk as they walked along and Kate wondered how someone who seemed the same outside could be so changed. They sat down on a bench in front of the lake and he gazed at it for a while. Suddenly he turned to her and kissed her passionately on the lips. He grabbed her so urgently that he gripped her arms too tightly and she felt herself shrink away from him.

'I-I-I'm sorry,' he said. 'Too, r-r-rough.'

'No, it's all right, Archie, really, it's all right. Just that it's been a while and . . .'

He stood up. 'L-let's walk,' he said.' T-t-tell me y-your news.'

She told him all about her brother and how the letters from the front took a very long in coming so it was all old news. She talked rather too quickly but felt the need to fill the space between them.

'He's fine, though,' she went on, 'no serious injuries apart from a few scratches and a bad case of trench foot.'

He nodded.

'Sounds awful,' she said. 'We've been knitting socks as fast as we can, Mrs B, Ida and I to keep their feet warm and dry. Miss Clara, she takes them to her charity and they get sent off to the likes of you and Fred.'

She told him about Mary leaving and how Ida was such a good person to work with, how Mrs B was the same as ever and kept them both on their toes. She tried to make him laugh by telling of the antics of the twins, how they'd got themselves locked in the storeroom one day when they were trying to avoid bedtime and Mrs B had told Ida to lock the door as there had been incidents of theft in the area. Archie appeared to be listening but she could see that his mind was really elsewhere. His eyes kept drifting away and he had a glazed expression. There was a new seriousness about him. The fun-loving Archie had disappeared. She didn't know much about medical things but she could tell when a person wasn't right and Archie wasn't right, he wasn't the same person as the one who'd gone off to war. He was holding back.

Archie remained silent, staring at the grass and flower-beds. Eventually he spoke.

'So p-peaceful here, so quiet. The-there's no g-grass, only mud,' he said. 'There w-were w-wild f-flowers, p-poppies but they all got b-blown to smithereens, Kate. Red petals everywhere.'

Kate reached out and held his hand. They strolled around the gardens until they found themselves outside the gardener's shed which had been Archie's once. He let go of her hand and traced his fingers over the warm, wooden panels. His faraway look told her that he wanted to touch that past, bring it back to himself and make the present disappear. A tear formed in the corner of his eye and he let it find its way down his cheeks until it soaked into his shirt. It was joined by another and another. The silent release of all the pain he felt inside made Kate put her arms around him and hold him tight. She couldn't take away what he had seen or stem the flow of memories that had taken his spirit of joy away from him. She'd thought, before she saw him, that she might tell him that he shouldn't hold out any hope for their future, but she knew now that she couldn't take that from him. It might be the only thing that he could hang on to when he had to go back.

He asked if they could meet once more, before he had to take his transport back and Kate agreed. His mother would be happy to make tea for them, he said. It would be the last opportunity next Sunday as he had to take the train the following Monday morning, his ten days' leave would be over.

Kate returned to Vanburgh House, troubled by what she'd seen in Archie's eyes. He was lost, the man who had courted her with such love in his heart. He needed rest and a return to a normal life but that was not about to happen. What was inevitable was that he would have to go back to the battlefield, despite the effects it had clearly had upon him. His body would recover but she feared for his mind. There was something broken inside him. She wondered about Philip and her brother and Carnforth too. What trials would they be going through? Would Philip be holding on to the memories of that one night spent with her or would the constant fight to stay alive make each day just like the other, a day to survive?

She wasn't sure if anyone here at home realized the damage being done to a complete generation of young men. It was all very well for gentlemen to raise their hats and ladies to smile their approval at a man in uniform, but they didn't have any idea of what these men were going through. She would go to meet Archie's mother, she decided, and wave him goodbye, for what happened over the following weeks and months was not to be guessed at. They must all live with no plans for the future, no hopes and no dreams.

# CHAPTER TWENTY-THREE

*September 1915*

Kate knocked on the door of the terraced house and Archie invited her in. She squeezed past the bicycle in the hall.

'C-careful of your dress, the ch-chain's a bit oily,' Archie said.

Archie's mother appeared, wiping her hands on her apron. Her round face settled on her double chin and her eyes fixed Kate's. Her smile made the creases between her eyebrows flatten and Kate could see that, in her youth, she had probably been quite attractive.

'Pleased to meet you at long last, Kate,' she said, extending her hand.

'Pleased to meet you too, Mrs Mabbs,' Kate replied.

'Archie, take Kate into the sitting room while I fetch the tea tray,' Archie's mother said.

'Please make yourself at home.'

Archie's mother laid on a special tea, neatly cut egg sandwiches, scones and jam and, in pride of place, a Victoria sponge. The tiny sitting room was crowded with furniture but everything was neat and tidy and a smell of polish permeated the air. Kate kept the conversation lively so that worries of Archie's imminent return would not dampen their spirits. She told them all about Micklewell, describing what a free and untroubled childhood she'd had wandering the country lanes and splashing in the streams. She reminisced about how her brother, Fred, had taught her to swim in the river, and how much she missed seeing her baby brother, Henry, grow.

Mrs Mabbs smiled and smiled all the way through the hour or so she was there and talked of happier days when Archie's father was still alive.

'He was a cab driver,' she said. 'Loved the horses, he did. Always said that he would move us to the country one day where the air was clean and we could have our own little garden. He would grow vegetables, he said, didn't he, Archie?'

Archie nodded. He didn't need to talk much, he told Kate later, 'cos his mum did all the talking for him. He walked her home to Vanburgh House and they said their goodbye. He asked if she would try to look in on his mother occasionally while he was away. Kate said she would.

'Sh-sh-she's worried about me, Kate. Y-y-you know, the st-st-st-stutter.'

'I'll visit when I can, promise,' Kate said.

They stood holding onto each other for a long while and Kate kissed him. Now was not the right time to show her doubts. He was going back and, as for every soldier going back, there was no guarantee of a safe return. It did no harm to give him the courage and the hope that he so needed.

'Look after yourself, Archie,' she said.

When she looked back he was still standing there. She smiled and waved and went inside.

It would be several weeks before Kate could keep to her promise. The next time she had a Sunday afternoon off Clara asked her to help at the Bethnal Green Hospital, to carry out non-medical duties and so 'release the nurses to do nurses' work', as Clara explained.

'I'm making a list of women who are prepared to do such work,' Clara said.

139

'Will you help, Kate? I know it's your only free time but we're desperate.'

'Of course, I'll help,' Kate replied without hesitation.

She penned a hasty letter to Archie's mother apologizing and explaining that she'd arrange something as soon as she was able to and pay her a visit. She hoped that she would understand. Kate was excited about the afternoon with Clara.

'Now, there are one or two things you need to know before we go, Kate,' Clara said. 'Firstly, you must prepare yourself to see some upsetting sights. Some of the men have horrific injuries. There are deep wounds and you will be asked to wash out bloodied clothes and bandages. There are men who have had limbs amputated, some lose their sight. What you are required to do is not to show any signs of fear or disgust. Do you think you can do that? These men have suffered enough without seeing horror mirrored in your eyes. Do you understand me?'

Kate nodded. 'I quite understand. I can do it. I'm sure I can do it.'

'Very well then. I will take you for your first introduction to Bethnal Green Hospital this Sunday.'

When Clara said that they would be going on an omnibus to the hospital, Kate felt a little flutter inside. She had never travelled on an omnibus before. They left the house together and boarded the bus. Clara asked Kate if she'd like to travel on the top. Kate was speechless, not just a bus but one that had an upstairs! What an adventure to write home about!

Kate held on to her hat as they began their journey towards Bethnal Green. They were not going so fast that it might have blown away but she wanted to make sure. The lurching movement and the stopping and starting made her hold on to the bar of the seat in front but, once she was settled with both hands securely clamped, she relaxed and took in her surroundings. She hardly spoke to Clara but was amazed at the view from her vantage point, taking in a bird's eye view of cyclists and pedestrians and seeing across walls into gardens.

'Bethnal Green Hospital,' the ticket collector called, and they descended the stairs.

'Now, Kate,' Clara explained, 'I'm not sure what the matron will need you to do but it's likely that you'll be asked to do some of the least pleasant tasks. There'll be bedpans to empty and floors to clean, bed linens to change and sick to clear up.'

'Not a lot different to what I'm used to then,' Kate replied.

'I suppose not.' Clara smiled.

As they entered the severe looking brick building, she wondered what awaited her and followed Clara silently to the area where the soldiers were being treated.

The Angel of Mercy ward was a long corridor of bed after bed. Nurses were moving amongst the white bundled shapes, under which some men were lying prone and others were sitting up and taking a drink or having their wounds tended to. A strong smell of disinfectant hung in the air, mixed with something sour and unpleasant which was unfamiliar to her. A screen was being pulled across a bed at the far end and there were shouts for assistance. A nurse was placing instruments hurriedly into a tray, a metallic clang accompanying each one.

Doors banged along another corridor somewhere and a doctor was being summoned. Kate was overwhelmed by the constant activity and wondered, for a moment, what she had agreed to.

One man, lying on a bed near the door, called out as they entered, 'Here we are then, another angel for us lads.'

'Now, Sergeant, just you behave yourself,' one of the nurses replied. 'Don't you mind him,' she said, addressing Kate, 'he's getting so much better that he'll be off our hands soon. Hello Clara, you've brought us another volunteer, I see.'

Clara was greeted by nurses and patients by name. Kate's eyes swept over the entire room and she could see that, although this particular group of men were very talkative, there were many who were too sick and injured to respond. One, whose thin body looked no bigger than a child's, groaned with every outgoing breath and his head was so bandaged that she couldn't see his face.

Kate turned back towards the nurse, her expression silently questioning what had happened to him.

'Gassed and bullet wound to the head,' the nurse whispered. 'I'm afraid the surgeons had to remove one eye. He's lucky to be here.'

Kate's realization of what she had volunteered for hit her. She expected that nursing the wounded would mean seeing injuries but she had not considered that some of those injuries might be so shocking to see, so life changing. She took in the rest of the ward. One soldier at the far end was calling out with such urgency for help that Kate looked around her to see if anyone was going to him. There was both pain and panic in his voice. A nurse pushed past them saying, 'Excuse me,' and rushed off, calling for assistance from the other nurses.

Clara said to Kate that they should let the nurses get on with their work and took her to find the matron. Before Clara knocked on Matron's door, Kate asked if the soldier who called for help would be all right.

'Some injuries are so bad, Kate, that the men don't survive. It's the sad reality of what we do here. Are you sure you want to do this?'

Kate thought of Philip and how she would want someone to be looking after him should he be lying in some hospital somewhere, a kind face and a helping hand to speed his recovery. She thought of Archie, heading back to the front, and Fred. These men she did not know, these soldiers, deserved looking after too.

'Yes, I'm sure,' she said.

Clara knocked, and a voice asked them to enter. The two women greeted one another and Clara introduced Kate.

'Good afternoon, Kate. Please sit down,' Matron said. 'I'm always pleased to meet another of Clara's young women.

We are particularly in need of extra help now, as we've just taken in another shipload of men. We've hardly enough beds for them all.'

Matron explained to Kate that she'd be given her duties each time she reported for duty by the ward sister and that there would be a certain amount of 'using her own good sense' when something needed doing.

'Oh, Kate is the most able person I know at taking the initiative,' Clara said.

'Well good, that's what I like to hear,' Matron replied. 'Now there are a few things I should mention about confidentiality. These are not normal circumstances, Kate, and we cannot have visitors on the wards. It's too distressing for all concerned. We get servicemen from all over and if local men were allowed visitors then the others would suffer and we believe they've suffered enough, as I'm sure you'll agree.' Kate did agree.

'Now, Clara will introduce you to Sister,' Matron said. 'I'll leave you to it.'

Sister Mathews welcomed Kate and then immediately passed the task of showing Kate the routines of the ward to an experienced volunteer called Jane. Jane introduced her to the clean linen cupboard and the dirty linen baskets, where to find the mop and bucket, the kitchens and the cupboard where the cleaning materials were kept. She showed her how to make up a bed according to Sister's strict requirements and where the collection of books and magazines were kept.

'Some of the men like to be read to, if you ever have the time,' Jane said. 'Main thing you need to know though is where to find the urine bottles and the bedpans.' She opened a tall cupboard door to reveal the rows of them. 'Right, next things next, this is the slops room. We spend a lot of our time in here,' Jane explained.

As soon as they returned to the main ward, Kate got her first call. 'Here's your chance,' Jane grinned. 'No time like the present, Kate! Sergeant Carter needs a bedpan and it looks like he needs it in a hurry.'

Kate fetched the pan and Jane helped her to assist the sergeant whose injuries made it difficult for him to raise his lower body. She waited, turning her face away and, when he had finished, removed the pan. Covering it with a cloth, she took the waste to the toilet area and disposed of it, unable to stop herself from wanting to retch.

As she came out of the slops room, where she'd cleaned and disinfected the pan, one of the doctors swept passed her. At the bed by the window, one of the nurses was calling for assistance. She was leaning over a patient and pressing down on his chest, beating out a rhythm. The doctor shouted for screens and Jane hurried across to Kate.

'Come on, Kate, help me,' Jane called, snapping Kate out of her shocked stillness.

'Will he be all right?' Kate asked.

Jane shrugged. 'Happens all the time in here,' she replied. 'Some of them survive and some don't. You'll get used to it.'

Kate wasn't sure of that but she knew that she must expect more and probably worse. The thought wasn't even cold in her head, when a cry of anguish snapped her out of it.

She turned to see one of the men slumped across the edge of his bed, contorted in pain. She went to him and could see that one leg was twisted under him. She needed to move him and called for Jane to help her get him on his back.

As they pulled back the covers and tried to right him, Kate noticed that his leg wound was bleeding out and had soaked his bandages.

'What on earth were you trying to do, Samuel?' Jane asked.

He managed to reply, his face creased and pinched with the effort. 'Needed to use the toilet,' he said.

'That's what we're here for,' Jane replied.

'You fetch the bedpan, Kate, and I'll get some clean dressings. Now you stay put, young man, and no more trying to get out of bed, do you understand?'

The soldier nodded and lay back exhausted.

Kate knew as she fetched her second bedpan of the morning that there was no room for squeamishness or embarrassment in this job. She knew that these men had suffered much and now they had to put up with the restrictions of being confined to bed and the loss of personal dignity. They had to get used to it and so would she.

# CHAPTER TWENTY-FOUR

*October 1915*

Kate had to put her own emotions to one side and get on with doing what was expected of her. Weeks went by. Her daily tasks went on and the routines took over. She hardly had time to think. She eventually paid her visit to Archie's mother and listened to her read through all the letters he'd sent. While Mrs Mabbs commented on the dreadful food he was getting and worried about him getting a bad chest, in her mind's eye, Kate constantly saw those men beneath the blankets on the ward and the true extent of their pain. As Mrs Mabbs talked about Archie and what a good son he was, Kate tried to make sense of what his words really meant and how much they were a true picture of what he was going through.

She felt uncomfortable listening to this mother who was worried that her son might have a bad cough when he could be lying badly injured in a field somewhere, his blood soaking into the earth. How little they all knew. When she felt she'd spent enough time to be polite, she thanked Archie's mother for her tea and tried to let her down gently by explaining that she didn't know when she would be able to come again. Mrs Mabbs said that was quite all right. 'I understand,' she said, 'you're a very busy person. You're a good girl, Kate. I always knew that Archie would choose a good one.'

She didn't feel like a good person. She had only made things more difficult for everyone by coming here in the first place. Continuing to write to Archie was giving him cause to hope when she was still thinking about Philip. But how could she let him go back to fight with the emptiness of rejection? She couldn't do it. Perhaps that was cowardly of her but there was no knowing what the future would bring. There was enough loss and pain in this war without her adding to it.

When she reported for duty at the hospital the following Sunday, she was pleased to be occupied with young men whose problems were far greater than hers.

'Kate, could you spare a few moments to talk to the soldier in bed number thirteen, please?' the sister asked her. 'He's just been admitted, transferred from Netley in Southampton and he's in a bad way. I think he could do with someone holding his hand.'

As she approached the soldier's bedside, she could see that he had a bandage around his head and an eye pad. There must have been injuries to his legs too because there was a cage lifting the bedclothes away from them. She didn't want to wake him and began to turn away. But something must have told him she was there because as she turned to go, he opened his eyes.

She leaned over to gently touch his forehead. He looked at her for a long time, frowns of pain and confusion distorting his face. After a while she removed her hand and he reached out to take it back.

'Where am I?' he asked.

'You're in Bethnal Green Hospital,' she said. 'Don't worry, you're safe now.'

She turned to get herself a chair so that she could sit with him.

'No, no, don't go,' he called.

'I'm not going anywhere, just to get a chair,' she reassured him.

She brought the chair to his bedside. She didn't know the full extent of his injuries and in all probability neither did he. If she had learned anything from her time at the hospital, it had been that patience and kindness were as important to the men recovering as the stitches in their wounds and the drugs to kill their pain. She smiled at him and sat with him while he drifted in and out of sleep.

She lost count of time and it wasn't until one of the nurses said that it was getting dark and shouldn't she be going that she realized she must leave him. As she stood up, two orderlies walked past her carrying a stretcher. The body, covered with a white sheet, was a reminder of the frailty of every human life. Beneath the loose covering, she could see the shape of a head, chest, knees and feet. Someone's brother, lover, husband, father. That soldier had made it back to England but his family still did not get to see him one last time. It made no difference whether the death was in France or in England, the loss for the families was just the same.

# CHAPTER TWENTY-FIVE

*January 1916*

Over the weeks that followed Kate spent as much time as she could with the soldier who she met on that first day. She discovered that his name was Charles and he was an officer in the Duke of Devonshire's regiment. Being close to him made her feel closer to Philip and to Fred and Archie. She still thought about Archie and hoped one day they would meet again. She could never love him like she loved Philip, she knew that now, but she still cared what happened to him, just like she cared for her brother.

The soldier's condition gradually began to improve. Slowly, the wound in his chest healed and he started taking a few steps with the aid of a stick. The operation he'd had on his damaged foot had been successful and the doctors had managed to save it, although he would walk with a limp now and Kate could see it still pained him.

On cold, bright days, Kate wrapped him up warmly in a greatcoat, with a blanket over his knees, and wheeled him out in the garden. The trips outside had lightened his mood and they began to really enjoy one another's company.

'Ah, here's my private chauffeur,' he said, as she wheeled the chair towards his bed one afternoon. He greeted her with a warm smile as she manoeuvred him into the lift and, when she knocked the wheel on the door, he jokingly said she needed more driving lessons.

'What a cheek,' Kate replied. 'Nothing wrong with my driving. I'll have you know. Perhaps I was distracted.'

'Busy looking out for those handsome young doctors, were you?' he teased.

'I've got enough to contend with at the moment, without that, thank you,' she said.

'Seriously though, Kate. Is there anyone special you think about . . . you know . . . over there?' he asked. 'I bet there is.' He smiled.

'Yes, there is,' she replied. 'Yes, my brother and three friends.'

'I'm sorry. I didn't mean to pry. Stupid of me,' he said.

'No, it's all right. I miss them all but that doesn't mean I don't want to talk about them.'

The afternoon sun was low in the sky but she could feel the warmth on her face. She pushed the wheelchair around the pathways and, although the trees were devoid of leaves and the flower beds were nothing but bare earth, she could feel Charles's joy at being outside.

'Look, a squirrel digging up his store of nuts,' he said. 'Such clever creatures, saving what is precious for hard times.

'Were there times when you had very little to eat?' asked Kate thinking of Philip and what might pass for meals in the trenches.

'Oh yes, plenty of times and when we did eat, it wasn't always entirely edible, just enough to keep us going.'

She wasn't sure how far she should pursue these questions. Perhaps he didn't want to think of what he had left behind? Perhaps it was better to let him enjoy the peace and recuperation time without troubling him with thoughts of his men? But she couldn't help but want to know what Philip and Archie might be living through now, at this moment. She decided to ask.

'It must have been so hard watching your men go hungry, on top of everything else they had to suffer.'

Charles didn't answer but shivered and instead said, 'Could we go back inside now? It's getting quite chilly out here.'

Kate determined not to pressure him into talking any more about the war. On the way home, she couldn't help but think that either Philip or Archie could be lying in a hospital bed somewhere in England and she would have no knowledge of them being there at all. She hadn't replied to Archie's last letter yet. She was putting it off. What would she say? Writing to one man whilst wanting another. On top of that, she hadn't kept her promise to visit Mrs Mabbs but she couldn't divide herself up into so many little pieces. At least she was helping one person. Charles was getting stronger every day. Soon he would be strong enough to go back. What a strange world they were living in, patching men up, making them whole, just to send them back to be torn and bloodied all over again.

Although Kate knew that Charles's departure was inevitable, when she returned to the ward the following Sunday, his empty bed gave her a shock. Being with Charles had helped her feel closer to Philip. Their experiences would be similar. They were both officers in charge of men.

Kate asked after him.

'He's been transferred to one of our recuperation houses for physiotherapy and convalescence,' one of the nurses, a pretty young woman named Rose, said.

'He said to make sure I gave you this.' She handed Kate a note.

*Dear Kate,*

*How can I thank you enough for helping me recover over the past few weeks? You have been my strength and the reason I can return to the battlefield. None of us can say*

*what our destinies will be but please know that the memory*
*of your sweet face and kind heart travels with me. I will get*
*stronger and eventually go back to the men in my battalion*
*restored and revived by your care.*

*With grateful thanks,*
*Charles Spencer*

Kate felt as if she'd been punched in the stomach. An emptiness and helplessness swept through her whole being. She hadn't said goodbye to him, just like she hadn't said goodbye to Fred. She didn't know where Philip was now or Archie, whether they were dead or alive. She needed something to hold onto and the only positive thing was her work.

Kate put all her energies into her work at Vanburgh House and at the hospital. Between the two places she had little time to herself but she was happy for it to be that way. She dreaded hearing about what was going on in this war. Every time she read the old news that came to her through Mr Winton's discarded newspapers, it seemed that another country had joined; this was indeed a world war. The names of places such as Turkey and Bulgaria fascinated her, places she would never visit and people she'd never meet. She wondered what some of these countries were like and why they sided with Germany against the British Allies. She wondered about those she cared for so far from home and when this war would ever end, when they would be able to return. Her head hurt with the thought of it all.

Whenever she voiced her thoughts to Mrs B she was told bluntly that the best thing she could do was to just get on with what she was good at and focus her mind on doing what little she could to help the men who were here. She could trust Mrs B to place her feet firmly back on the ground!

\* \* \*

Ida came into the kitchen and placed an envelope on the kitchen table. They'd just cleared the remainders of the breakfast away and were enjoying a quick cup of tea before the morning tasks took over.

'This one's for you, Kate,' Ida said. 'Post was early today. Must be a new postman. Old Jones must've retired. About time, I say. He could hardly get up the front steps most days.'

Kate looked at the handwriting. It was her mother's. She opened the letter eagerly for news of home. She wanted to hear of how Henry had grown. Whether the top of his head had overreached the markers on the outhouse wall for her and Dot and Fred at the age of five. Five years old and she had hardly spent any time with him at all. Her eyes hurriedly scanned the page but the words they settled on were not the ones she wanted to read.

*heartbroken . . . your dear brother, Fred . . . killed in action . . . come home, Kate, please come home.*

Kate's arms fell into her lap. The only words she could find stuck in her throat but her brain kept repeating them. 'Oh God, no, not Fred, please God, not Fred.'

'What's wrong, Kate?'

It was Mrs B's voice reaching out to her through the mixed muddle of muted sounds that ran through her head. Ida was standing in front of her saying something, but although her mouth moved, Kate could make nothing out. There was a ringing in her ears and a sudden heat flowed up through her body until she felt she was drifting away from them.

When she came to, she was being supported by Ida and Mrs B either side of her. Her head was down between her knees and she let out a groan that came from deep within her. She slowly sat upright, her head was pounding. She tried to speak but the dryness in her mouth made speech impossible.

'Get her some water, Ida,' Mrs B said.

Kate sipped the water and gradually the room came back into focus.

'You almost fainted,' Ida said.

'Feeling a bit better now, love?' Mrs B asked.

Kate nodded.

'You went as white as a sheet. It was a good thing Ida held onto you or you would have ended up on the floor,' Mrs B said. 'Was it bad news? In the letter?'

Kate looked up at her unable to respond for the choking sensation in her throat.

'You don't have to talk about it if you don't want to,' Mrs B said reaching for Kate's hand.

A silent flow of salt tears trickled down into her mouth. 'My brother's dead,' Kate said. Three stark words. The painful truth. 'I must go home.'

Mrs Winton understood, of course she understood. She had a son serving in the army, a son that could be taken from her any day. The news that no parent wanted to hear could be hers and the master's at any moment. Kate felt the flow of deep sympathy pass from Mrs Winton when she said that Kate must go immediately. 'Without delay, Kate. Your family needs you.'

'Thank you, ma'am,' Kate replied.

# CHAPTER TWENTY-SIX

*April 1916*

The woman who walked beside the brook in early April 1916 had forgotten the girl who had left Micklewell three years ago. Where had she gone? As Kate entered the village, she expected to see through the same eyes, feel with the same heart but it felt as if she was walking through treacle. So much had changed since she was last here and she herself had changed too. How could she not? She had experienced the effects of the war first hand, seen the suffering. She was pushing against a force that was sucking her down.

She listened, but the brook did not talk to her, she looked but her vision was blurred. The street was quiet and there was a solemnity in the air. It was the day before Palm Sunday and on a Saturday afternoon the children would usually be celebrating their freedom, playing leapfrog in the field, throwing balls against the wall of the Queens Head, being chased off by the landlord. The quietness unsettled Kate.

As she passed Addison Farm, where she used to work lifting and bagging potatoes, she paused, trying to recapture what that younger Kate thought about then, her nails clogged with earth. Her hands were busy but where would her mind have been? Certainly not preoccupied with the thoughts that tormented her now. Her heart was divided. Her loyalties strong. The comfort she could give to her family would be short-lived. She would only be here for a short time and then she would be going back to her new life in Forest Hill. She couldn't stay with them. A wave of uncertainty swept over her. How could she help them? The pain of the loss of their dear Fred was raw, it cut through to the bone and, as much as she ached with it, her mother and father's suffering would be so much worse. And what of Dot and little Henry? He was too young to fully grasp the meaning of it all but once she had gone back to London, Dot would be left to cope with the emptiness of their grieving parents alone.

She looked past the farmhouse to the fields beyond. In the scoured patterns of the ploughed land, patches of green were emerging. New beginnings. Which crop were they growing in the fields this year, she wondered? How many young men of the village would be here to eat it come harvest time?

She stopped at the five-bar gate and looked for the horses that were usually grazing there. She needed a few minutes to prepare herself for what, she knew, would be such a painfully sad greeting. There should have been such joy in her homecoming. She hadn't been back for many months and now there would be no laughter, only tears.

She noticed a mare in the far corner of the field and, beside her, the wobbly form of a newborn foal. A smile crept across Kate's lips as she watched the rubbery stilts fold and reform under the foal's chestnut body. He staggered about around his mother, her gentle nuzzling encouraging him, as he tried to find his feet.

She was reminded of Fred teaching her to ride a bicycle. How he ran along behind her and held onto the saddle. How she had shouted, 'Don't let go, Fred.' And he'd not replied. So, she'd looked over her shoulder and promptly fell off. As he ran and picked her and the bike up, he'd said, 'See what happens when you doubt yourself, Kate? You were doing it before you thought I wasn't there to catch you. So, you can do it without me then, can't you?'

'I can do it, Fred. I can do it,' she said to herself now.

The backyard was quiet. No Ma hanging out the washing. No sign of Dot or Henry. Pa's bicycle leaned against the back wall of the house, waiting. Kate opened the kitchen door. Her parents sat either side of the kitchen range, staring into blankness. As Kate entered the room, her mother looked up, her eyes red and her mouth trembling. She opened her lips to speak but what came out sounded more like an animal caught by the jaws of a trap. Her mother tried several times to find words that would not form, the sobs of a child struggling for breath, distraught and inconsolable. Her strong, capable mother crushed and bleeding inside with a flow of grief so powerful it overwhelmed her. Kate went to her and knelt in front of her, resting her head on her mother's knees and holding onto her skirts like she used to do as a child. They both let their grief engulf them. Kate felt her mother's hand touch her hair and her back in slow, even strokes until their sobs subsided.

Kate eventually pulled away and turned to her father who stood and wrapped Kate in his arms, his hold so tight she thought her back would break and her lungs be emptied. She felt his huge shoulders heave with the weight of what he carried. They stood together wrapped in a shroud of sorrow until the strength seemed to go out of him and evaporate into the air. He wiped his face on his sleeve and sat back down in his chair, his broken body limp and his broad chest heaving.

They did not need to speak. Kate's mother pulled a piece of paper from her pocket and held it to her chest. She grasped the printed message that every mother fears, as if it could bring her dear son back. Fred was gone. Her sweet brother would never hold her hand or run with her through fields of buttercups again, would never weave a daisy chain in her hair or tease her about her admirers at the May Fair. He would not be there when the other boys came home. A hole opened up in her chest that ached. She sat down and joined her parents in a silent prayer that faded on her lips.

After what seemed like an age, her mother handed her the telegram. The typed words swam through her tears. *Deeply regret to inform you . . . Fred Truscott died in action.* There was a date and a place, his regiment, rank and number, but none of this was significant to Kate. She'd seen the wounds that men received from battle, she'd listened while men suffered in body and mind, she'd tried to make sense of it all. But all she could see now was Fred's face and then Philip's and Archie's and Carnforth's, until they all mingled into one. Is that all they were in the end, a number amongst hundreds and thousands of others? Fred was gone and he would never return. How could that be?

\* \* \*

After sitting in silence for quite some time, Kate asked where Dot and Henry were.

'At the church,' Kate's father said. 'She's taken him to help decorate the church for Palm Sunday. They'll be a while because they're calling at the farm, for eggs, on their way back.'

Kate suggested that her mother went to lie down for a while and that she would get on with preparing the dinner. Once she had gone out of the room, Kate asked her father, 'How's Dot taken the news? Have you told Henry?'

He shook his head and then slumped over with his head bowed, his arms lifeless in his lap. 'We've told Dot but how can you tell a small boy that his brother's never coming home?'

He clenched and unclenched his fists, and then rose from his chair. He walked out into the back yard, closing the door behind him. Kate stood at the window and watched as he took his axe from the shed and placed a huge log on the chopping block. With one swift movement he swung the axe above his head and brought it down, splitting the log in half. He threw the two pieces to one side and took another from the pile. In fifteen minutes, he had worked his way through

158

what was there and the sweat dripped from him. He sat down on the block and put his head in his hands. He came into the kitchen and grabbed his shotgun from the cabinet.

'Where are you going, Dad?' Kate asked.

'Where does it look like?' he snapped.

His bitter anger hung in the air between them. He stopped with his hand on the latch. He turned and gave one brief nod of his head, his eyes empty and his skin pallid. For the first time Kate saw him as an old man, the folds of skin around his mouth and jaw, his scarred and pock-marked hands, his thinning hair and grey stubbled chin. It was as if the years had been compressed into one day, his youth and vigour gone, his strength sucked from him and bones and gristle spat out. The sparse remains of the man she knew as her father had disappeared from view, the shadows had taken him.

Kate knew what she must do but how to do it? Dot was now twelve and perfectly able to understand, but Henry, at just five years old, would not. She had barely time to think of how to explain when the back door opened and Dot ushered Henry into the kitchen.

She put the eggs down and immediately ran to her sister.

'Kate, you're here,' she said hugging her tight.

The two sisters held onto each other and Kate whispered into her sister's ear, 'I love you, Dot.' They pulled away and looked at each other with deep sorrow. Kate cast her eyes down at Henry who was hiding behind Dot's skirts. Dot pulled him out and lifted him up.

'Say hello to your sister, Kate,' she told him.

'Do you remember me?' said Kate gently.

'Of course he remembers you,' Dot said. 'Come on, silly. Say hello.'

Henry mumbled hello and then announced he was hungry.

'Dinner won't be long,' Kate said. 'It's cottage pie.'

Henry looked at Kate expectantly. She knew what he was waiting for.

'I'm sorry, little man, but I came in a hurry. I didn't have time to bring you anything but I'll make up for that by making the best dinner ever. A little bird told me cottage pie is your favourite.'

'Fred likes cottage pie too. Is he coming?'

The two sisters exchanged glances. Dot sat down and lifted Henry onto her knee. Kate sat opposite them, ran her fingers over her face and lips and breathed deeply. Should she tell him the truth? Would her parents be angry that she told him? The moment was now, Kate thought. She didn't let the moment pass.

'Henry, Fred went away to fight. You know that, don't you?' Henry nodded. Dot looked at her, wide eyed. Kate was about to say what her parents and her sister had been unable to say.

'Sometimes in a really bad fight, people get badly hurt. So badly hurt that they can't come home.'

'Is Fred hurt?' Henry asked.

'Yes,' Kate whispered, her voice cracking.

'Do you remember the baby rabbit that the cat caught, Henry?' Dot asked, her eyes filling with tears.

'It died,' Henry said.

The two sisters waited.

'Did Fred die?'

'Yes,' they both replied, their hearts heavy with the knowledge that they would never see their brother again.

'We'll all miss him so much, won't we, Henry?' Kate said. 'We're all so sad. It's all right to be sad.'

Henry looked from one sister to another, then he hugged Dot, wriggled down from her knee and went to Kate. She lifted him up and he placed his arms around her neck. She held him close, his warm breath on her neck.

'We'll pray for Fred when we go to church on Sunday,' Kate said. She let Henry rest his head on her breast for a while and breathed in the warmth and the closeness of him until she sensed his desire to get down. She let him go and turned to her sister.

'Let's leave Ma a little while longer yet. She needs the rest,' she said. 'Shall we go and see if the chickens have laid any more eggs, Henry?'

The three of them went to the bottom of the garden and Henry carried the only two eggs carefully back to the house. They collected potatoes and onions from the sacks in the outhouse, counting them out with Henry as he placed them in a bowl. The two sisters then began the dinner while Henry played with his old wooden car with the wobbly wheels that Pa had made for him. As they settled to food preparation, they fell into the old ways of dividing the tasks between them and chatting as they worked.

'You peel the potatoes,' Dot said, 'and I'll chop the onions. If Ma comes down, she'll complain about the thickness of my peelings.'

'Leave us some potato. We don't want marbles,' Kate said, mimicking Mrs B, and exchanged a smile with Dot.

The potatoes were set to boil on the range and Dot retrieved the mincer from the cupboard and screwed it to the edge of the old wooden table.

'Me help,' Henry said, jumping up.

'All right,' Dot replied. She brought the chunks of left-over cooked meat from the pantry and let Henry turn the handle of the mincer while she fed the meat through.

Once the potatoes were mashed and the pie assembled, it was placed in the oven. Their mother came downstairs, bleary eyed from her sleep and complaining that they should have woken her, but when she'd drunk a cup of tea her good-humoured nature returned.

'You are good girls,' she said. 'Smells good,' she continued, inhaling the rich meaty smell. 'Where's your father? I hope he's back soon. It will soon be time to eat.'

'Sounds like him now,' said Kate. 'I hope he's brought some cabbage from the allotment.'

Jim Truscott came into the kitchen and placed a cabbage, a bunch of carrots and a brace of pigeons on the table. Kate knew that he took pride in being able to put food on the table for his family and, although he still wore a deep furrow between his brows, the physical labour and time alone to gather his thoughts had clearly helped him to calm himself. Kate was aware that his silent contribution to the evening meal was his own way of saying that grief may be gnawing away at his insides but he had a responsibility to the living.

# CHAPTER TWENTY-SEVEN

*April 1916*

Leaving was so painful. The hugs and the held-back tears said everything that needed to be said. There was no alternative; each had to hold on to their own grief. Belonging to a family gave Kate such great support, knowing that she was loved. She loved them all back, but she had to return to Forest Hill, alone.

As she gathered up her bags and Dot held the door open, she knew that she had no choice but to leave them. Dot kissed her on the cheek and held Henry up to kiss her goodbye too. Her mother pressed a small, wrapped meat and potato pie into her hands.

'For the journey,' she said and the two women kissed each other.

'And this is for all of you,' Kate said, handing over a purse of money to her father.

'Kate, you don't need to . . .' her father began but Kate interrupted him.

'I don't need to but I want to,' she replied. 'Take it.'

He nodded. 'Thank you. Look after yourself, Kate.' He held her tightly in his arms. Tears welled up in his eyes and she knew that he was hurting deeply, his first born, his son, taken from him and buried in the muddy fields of Flanders. As she walked away from them she let her own tears fall, for all that now could never be.

The walk to the train station at Hook would take Kate an hour at least, so she left plenty of time. As she walked down past the school, her feet dragged and she felt a compulsion to turn around and run back home. Her sight was bleary and she stumbled over some stones in the lane.

'Careful there, Kate,' a voice said. It was Miss Clarence the schoolmistress. 'How are you, Kate? Your sister tells me that you're quite the Florence Nightingale now, as well as a nursemaid. Have you been visiting?'

'Yes,' Kate replied, trying to cover her red face. 'I'm on my way to catch the train back to London now.'

'What a shame we didn't get to see each other, Kate . . .' Miss Clarence paused.

'I was so sorry to hear about your brother. If there's anything I can do to help?'

At this kindly offer Kate couldn't contain her sorrow anymore and she released all the force of her sadness. Miss Clarence stepped forward and took Kate's bag from her hand.

'Come with me,' she said.

'But my train . . . ?' Kate sobbed.

'There'll be another,' Miss Clarence said. 'You need some time. Don't worry. I'll arrange things.'

When they were inside Miss Clarence's schoolhouse, the teacher put down the bag and drew Kate to her, her arms folding Kate close, her breasts absorbing the force of Kate's sobs, her voice whispering words of comfort.

'What is it, Kate? What has upset you so?' she asked.

Kate struggled to reply, her chest refusing to stop heaving and her breath coming in shorter and shorter gasps.

'Please, sit down for a while,' Miss Clarence said. 'You don't have to say anything, Kate, if you don't want to. Just take your time. I'll fetch you some water.'

Miss Clarence returned and, after drinking the water, Kate managed to say a few words.

'It's Fred,' she said, her voice hardly perceptible. 'He's dead . . . killed in action.'

'Oh, Kate, I'm so sorry. I didn't know. No wonder you're in such a state. Please rest a while. Must you go today?'

'I'm expected back this evening,' Kate replied. 'In fact, I should be going now or I'll miss my train.'

Miss Clarence said that she would hear of no such thing. 'I'll arrange with Florence Taylor for young Jamie Stephens to drive you in their pony and trap. I'm sure they'll be only too happy to help,' she insisted. 'Now, I'll make us some tea. I'll leave you with this to read.' She handed Kate a magazine. 'I think you'll find it both interesting and extremely moving.'

The magazine was opened at a specific page. It had been well thumbed and the pages were beginning to separate from the binding. Kate thanked Miss Clarence and, when she was left on her own, took a moment to take in her surroundings. The room was comfortable and the walls carried many pictures and a huge bookshelf which ran from floor to ceiling. There was a desk in the bay window with writing materials and a brightly coloured shawl hung over the back of the chair. A side table held a vase with a bright bunch of daffodils which drew the sunlight into the room. The whole feeling was one of lightness and calm.

Kate looked down at the magazine. The main article on the page was a poem called 'In Flanders Fields'. It spoke of poppies and larks and guns. She read and reread the poem, seeking some meaning for herself. She looked again at the second verse.

*We are the dead. Short days ago*
*We lived, felt dawn, saw sunset glow;*
*Loved, and were loved — but now we lie*
*In Flanders Field.*

Kate knew that Fred lay side by side with these men that the poet talked about. It didn't make her feel better to picture his body twisted and torn, next to another who had suffered the same dreadful fate, but the words 'loved and

165

were loved' gave her new strength. For whatever this war took from her, it couldn't take the precious memories of a brother who always had time for her, no matter what else he had to do. He would listen to her as she prattled on about the latest book she had read or her dreams to become a teacher. When he set up his shaving kit in the kitchen, he would let her lather up the shaving soap and wait patiently while she applied it to his chin. He let her watch as he pulled the cut-throat razor across his chin and joked about how lucky she was not to have to perform this particular ritual.

She was grateful to the young poet who had brought the experiences of serving in the trenches to those who remained at home. The words of the poem made the harsh realities of life and death on the battlefield clear, but there was also some comfort in knowing that he didn't die alone. As she read it through again, she knew that there would be many more families who'd receive the same terrible news as hers. There would be many broken hearts and empty arms across the country and there'd be no respite until this war was over. She thought of Philip, Archie and Carnforth and wondered if they were, at this very moment, lying in a Flanders field. She hoped beyond hope that they were still alive.

'What did you think of the poem?' Miss Clarence asked as she returned with the tea tray.

'Such beauty in words and yet such a dreadful source of inspiration,' Kate replied. 'How could he write about such horrors?'

'How could he not?' Miss Clarence said. 'He writes because it is the only way he can make some sense of it all. He writes to show us what he and so many other young men are experiencing. To bring us the painful truth. We all do what we can in times of crisis, Kate. You can't help your brother but you can do something to help those young soldiers who need you.'

Miss Clarence was right, Kate thought. She must get back to the hospital. She would return to London and do what she could.

\* \* \*

The train stopped at Woking station, a few passengers got off but more crammed on. The train became crowded and Kate was squashed against the window by a noisy, bickering family with four children. She tried to close her ears to the clamour of their voices. They were just a normal family, doing what families do, but their vital presence only underlined her loss. She wanted to be alone with her thoughts and memories of her brother but she was trapped in the present.

Kate began to feel unsettled and shifted uncomfortably in her seat. Her head began to swim. The air was suffocating. She couldn't breathe. A shudder passed through her and lodged itself deep in her gut. Beads of sweat formed on her upper lip and her hands began to shake. The child next to her was staring, so she put her hands in her pockets to hide them from view. Her fingers touched the bunched and pleated shape given to her at church, the palm leaf. She slowed her breathing and tried to calm herself. What had brought this on? She wanted this journey to be over. She wanted this war to be over.

The squealing of brakes announced her arrival and she lifted her bag down from the rack. As she was jostled along the platform and moved with the flow of bodies, she wanted to get away from all these people, to get back to Vanburgh House. She walked quickly, her shoes tapping rhythmically on the pavement. The sooner she got back, the sooner she could immerse herself in her work.

# CHAPTER TWENTY-EIGHT

*September 1916*

The Battle of the Somme began on 1 July 1916. News of the advance reached England. *All Goes Well for England and France*, the headlines read. *Sixteen miles of German front trenches captured . . . our gallant soldiers . . . many German prisoners taken . . . the great British offensive, for which we have waited so long, has started well.* In the two months since there had been nothing except positive news. *Million shells daily fired by British. German Lines Broken.*

'That's what they tell us,' Clara said. 'But is it the truth?'

'Would they tell us lies?' Kate asked.

'Lies are not the same as holding back on telling the whole story,' Clara replied, 'and I'm not sure we're getting the whole story. Carnforth's letters arrive with sections blacked out, for security reasons they say. The only people who will know are the men themselves, Philip and Carnforth, and at the moment we're not getting any letters, no information at all. We only get to know when one of our own has . . .' Clara stopped herself. 'Oh, I'm so sorry, Kate, I didn't mean to . . . your poor brother . . . I haven't even asked you how your mother and father are coping . . . such sadness for you all.'

'They just have to go on,' Kate said, tears forming. 'We all do.'

'I can't imagine what it must be like to lose a brother,' Clara said. 'I think about Philip every day. Where he is, what's happening to him.'

Kate felt her stomach clench. Her face surely betrayed her. There was an awkwardness between them.

'You are very fond of Philip, aren't you?' Clara asked, in a probing tone. 'It's like he's your brother too,' she added, looking directly at Kate.

Kate faltered. How much should she confide in Clara? She so wanted to tell her the depth of feeling she had for Philip. She didn't know what to say and, when she found the words, they sounded so inadequate to her own ears.

'Yes,' Kate replied, 'I'm very fond of him.'

'What about that young man you were seeing? Have you heard any news of him at all?' Clara asked.

'Archie? No news recently. I hope that means he's all right,' Kate replied, pleased that Clara had changed the subject. She felt the flushing in her cheeks subside and a sense of relief that Clara hadn't pressed her about her affection for Philip. The two men both occupied her thoughts daily, although perhaps not equally.

'I must tell you something,' Clara said. 'I've volunteered for a new project. The Relief Fund needs women to supervise the running of a knitting factory and workrooms over in Woolwich. I'm going to recruit the workers. I need to stay in that area for a while.'

'Where will you live?' Kate asked.

'Oh, the fund has plenty of contacts in that area. I'm staying with friends of the Astor family, Colonel and Mrs Gardener. It will save all the travelling back and forth. Will you miss me?' Clara said.

'Of course I will,' Kate replied.

* * *

169

Clara had only been gone a week or so when Kate came down to the kitchen, one Saturday morning, to a commotion.

'What's the panic?' Kate asked Ida as she scurried about answering Mrs B's demands.

'It's Mr Philip,' Ida replied. 'He's been badly injured and they're sending him home from the hospital to recuperate. Mistress says that his room hasn't been used in so long it must be given a thorough clean and we're even to take the summer curtains down and put the winter ones up, says they'll keep the room warmer.'

Kate's heart plummeted at the words 'badly injured'.

'How badly?' she asked.

'No one knows 'til he gets here,' Ida said. 'Or if they do they're not telling us anything. It's a big job, getting the curtains down out of the loft and giving them a good brush down,' she added.

'Well, you'd better get on with it then,' Mrs B said, overhearing Ida's complaints.

The rest of the day Kate found herself running between the nursery and the kitchen without time to take a breath. Her feelings lurched from excitement to trepidation, expectation to fear. She wanted to see him but she knew they couldn't be together. They would be under the same roof but separate. By the time the evening came she was ready to collapse with physical and emotional exhaustion.

'He's here,' Ida announced. 'At least I think it's him.'

'What do you mean, you think it's him. Either it is or it isn't,' Mrs B said.

'Well he looks different. He's so thin and his face is . . . is . . .'

'Spit it out, girl, what about his face?' Mrs B snapped.

'I'm sure the doctors did their best but . . .' Ida began.

'He's scarred?' Kate asked.

Ida nodded.

The atmosphere in the house was subdued. What should have been a cause for celebration had turned into the grim reality of the true meaning of this war, the sacrifices that were being made. Kate was desperate to see him, but the family had asked to be given their meal and their coffee and then not to be disturbed.

Kate hadn't been called to help in the dining room and had therefore not seen Philip's injuries for herself but, as she came out of the kitchen late in the evening, she watched him, from a distance, painfully climbing the stairs. She hated to see him in this state but at least he was safe, he was home.

Just as she was retiring to bed and turning off the lamps for the night, she passed Philip's room and could hear him sobbing. The sound cut her deeply. She stood and listened for a while, unsure of what to do. Thoughts crowded her mind. He was suffering, alone, racked with the wounds inflicted on both his body and his mind. She knocked gently on the door. When no answer came, she opened it quietly and whispered, 'Philip, Philip, it's me, Kate. Is there anything I can do?'

A low triangle of light lit up the floor. A shape moved beneath the bedclothes.

'Sorry to disturb you. I was wondering if . . .'

'Come in, Kate,' Philip said, in a broken whisper that hardly reached her.

She stood just inside the door and waited for him to speak again. She could see that there was a very pale light coming from a bedside lamp turned down very low. The yellow glow gave the room a sickly tinge.

'Come . . . closer . . . come,' he said. His voice was weak and punctuated with deep intakes of breath.

'I thought perhaps you might like something to drink,' Kate said. 'Some warm milk perhaps with a little brandy?'

The bitter laugh that escaped him then was a shock to Kate.

'Some brandy, yes, that will do it!' he said choking over the words. 'That will make it all go away.'

She knew from his tone that he was mocking her. It frightened her.

'Well, if there's nothing you need then I'll . . .' Kate began to move slowly back towards the door.

Philip sat up in bed and said more calmly and slowly this time, 'I'm sorry. I'm so sorry, Kate. You're only trying to help, I know. I have these times when I just don't know what I'm saying. There's an anger inside me that has to come out. I would like a drink, yes, if it's not too much trouble. I'm having difficulty sleeping.'

Kate went downstairs. The house was quiet; all had retired to bed except her. She entered the room again with the drink and placed it on the bedside table.

'Will you stay a while?' he asked.

'I don't know. I don't think it would be . . .'

'Proper? It wouldn't be proper. Tell me what is proper in the current world as we know it?' Philip spat the words out at her, making her feel uncomfortable. She didn't know what to say. He was silent for a while until he was finally able to gain control of himself. Then he spoke again. 'There, you see, it comes at me just like that. I can't seem to stop it. I'm so . . .'

'No need to apologize,' Kate said. 'I've seen what this war can do to people.'

She tried not to stare at him. In the low light, with his face turned slightly away from her, she couldn't see how badly he was hurt. She could tell from his outbursts, though, that he'd been through the unthinkable and unimaginable. She gently touched the side of his face. The torn and patched ridges of his scars under her fingertips made her start but she wanted him to know it made no difference to her and she leaned over to kiss him.

At the touch of her lips he turned towards her. She took his hand.

'He wanted to know all about it, my father,' he snapped. Kate could feel the anger returning. She let him talk. She didn't interrupt or try to calm him down. She just listened.

'He kept saying what a great honour it was to serve and how well our boys are doing. He knows nothing. Mother just kept on looking at me and weeping. I don't want their adoration or their pity, Kate. I just want to be left alone. I'm here to recover so that I can go back. I have a job to do. I need to get better and get back to my men. I need to . . .'

Kate stepped forward to take his hand. She sat down on the bed beside him and said she would stay with him for a while.

'Don't be kind to me, Kate,' he said. 'I just want you to listen and to be there but don't be kind to me or I won't want to go back and I must,' he said. 'I can't get too comfortable here.'

'But you can rest and I can help nurse you, if they'll let me,' Kate said.

He suddenly lurched forward and grabbed hold of her by her shoulders, thrusting his face up close to hers.

'Look at me, Kate, look at me. That's what shrapnel can do,' he cried, his voice rasping. He began to cough and struggle for breath.

'And that's what . . . gas . . . does to your lungs,' he said. The tears began to flow, tears of anger and frustration. The sobbing and coughing racked his chest and she drew him to her, letting him rest upon her breasts.

Eventually a calmness came over him, he pulled back and said, 'You're a good person, Kate. Has anyone ever told you that?'

She smiled at him. 'Try to sleep now,' she whispered.

She wondered if anyone had held Fred while he died. She hadn't been with her brother when he needed her, she couldn't be there to soothe him and comfort him, but she could be with Philip. He was here, he was real and his pain was real. She could help him. She handed him the milk and brandy and watched him drink.

'It'll be cold,' she said.

'But you're warm,' Philip replied.

They sat for a while in the darkness until the cup began to tilt in his hands and his head dropped onto his chest. His anger had finally dissipated and his body relaxed. She held onto the back of his head with one hand and took the cup with the other. She placed his head gently back on the pillow and then crept towards the door.

'Don't leave me,' he whispered.

She went back to the bedside and sat smoothing his forehead, just like she did for the children when they were sick. Her fingers traced the raised and puckered flesh. His whole body began to shake and she lay down beside him. He kept repeating, 'Cold, cold, cold.' She put her arm over him and held him close.

They lay together, her breasts to his back, her knees tucked behind his knees, her arm across his chest. She didn't dare move for disturbing him but couldn't stop her shivers as the cool evening air filtered into the room. Philip shifted as he sensed the ripples running through her body. Slowly he turned towards her and took her hands in his and kissed them. He threw the covers back and then he rolled her towards him. She let her body fall into his. He carefully pulled the covers over them and they held each other close, until her breath merged with his breath and his lips touched hers. She let her mind drift into a place where there was no time, no demands to call them, no walls to divide them. They were here, together, now.

When the morning light crept around the edges of the curtain, Kate's eyes flicked open. She was still in his embrace. She was warm with his love. She peeled away from him and slid silently onto her feet. He rolled onto his back but his breathing was heavy and rhythmical; he slept peacefully, one arm thrown above his head. She could still feel the heat of the passion between them. He had entered her oh so gently and taken her to a place where she felt as if her whole body would burst with the sheer joy of him. She would hold the memory of this night in her heart. Nothing and nobody could take this away from her.

# CHAPTER TWENTY-NINE

*November 1916*

Every time Kate passed his room to and from the nursery she looked at the closed door. She prayed that the Philip she knew and loved would heal in mind as well as body. When the children were with her, they asked to be able to go in and see him.

'But why can't we?' Simon asked.

'Because your brother needs his rest,' Kate replied.

'When will he be better?' Sophie asked. 'Will he be able to play hide and seek with us soon? He's so good at finding places to hide.'

'Try to be patient, children,' Kate said. 'He will get better but it's going to take a while longer yet.'

She didn't expect them to understand, she struggled to understand herself, even with the sights she had seen at the hospital. The bodies she had seen patched up, repaired and sent to fight again were only part of the man that lay inside, she knew that. What she could never know was how that felt. Philip was broken and she was helpless. Only time could help him mend.

Clara came home as soon as she heard of Philip's arrival but she couldn't stay long. She was needed to continue with setting up the factory. She came to find Kate before her departure and they talked of their worries for Philip.

'We've seen so many men with such horrific injuries,' Clara said. 'But nothing prepares you for seeing your own brother in such a . . .'

Kate took her hand and said, 'He's home, Clara. Take comfort in that.'

Clara inhaled deeply and wiped away her tears.

'You'll be a sister to him for me, Kate. I know you will,' she whispered.

Kate wanted to say that she wanted to be so much more than a sister but this was not the right time.

Over the following days and weeks, Kate snatched every moment she could to be with Philip, offering to take trays up to him and staying as long as she dared by his bedside. She told him about her volunteering work at the hospital and how pleased she was that Clara had encouraged her to go and help.

'Sounds like my sister,' Philip said. 'Right in the thick of it.' He paused then and she wondered what was occupying his thoughts.

He finally said, 'You're doing a good job, the two of you. An important job.'

She took that as a sign of encouragement to tell him more but when she started talking about particular patients, however, he stopped her by saying he was tired or he needed the bathroom. Kate realized that it was too painful for him. It was like revisiting the battlefield and she found other things to talk about, simple things like the antics of the twins and the news from her Hampshire home.

It was over a month before he was able to come downstairs for meals and spend some time with the family, but then he didn't seem to spend very long before he went back to his room.

'They exhaust me, Kate,' he explained to her, 'with their constant attentions. At least you don't crowd me and fuss over me. Your hospital training perhaps?'

Little by little, as time progressed however, his mood swings became less frequent and he talked more. He tolerated the excitements of the twins and asked Thomas to come and read to him from one of his nature books. When they could snatch a few moments alone, Kate and Philip sometimes dared to embrace. Stolen kisses were not enough but it was all that they could have.

'Walk in the garden with me, Kate,' he said one sunny afternoon. 'I want to feel the fresh air on my face.'

'I'm not sure it would be right for us to be . . .' Kate began.

'To be seen together?' Philip said.

'Won't your parents think—'

'I don't care what they think,' Philip replied. 'I'm past caring what people think. I may not come back from this, Kate. We should spend every moment we can together, shouldn't we?'

Kate nodded and fetched Philip's coat and scarf and a walking cane. They walked together in the autumn sunlight and when they were out of sight of the house, they held onto each other and kissed. She felt the passion in his searching mouth and the urgency in his breath. This is how it should be, Kate thought. But their closeness didn't last for long. When they heard voices, they pulled apart from each other and Kate felt his aching for her as she ached for him.

\* \* \*

All too quickly Philip left to rejoin his regiment. She had hoped that he would be medically discharged but, with rest and all the loving care he received at home, his strength had come back and the Philip they all knew so well returned. The rages subsided and the scar on his face was healing. As Kate said goodbye to him, the night before he left, she had to believe that he would come back. He kissed her tenderly on the lips and promised that they would be together again.

'But how?' Kate asked.

177

'We will think of a way,' he replied.

For several days after he left, Mrs Winton retired to her bedroom and emerged only for meals. She didn't even want to see the children. Mr Winton spent longer and longer at the bank and barked instructions to everyone when he got home. Kate found herself losing patience with the children more easily and Mrs B was in a constant state of agitation. As the weeks went by, after Philip's departure, the news of British casualties in France caused more and more concern. Every time the post arrived, Mrs Winton would ask Ida to check if any official looking envelopes had arrived. Her relief when the answer was no, was clear. Simon and Sophie wanted to know about the war and asked lots of questions about what it might be like to be shot. Simon played games with his soldiers in which the British always won and took German prisoners. Kate wished that the reality matched the game.

The first indications came when she didn't bleed that month. Was she pregnant? Could she be carrying Philip's child? If she was then she would lose her job. How could she tell her parents? How would they bear the shame? She didn't really want to think about it or what she would do if she was. She told herself that it was the worry of having lost her brother and Philip's insistence that he must return to France.

She knew the signs of pregnancy, of course. She'd been old enough, at the age of eleven, to understand that her mother's retching every morning for weeks was not a usual occurrence. When her mother's belly began expanding and she found bending difficult, when she became short-tempered with her father, and fell asleep in the afternoons, Kate knew that a baby was growing inside her mother.

Kate didn't have to ask the questions. Her mother, sensing that her eldest daughter's own body would soon be fertile and ready, prepared her for the arrival of her monthly bleeding. So, when the red stain arrived in her underwear, Kate would be ready. Kate really began to grow up during the time of her mother's pregnancy with her third baby. The innocence of childhood had gone forever.

When her little sister was born, she recalled the desperate shouts of her father to fetch the midwife, the panic, the door closed in her face. She heard the screams of pain, the words of encouragement, the pleas of desperation and exhaustion and then, the awful silence. Baby Ellen did not survive. There was no cry as breath entered her tiny body, no movement in fingers or toes, no sweet sighs of joy from her mother's lips, so still, so quiet. The tiny bundle, swaddled in white, was carried out of the house by her father, his head bowed as he hugged his lost daughter to his chest.

Carrying a child to full term and then losing it must be more than any mother could bear, but no one else could carry the burden of that pain. If she was carrying Philip's child then she must face up to the facts and face the future whatever it might bring.

PART THREE

# CHAPTER THIRTY

February 1917

Kate lay with her eyes wide open. It was dark in the room and she'd been awake for hours, listening to the soft breathing of dear Ida. She wished for the arms of sleep to hold her and take her to another place but they were not open and she could not fall. Her hands wandered to her belly and stroked the taut skin. It wouldn't be long now before the mistress noticed. She had birthed five children of her own; the signs would not escape her. She'd been lucky not to have the morning sickness.

Kate had managed to keep her widening waist from all except Ida, who had noticed the safety pin holding her skirt together and observed the absence of Kate's monthly rags. Ida said that her secret was safe with her but that eventually the truth would be obvious. Kate knew she was right but she needed time to think.

What was she to do? Her condition would not go unnoticed for much longer. The time was coming and coming soon when she'd no longer be in the employ of Mr and Mrs Winton. How could she go home and place the burden of her problems upon her mother's shoulders? She'd had news that her mother was pregnant again. Her father and Dot could not be the only providers for their family, Fred had gone and the prospects of her being able to find work with a child to look after were slim. Kate's mind surged with the swell of all that she had done and all that she could not do. Every direction she thought to turn in seemed barred to her.

Ida stirred and sighed. A whisper of light from the street lamp appeared in the corner of the window and Kate could see that the creeping fingers of frost were grasping at the panes. She pulled the blankets up to her ears and stretched her legs. The night cramps were a curse, they were always the thing that woke her and there was nothing to do but squeeze and flex her toes and wait for the pain to pass. At least she could still reach her toes, for the time being anyway.

'You awake, Kate?' Ida croaked. Ida had been suffering with a cold and sore throat for several days but there was no lying in bed with a hot water bottle and beef tea for the likes of them. The servants had to keep going through all their ailments, mild or more serious. There were plenty of others waiting, ready to step into their shoes if they faltered, as Mrs Bowden often reminded them.

'Yes, I'm awake,' Kate replied.

'Time for us to get going then,' Ida said, throwing back the covers and getting out of bed. She threw a shawl around her shoulders, then poured water from the jug and splashed her face. She shivered and flung off her nightgown, dressing as quickly as she could whilst keeping up a steady stream of chatter. Kate wondered where she got the energy from first thing in the morning.

By the time they were both dressed, Ida had stopped talking and Kate could feel that she was building up to saying something important. As Ida handed Kate her apron, she looked first at Kate's swollen midriff and then at her face.

'We have a few moments before we need to light the fires. We have to talk, Kate,' Ida said.

Kate took in the sudden change of tone in Ida's voice and the seriousness of her expression. Ida reached for Kate's hand and sat her down on the bed next to her.

'I've been asking a few questions on your behalf,' she said to a worried Kate.

'Questions? What about?'

'The workhouse,' Ida replied. 'It's not far away. It's in Greenwich. What else are you going to do? We agreed that you can't go on much longer.'

'But the workhouse! I could die there, Ida, and no one would care,' Kate whispered.

'I would care,' Ida said.

Kate felt the slight pressure of Ida's hand. Her attempts at reassurance were a sign of her true friendship but Kate knew that she would have to go through this alone. No one could help her now. She was to become a mother and she'd have to give birth in a strange place with strangers, instead of in her own village surrounded by her own family. She couldn't tell them, she couldn't go there. How could she? The thought of her own mother, now pregnant with her sixth child, made Kate catch her breath. She tried to stem the flow of her tears but they would not be stopped. She leaned her head against Ida's breast and wept for everything that she must lose and the fear of what was to come.

'Come,' Ida said, 'we must go and tell Mrs Bowden.'

Kate wiped her eyes and stood upright. She pulled back her shoulders and took a deep breath. She knew she just had to get on with saying it and hoped Mrs B wouldn't take it too badly.

When Mrs B saw the serious expressions on Kate and Ida's faces as they entered the kitchen, she asked, 'What's up with you two? What's happened? Tell me now. Whatever it is, it can't be that bad.'

'It is,' Kate said. She looked straight at Mrs B. 'There's no way to say this gently. I'm pregnant.'

Mrs B flopped down in her chair, her face pale and her hands wringing her apron. She remained silent for a long time and Kate braced herself for the onslaught, but Mrs B simply let out a huge sigh and said, 'Well, there's nothing to be done then.'

Kate and Ida looked at each other and waited. Finally, Mrs B broke her silence.

'My sister had an illegitimate child,' she said. 'My nephew is a lovely boy. He's grown up to be such a lovely young man, looks after his mother so well. But she had a hard time of it. You'll need all the help you can get. I suppose the father's not around?'

Kate looked down.

'I'll ask you no questions and you can tell me no lies, Kate. No doubt you'll get enough of a stripping down from the master and mistress but you must tell them and very soon. They are not going to take it well. When's the baby due?'

'End of June,' Kate replied.

'Further on than you look then. And I thought I had a second sense for these things. You're not showing much.'

Kate and Ida exchanged glances. Without Ida's help she couldn't have hidden the truth for so long.

'You know it will mean you'll have to leave, don't you, Kate? Can you go home to Hampshire?' Mrs B asked.

'They've got enough mouths to feed. I can't add to their struggles,' Kate replied.

'Well, the only alternative is . . .'

'I know, the workhouse,' Kate said.

'I wouldn't wish that on anyone. Is there no one else you can go to?' Mrs B said.

Kate shook her head.

* * *

The meeting with Mr and Mrs Winton went as badly as Kate expected it to with shouts of recrimination and demands to know who had fathered this child. Kate wouldn't say. The deep sense of guilt inside her felt like boiling oil erupting over raw skin, her secret must stay within for no good could come of voicing the truth. She would not be believed.

'Well, there's nothing for it but to give you your notice,' Mrs Winton said. 'You bring shame upon this household and upon yourself.'

185

Mr Winton was not as sparing with his words. He called her all sorts of unpleasant names and hurled abuse at her.

'You're no better than a street walker,' he said. 'You must leave immediately. You're a bad influence on our children and I can't have you under this roof. Those who behave like guttersnipe will end in the gutter. You mark my words.'

Mrs Winton winced at her husband's anger and looked at Kate with great sorrow. She expressed her disappointment in her but implored her husband to at least let her stay until they could find a replacement.

'I will give you one week to make arrangements to leave,' Mr Winton said storming out of the room.

'You must find a way to explain your departure to the children,' Mrs Winton said. 'This is a sorry mess, Kate. Now get Ida to bring me some of my medicine, I have a headache coming on.'

Kate was angry at the way Mr Winton had spoken so cruelly to her but she was also sorry to have let Mrs Winton down. Mrs Winton had been so kind to her. Yet she had no regrets about having given herself to Philip. She had no regrets for loving him with all her heart. She waited that evening until the whole household had retired to bed and then sat on her own in the kitchen reliving the happier times she had spent here and trying to work out what she would say to Clara and the children. She wasn't looking forward to it, neither was she looking forward to the workhouse. She prayed that there was some other way.

Kate decided that the best place to inform Clara was away from the family home, at the hospital. So, on what was to be her last Sunday there, she took Clara to one side and told her about the baby. Clara's initial reaction was one of total surprise.

'I can't believe that I didn't notice, Kate. I must be so preoccupied with myself and my work that . . .'

'You've been busy. My clothes are loose and I've done a good job of hiding it.'

'You have but who's the father, Kate? Have you told him? Is it your soldier chap you've been seeing?'

Kate didn't reply. Clara looked at her.

'Whoever the father is, you must tell him. He has a responsibility,' Clara said. 'You can't face this alone.'

Kate looked at Clara and a tear trickled down her cheek. She couldn't say it, she couldn't say his name, even if it meant losing her friendship with Clara.

'All right, well I can't force you to tell me,' Clara eventually said, 'but I'm concerned for you, Kate. I presume you've told my parents?'

Kate's tears were flowing freely now. She tried to answer but all that would come were sobs. Eventually she managed to whisper, 'Yes'.

'Oh, Kate,' Clara said trying to console her friend. 'There's so much we women still need to achieve to take control of our futures. A woman's body can be a joy but it can also be a burden. We are governed by our monthly cycles, which are a nuisance when they are here but can cause such chaos in our lives when they don't arrive. What can I do to help? Tell me, Kate. I can't just abandon you.'

'I'll not be abandoned,' Kate replied, trying to reassure herself as much as Clara.

'Will you go home to Hampshire?' Clara asked.

Kate's mind was racing, confused. Her heart thumped. Was it the right thing to do? What should she say? The thought of the workhouse terrified her but Hampshire was so far away and how could she take her problems to her family's door. The shame of what she had done on top of their son's death was too much to ask. But the workhouse? If she told Clara about the workhouse, Clara would try to help her and in helping her, anger her parents if they ever found out. She had caused enough problems for everyone already. She had to tell Clara something, anything. The words were out before she'd formed them clearly.

'Yes, I'll go to my family,' she blurted. 'Please don't worry about me. I'll be all right. I'm not the first woman to be in this predicament and I won't be the last and the child will not be the only one without a father. Before this war's over, there will be many.'

Kate needed to give herself some thinking time. Should she tell Philip he was going to be a father? Should she ask Clara for his regimental details, so that she could write and tell him? No, that would immediately arouse suspicions. Clara was no fool. Should she go straight home to Micklewell? If she did that straight away, it would be difficult to come back.

'If you think that's best,' Clara said,' but you will write and tell me when the baby's born, won't you and how you are?'

Kate agreed. The two friends hugged each other.

'Look after yourself, Kate. I'm going to miss you,' Clara said.

'And I'll miss you . . . all of you . . .' Kate said, taking a deep breath. It was for the best, she kept telling herself, for the best.

As soon as they parted, Kate began to worry about what she'd done but she just couldn't tell her. Perhaps the passing of time would help her to see the way. What was it Clara had once said about a knot? It had a special name. She couldn't remember what it was. Her stomach was rolling and her head ached with weaving and winding. She couldn't unravel what she couldn't control.

When the children were playing in the nursery the following evening, she sat them all down and explained that she must leave. Thomas took it in his stride, as she expected. The twins wanted to know more. 'But why?' Sophie asked.

'Who will take us to school now?' Simon added.

'And who'll plait my hair?' Sophie said, a note of frustration in her voice.

'I have to go home for family reasons,' she said. 'A new maid will look after you.'

'We don't want a new maid,' Sophie said, stamping her foot. 'We want you.'

They were cross with her, but after much reassurance and promises that Ida would make sure the new maid was kind to them, they accepted what she had to say. She felt a deep sadness that this time in her life was about to end. She would miss them all.

\* \* \*

So it was, that Kate found herself standing at the doors of Greenwich Union Workhouse in the bitter cold of a February morning, one small carpet bag in her hands, holding all that she possessed. She'd packed her only two work dresses, night clothes and underwear, a few items of baby clothes Ida had managed to get from her family and the enamel-backed hairbrush that her mother had given her that belonged to her grandmother. Her winter coat barely kept out the biting winds and her ears were nipped and blue, her only hat serving little purpose, being more a case of respectability than warmth.

The workhouse appeared from the outside as forbidding as she expected it to be on the inside. The pale brick building rose above her, faceless and grimy. The windows gave no sign of life, shuttered against the outside world. As the workhouse doors opened and she stepped inside, she felt as if a black hole had opened up and swallowed her. What would become of her over the next weeks and months? She tried not to think of it, for what was there except the perpetual turning of night and day and the grinding down of her self-respect? Her spirit was nearly broken and her body would follow, soon to be split asunder by the demands of the factory floor and the birth of a homeless, fatherless child. She mustn't think on it any more but greet each breaking day as it dawned and stumble on, or she would surely sink beneath the oncoming tide.

Kate went about her work every day as best she could. Her bulk was making her tired as she heaved her swollen belly out of bed each morning and reported to the laundry room. Her hands were red raw with scrubbing and her legs ached with the constant standing. She'd asked to be put on different duties where she could be seated for some of the time but was told there were no vacancies and she must continue in the laundry or go elsewhere.

She constantly thought of going home to Micklewell but the shame that would bring upon her family was unthinkable. Kate was on her own!

# CHAPTER THIRTY-ONE

*April 1917*

One evening, wrapped in her coat for warmth, she put her hands into her pockets and felt something that had dropped into the lining. She lifted it out and saw it was the card from Carnforth. It seemed like a lifetime ago that he'd given it to her. Both he and Philip would probably still be fighting in France but her situation was becoming desperate. The baby could arrive any time now; she was nearly seven months pregnant. She needed to get a message to Philip. Carnforth would know how.

The address on the card said: Stratheden Road, Vanburgh Park. The same name, Vanburgh, it couldn't be so far away. She would find out how to get there! She managed to get hold of pen and paper and wrote a brief letter explaining her situation and her need to tell Philip as soon as possible. She would go to the address on the card and hope he was there on leave or that a message could be left for him. She recalled his words, his offer of help should she ever need it. Well, she needed it now. At the end of her daily shift, she took the letter and set out to find Carnforth. The gatekeeper was helpful, at least, and pointed her in the right direction.

The streets were gloomy in the fading light and she had to ask her way several times. She hoped that she would be able to find her way back in the dark and that the night watchman would let her back in to the workhouse. She had taken the precaution of retrieving what little money she had left from its hiding place, should she need to persuade him of her right to enter.

The Carnforth house was lit up and the shapes of several people moved in front of the windows on the ground floor. The family must be entertaining. She couldn't possibly knock on the front door, she would be taken for a beggar and be driven away by whoever answered. The only way was to seek help from her own kind. She walked around the side passage, hoping that she could find a way into the kitchens. A tall, ironwork gate barred her way; she tried the handle but it was locked. She waited, moving her weight from foot to foot and pressing her aching back against the wall. She couldn't draw attention to herself by shouting. Who would she call for? She was about to give up when a young woman came out of the back door carrying a bucket which she began emptying down the drain.

'Excuse me,' Kate whispered.

The young woman was so startled she dropped the pail and stood up looking in Kate's direction.

'My God, you scared me!' she spluttered. 'What are you doing there?'

'Is this the Carnforth residence?' Kate asked.

The girl stepped forward. 'Who's asking?' she said.

'My name's Kate. I know Mr Edward Carnforth.'

'Oh, you do, do you?' the girl sneered, looking at Kate's swollen belly. 'And does he want to know you?'

'All I want to know is if he's all right. Is he here or still in France?'

'What business is that of yours?' the girl asked.

'What's taking you so long, Bessie?' a voice asked from inside.

A tall young man in a butler's uniform came out, chastising the girl for time wasting. When he noticed Kate, he stopped mid-sentence.

'Who's this?' he asked.

'Says she knows Mr Edward. She's in the family way,' the girl replied.

'I can see that,' the butler replied.

Kate's shivering became uncontrollable, her head started to swim and her legs gave out from under her. She hung onto the gate and put her head down to stop herself from fainting.

'Get the key, Bessie,' the young man ordered. 'Can't you see she's not well?'

'But . . .'

'Don't you but me. Do as you're told,' he snapped.

Kate could feel the arms either side of her holding her up, but she couldn't see their faces. Her eyes moved in and out of focus and there was a buzzing in her ears. People were talking to her but she couldn't work out what they were saying. They guided her to a chair and sat her down. A cup of water was put to her lips and she tried to sip but her throat wouldn't swallow. Someone dabbed her mouth with a cloth.

She felt air moving across her face.

'Seems to be working, Mrs Fitch,' a voice said and she opened her eyes to see a round-faced, broad-hipped woman flapping a tea towel at her.

'There that's better,' the round-faced woman said. 'Now, Bessie, fetch me my smelling salts from the wall cupboard. They'll do the trick.'

After several inhalations of the smelling salts and some water, Kate felt better and could answer some of the questions that were being thrown at her. Yes she really did know Edward Carnforth and he had told her to find him if she ever needed help.

'Seems like you do now, right enough,' the young man said.

'I think this is a problem for Mr Jenks to deal with,' Mrs Fitch said. 'Go and find him, John, he'll be finished serving the port soon to the gentlemen in the library.'

Kate was given a hot cup of tea and some fruit cake, which she ate with relish. She hadn't tasted anything so good since she'd left Vanburgh House. Mr Jenks was a serious looking man with deep-set eyes and heavy brows that gave him a forbidding look, but when he sat down next to Kate and spoke to her, his voice tenderly belied his appearance.

'Now, my dear, John here tells me that you wish to see Mr Edward,' he said.

'Well, he's home but he's not well enough for visitors as yet,' Mr Jenks explained. 'Come back in a few weeks and I'm sure he'll be able to talk to you. The family are hoping he'll be well enough to join his sister's wedding party. That's what's going on upstairs, the pre-nuptial celebrations.'

Kate was devastated. It had been difficult enough for her to get here this time. In a few weeks the baby could be here. She felt in her pocket for the letter and entrusted it to Mr Jenks, hoping that Carnforth would soon reply. If Carnforth was a man of his word, he would help her, if not for her sake, then for Philip's.

If she could have witnessed what happened an hour later in the Carnforth household, that hope would have died in her breast. As Kate returned to the workhouse, Mr Jenks carried the note through to Mr Carnforth Senior. Mr Jenks might have shown Kate some kindness but when he weighed up the repercussions of delivering the letter to Mr Edward in his current condition and incurring the potential wrath of his employer, he decided upon an entirely different course of action.

After bidding his guests goodnight, Cecil Carnforth sat and smoked for a while in the library. When Jenks entered with the letter, he listened to the explanation of how it had arrived and who it was intended for with only partial attention. Two glasses of port after a full meal with liberal glasses of wine had made him sleepy and clouded his thoughts.

'A young serving woman, you say?' he asked Jenks.

'Yes, sir. She insisted she and Mr Edward know one another,' Jenks replied.

Cecil Carnforth placed the note on the side table.

'Thank you, Jenks, that will be all,' he said.

After finishing his cigar, he stood and picked up the note. Without even opening it, he screwed it into a ball and threw it into the dying embers of the fire.

# CHAPTER THIRTY-TWO

*June 1917*

Kate's waters broke on the laundry floor on 28 June, 1917. She was emptying the dirty water away for the next rinse, when there was as much water gushing between her legs as she was tipping down the drain. One of the other workers noticed the wet patch on the back of her skirt and said, 'Best you get yourself off to the infirmary. Looks like your time's come.'

Kate staggered up the staircase, stopping every few steps to gather her strength. She hadn't been sleeping well the last few weeks, what with the baby moving and her mind churning. Despite all her best efforts, this baby would be born in the workhouse after all.

She eventually made it to the top floor when the first pains started. She held her arms under her belly as if to stop the baby falling out. She could feel her stomach muscles hardening, preparing for the arrival of her child. She knew that babies often took a long time to come into the world. She'd heard her own mother's moans often enough. Very soon now they would both be mothers, for at the end of May, Ida had brought a letter to the workhouse announcing the birth of Tilly, a new baby sister for Kate. How could she go to them now? If she arrived at their door with her child and no money there would be two more mouths to feed. She couldn't do it to them.

'Ah, I wondered when you'd be coming to us,' a grey-haired old woman said as she saw Kate enter the ward. 'So, he's ready to join us then, is he?'

Kate hoped it would be a boy, a part of Philip to be with her always.

The woman hobbled towards Kate on ulcerated legs, her two crooked teeth visible through cracked lips. Kate instinctively drew back from her.

'She might not look pretty but she knows how to birth a babe,' a voice called behind her.

Kate turned. A younger woman with her sleeves rolled up and wispy, pale hair falling across her face was changing sheets.

'Been seeing nippers into the world since you were in your own cot,' the young woman said, standing upright. 'I'm Sara and that's Old Alice. We'll be by your side when you push yours out, don't fret.'

Kate looked around her. The infirmary was just one ward, with beds lined up on either side of the room. No screens or curtains, no privacy. She'd be in labour in full view of all the other inmates.

Her thoughts must have been etched on her face, for Sara came to her and whispered, 'Don't worry, we'll put you in that end bed, so that when the final stage comes, you're as far away from the rest of them as possible. You're lucky that no one else is ready to pop today!'

Kate didn't feel lucky. She prayed silently to herself that the labour would be quick.

Ronald Philip Truscott was born six hours after Kate felt the first birth pangs. Old Alice placed his little form gently in her arms and said, 'Welcome to the world, little man, though what a world it is!'

Kate looked down at his screwed-up face and held his tiny hand in hers, looking at each perfect pink fingernail. She raised his hand to her lips and kissed it. He began to whimper and she stroked him tenderly on the forehead smoothing his puckered brow, her fingers holding memories of Philip's scars.

'Sssh, sssh my little one,' she whispered. 'It's all right; everything's going to be all right.'

Part of her knew that she shouldn't promise what she couldn't deliver, but one thing she did know was that she was never going to let this baby go. She would cling on to him just as he clung on to life. If only his father could be with her now too!

Just a few days after giving birth, Kate was sent back to work. She had lost a lot of blood and was continuing to bleed heavily. There was too much heavy lifting in the laundry. The work master said he didn't want to have to call any doctor, so she was to go to the rope workshop. Here the women were tasked with unpicking the oakum, pieces of old rope which had to be untwisted and pulled apart to repair holes in wooden boats and ships. Her fingers were shredded and sore with the picking and unravelling but Ronnie could be with her, swaddled to her breast.

Most of the time Kate kept herself to herself but sometimes, when the women worked, they told one another stories of their past lives and how they longed to be free to return to their previous existence. Kate never talked about Philip and the assumption was that she was yet another young woman who had to suffer the consequences of an employer's lust. It was during one such session that Kate was warned of what would happen when Ronnie was weaned.

'Ya need to get out of 'ere before they takes him from ya,' sniffed Peggy, wiping her nose on her sleeve.

'Don't frighten her, Peggy. They don't always,' Joan said.

'They do. They take 'em and they sell 'em for adoption or keep 'em in the nursery until such times they're old enough to work,' Peggy continued. 'When they're still small they can fit inside the cooking vats to clean them out. Or they're set to work scrubbing potatoes or floors, whatever it is that needs doin'. If they're lucky, when they gets older they'll be taken for a 'prentice.'

Kate didn't want Ronnie scrubbing vats and floors. He was going to be better than that and she was going to see to it that he had the opportunity. And no one was going to take him away from her either. That was not going to happen. The workhouse had served its purpose, a temporary shelter for them both, but now she must get away as soon as she possibly could. Why hadn't Carnforth replied to her letter? Where was she to go now?

# CHAPTER THIRTY-THREE

*August 1917*

Kate so wanted to go home but she couldn't just arrive in Micklewell unannounced, with a babe in her arms. She must go to the only people who would help her, Mrs Bowden and Ida.

'You can't walk all that way, with a babe,' Sara said. 'I'll pull a few strings for 'yer. The carters go that way once a week, taking the laundry to the military hospital in Lewisham. They takes the clean and picks up the dirty.'

Kate thought of the blood and sweat of those poor soldiers that she had been washing and rinsing away in her time in the workhouse. Well, no more. She accepted Sara's offer as it would cut her journey time in half. So, the following Monday she stepped onto the cart and turned her back on the workhouse, she hoped for the last time.

The remainder of the walk took her about an hour and, thanks to Sara, she arrived without feeling too exhausted. She needed all her courage to come close to the house again. Should any of the family spot her, she didn't know how she would be received. She waited outside the gates for a while, watching the front door and the windows for any sign of life, until she was sure that she could enter the side passage unseen.

The smell of baking reached her nose before she got to the kitchen door. She inhaled the scent of spices, cinnamon and nutmeg. She hadn't tasted cake for months. As her mouth began to water, Ronnie began to cry. She pulled the shawl around him and hugged him to her breast.

'Shhh,' she whispered, rocking her body to the rhythm of his whimpers.

The back door opened and Ida stepped into the yard.

'Kate,' she exclaimed, 'I thought I heard something. Come inside, quick now before he kicks off good and proper.'

Once they were safely inside, Ida said, 'Look who's here Mrs B.'

'Oh, my good Lord, Kate!' Mrs B gasped. 'Sit down, sit down, for goodness' sake. How did you get here? And who's this?' she asked peeling back the shawl.

'This is Ronnie,' Kate said, smiling down at her son, 'and we've walked from Lewisham. We got a ride from Vanburgh Hill so it wasn't so far.'

'A little boy and a bonny one too,' Mrs B said, taking him from her. 'Ida, put the kettle on. No doubt our mum here could do with a drink and so could this little man, by the look of things.'

She handed him back and Kate unbuttoned her blouse and lifted Ronnie to her breast. 'Where are you on your way to?' asked Mrs B, once they'd all had some tea and relaxed into one another's company.

Just like the old days, thought Kate. Except the old days could never return.

'Well, that's just it. I don't know,' she replied. 'I had to get us out of that workhouse, that's all.'

'Mmmm!' said Mrs B, folding her arms over her chest and letting out a long sigh. She sat in that position for quite some while, sucking her teeth until she finally got up and said, 'Ida, put on your coat, you're going on an errand.'

'Where to?' Ida asked.

'To Mrs Philpott, the housekeeper two doors down. Her son is serving out in France and his wife's just had a baby. She's all on her own and not coping too well by all accounts. Her family don't live close by. It's a lonely time for new mothers just after a birth, as you know full well, Kate. I'm sure she'd be pleased to have some company for a while. Now you tell Mrs Philpott about our Kate and ask her if, in exchange for a little financial recompense, her daughter-in-law would like a lodger for a few days.'

'I don't have much money, I'm not sure . . .' Kate started to explain.

'Don't you worry about that. I'll see to it,' Mrs B said. 'I should never have sat by and watched you go to that place, but the master and mistress were so angry. I've regretted it every day, but I can help now. Let me help you and Ronnie, Kate, please.'

'But you can't . . .'

'Yes, I can and I will,' Mrs B snapped. 'What else have I got to spend my money on?'

After Ida had gone, Mrs B fetched a pen and paper and said, 'Now, you give me that little one and get on with writing to your parents. From what you've told me, they're a good sort and I'm sure they wouldn't see their lovely daughter and grandson out on the streets.'

While Kate wrote, Mrs B nursed Ronnie and talked.

'It's a real treat to see you, Kate,' Mrs B said. 'And Ronnie too, of course. He's the best news we've had in a long time. Goodness knows, we need some. The whole house has been on tenterhooks waiting for any word from the front. There's not been a letter from Master Philip in weeks. Then we heard the news that his friend, Mr Carnforth, was badly injured. That's made the mistress even more jittery. Living on her nerves, she is.'

Kate swallowed hard and concentrated on her letter. Was there no end to the loss? She just had to hang on to the hope that Philip was still alive.

* * *

When Ida entered the kitchen, half an hour later, she was so excited she couldn't get the words out fast enough.

'It's good news, Kate, but you'll have to get yourself over to Brook Street right away if we're to beat the curfew. Mrs Philpott says that she's sure Edith won't turn you away, that's her daughter-in-law. There's no time for me to go and ask her if it's all right and get back in time to serve supper, so we must go now. She's told me how to get there. I'll come with you.'

'Oh, you will, will you?' said Kate.

'If that's all right with you, Mrs B?' Ida asked looking expectantly at Mrs B with just a hint of pleading in her eyes.

Mrs B paused just long enough to make it seem as if she was in charge and then announced, 'Well get along with you then. I suppose I can manage until you get back, Straight there and back, mind. I don't want to have to ask that Dora to help me. She's not a patch on you, Kate, a right dopey-drawers!'

Kate smiled, pulled on her coat and hugged Mrs B.

'Thank you, Mrs B. I'll never forget your kindness,' Kate said, taking Ronnie.

'Oh, go along with you,' Mrs B replied, through misty eyes. 'Now get on your way and all the best to you, Kate and your Ronnie, God bless him. Oh, I almost forgot. We've been keeping a letter for you. It arrived a few days ago. What was the woman's name Ida? Marks, was it?'

'No, Mabbs, Mrs Mabbs,' Ida replied.

'Now where did I put it?' Mrs B said.' Ah, yes, on the dresser.'

As Kate took the letter, she noticed a tear slip out of the corner of Mrs B's eye. Kate placed the letter in her skirt pocket and took Mrs B's hands in her own. They stood for a while, looking at each other until Ida reminded them it was time to leave.

'Look after that little one,' Mrs B said.

'I will,' Kate replied. The streets were busy with people rushing home. They took so many twists and turns that

Kate's head was all of a confusion. Ida walked quickly and Kate found it hard to keep up. They eventually arrived at number thirteen Brook Street and Ida knocked on the door.

A young woman answered with huge black circles under her eyes and a baby could be heard howling somewhere behind her. She swiped her straggling hair out of her eyes and asked them short-temperedly what they wanted. Ida explained that Mrs Philpott had sent them and that Kate needed a bed and lodging for a few nights. The young woman looked as though she was going to close the door on them, so Ida took out the purse.

'We're not expecting you to do it for nothing,' Ida said.

The young woman grabbed the purse, stepped back and held the door open.

'You'd better come in then,' she mumbled.

Ida hugged Kate and kissed Ronnie on the forehead.

'Take care of yourself and your little Ronnie,' she said. 'I'll be back to see you in a few days.'

'I left a letter to be posted, back at the house, to my parents in Hampshire,' Kate said. 'Could you please make sure you put a stamp on it and post it for me?'

'Don't worry, I will,' Ida replied.

Kate was so relieved to be out of the workhouse that she didn't mind Edith Philpott being snappy and unfriendly. Edith said that she would have to make do in the spare room which was all cluttered up at the moment because she hadn't had time to think.

'He insisted we got married before he went off and then he left me with a load of his stuff to sort out and a swollen belly. God knows when I'll see him again. Three shillings and six pence a week, that's what I get. How's a person to live on that, with a babe to look after and all?'

Kate thanked Edith and said she was happy to sleep anywhere.

'You'll have to empty one of the drawers of the chest and put him in there to sleep,' Edith said, pointing at Ronnie. 'I hope he's a better sleeper than she is, little madam. Has me up all hours, that's why I look the way I do. Used to be a looker, I did, look at me now!'

Kate took Ronnie upstairs, cleared a place on the bed and fed him. She laid him gently down and positioned two pillows either side of him. She unpacked her few possessions and placed her hairbrush on top of the chest. She emptied one of the drawers to make a bed for Ronnie as Edith had suggested. The room was small and the bed filled most of it but it was warm and dry and a roof over their heads.

Once Ronnie was settled, Kate reached into her pocket for the letter. She sat with the envelope in her lap, frightened to open it. There could be only one reason that Mrs Mabbs had written to her. She slowly turned the envelope over and tore it open. She took the letter out and unfolded it. The carefully formed writing flowed across the page and Kate stared so hard at it, that it began to move before her eyes.

*Dear Kate,*

*This is the letter that I hoped I would never have to write. I received a telegram a few days ago to tell me that my dear Archie has been killed in action. I know he loved you dearly and it was his intention to propose to you when this dreadful war finally comes to an end. He would have been a fine husband to you but now that will never happen. My only son has been taken from me and I will never see him again. There is nothing more I can say except you know you can visit me here at any time.*

*With best wishes,*
*Violet Mabbs*

Kate folded the letter and put it back in the envelope. She placed it carefully in the drawer, underneath her clothes. She pushed the drawer back and stood gazing at the wall, unable to cry. So much death. A shiver rippled through her body and she felt empty. She knelt beside Ronnie's makeshift cradle, kissed him lightly on the forehead and stood silently watching him and listening to his breathing.

'I have you,' she whispered. 'We are alive and I have you.'

Edith's baby was still crying by the time she went downstairs and Edith was trying to rock her with one arm while stirring a pot with the other.

'Let me do that,' Kate offered.

'I'd rather give you her, she's driving me mad,' said Edith.

Kate took the baby and asked her name.

'She's Grace, though she's anything but gracious,' Edith said. 'He wanted her named that. Grace if it's a girl and Graham if it's a boy. So, she's Grace.'

As Kate placed her on her shoulder, the baby let out an almighty burp.

'She's got wind,' Kate said. 'Have you tried sitting her up after a feed and rubbing her back until she brings it up?'

'Well, that midwife is always in such a hurry to get out of here I never get a chance to talk to her. She might have told me.' Edith sighed.

'Try it next time you feed her and don't stop until she lets that wind out.' Kate smiled.

From then on she and Edith got on really well. They took the babies out, top and tail in the pram. They cooked together. Kate helped Edith to write her letters to her husband, Stan, while Edith helped Kate to sew Ronnie rompers for when he was older.

Kate didn't know whether to envy Edith because she had a husband, or to pity her because she had to wait each week to see if a letter arrived back. She tried not to think about the distance between her home in Hampshire and London and whether she and Philip would ever find each other again. When he returned home to find her gone, would he even want to be with her? By returning to fight, he was opening himself up to more of the same destructive forces that had changed him in the first place. Perhaps he was changed forever but then this war had changed everything. She had changed. She'd given birth to a child, without him. She'd survived the workhouse, but for now she and Ronnie were

206

safe. So many of the men who went to war didn't return. There was no way of knowing if Philip would.

She tried to console herself with the thought that this war couldn't go on forever, but it was showing no signs of coming to an end and uncertainty was a feeling everybody lived with every day. There was no point in making plans. Ronnie was her first concern now, everything else must wait.

The following day Edith answered a knock at the door. Kate heard her greeting Ida but she didn't hear Ida's voice at all. Ida came into the kitchen and looked across at Kate, a darkness in her expression. No words of explanation came.

'Ida? What is it?' Kate asked, going to her.

Ida just looked at her, wiping away the wetness on her cheeks with her sleeve. Kate reached across and took Ida's hand.

'Ida?' she said again.

Ida sniffed away her tears and pulled a handkerchief out of her pocket.

'It's Mr Philip,' she said. 'Mrs B sent me, she said that you would want to know.'

'Yes?' Kate prompted her, not really wanting to hear what she feared was coming next.

'He's . . . he's . . . been killed,' Ida sobbed. 'The telegram arrived yesterday.'

A coldness crept through Kate's body. Her breathing slowed, her vision blurred and her legs felt as if they could not hold her up. Someone was calling her name, someone was speaking to her, but it was far off. There was a humming in her ears that blotted out the words and she felt as if water was flooding into her mouth, choking her.

Then she heard it, a cry but who was crying? The ache in her chest surged up through her throat and then she let it loose.

'Ronnie, I must go to Ronnie,' she said.

# CHAPTER THIRTY-FOUR

*August 1917*

'Here's a letter arrived from London,' an excited Dot said as she ran into the kitchen with the envelope.

'It'll be our Kate,' Ada Truscott said, placing a sleeping Tilly into her cradle and rocking it a few times to be sure.

'About time, haven't heard from her in months,' Kate's father, Jim, replied.

'Let me see,' clamoured Dot, leaning over her mother's shoulder as she opened the letter. 'What does she say, what does she say?'

'Give a person time to look,' Ada scolded and sat down to read the letter in private.

Jim watched as the expression on his wife's face changed. Her wide, kindly eyes narrowed and the corners of her smiling mouth tilted downwards.

'Haven't you got jobs to do, young lady?' he said to his daughter.

'Yes, but . . .'

'Never mind "yes but", let your mother read the letter in peace. You'll be told the news soon enough,' Jim said with a firmness in his voice that could not be misunderstood.

Dot, eavesdropping just outside the back door, caught the main gist of her parents' words and knew at once that her sister was in trouble. She shifted uneasily and knocked into the tin bath which scraped along the wall.

'You might as well come in, my girl, for we know you're there,' Ada said.

Dot sheepishly appeared and responded, without hesitation, when her father told her to sit down.

'Now see here, what you've just heard goes no further than these four walls. Do you understand?' Ada said.

'Or you'll know the consequences,' her father added tapping his belt.

Dot had seen him take the belt off and strap Fred when he'd overstepped the mark, but she'd never received more than a scolding and been sent to bed without her supper. She wasn't about to challenge her father's authority though, so she simply nodded her compliance.

'The village gossips will find out about this soon enough,' Ada said. 'But we need to keep this to ourselves for a while. We need to think about what's best to do.'

Tilly murmured in her sleep and Ada's eyes went straight to her. She knew the joys and pains of motherhood all too well and now her eldest daughter was to face them without a husband to provide.

The family sat in silence for a good while, each absorbing the information about Kate and the baby. It was Jim who eventually spoke.

'Well, this is a fine mess. My daughter wants to come home here with some man's child who we know nothing about. Two more mouths to feed, Ada. My pay from the smithy is barely enough for the five of us. How are we to manage?'

'There's my money from the school too,' Dot said cautiously.

A family discussion ensued which veered from expressions of anger that Kate could have got herself in this mess, to accusations of her being taken advantage of, to sympathies for her poor babe without a father. Ada moved from being disappointed in her daughter, to defending her and Jim threatened to show the culprit the barrel of his gun until Dot reminded him that the father must be a London man.

'That's what city people are like,' Jim fumed. 'All chancers, you can't trust them!'

In the end the family agreed that the best place for Kate and her baby was back in Micklewell. Jim was accepting of their decision but sat with a worried frown on his face.

'Whichever way you look at it though, Ada, there's still the problem of how we can all live on so little. So, what's to be done? How will we manage?' Jim eventually said.

Ada was never one to be defeated and had an answer for him. 'We should pay the Taylor sisters a visit,' she replied, 'They might be able to help. They're known for their generosity and good sense.'

'Then you and Dot go, that's women's work,' Jim announced putting on his cap and heading for the back yard.

'Oh no you don't, Jim Truscott!' Ada said, holding firm. 'You're her father. What happens to her is your concern too.'

It was Nora who opened the door to the family that day. She greeted them with surprise.

'Why Mr and Mrs Truscott, good morning, and Dot and young Henry and baby Tilly too,' she said in a breezy voice. 'How may I help you on this fine morning?'

When she received a muted reply and noticed the slightly bowed heads and serious faces of Ada and Jim Truscott, however, she altered her tone.

'Is it Florence you've come to see?' she asked, as it was usually the eldest Taylor sister people came looking for if there were problems and the family certainly looked as if they had a dilemma that needed Florence's kind and steady nature to resolve. Just then, Florence herself appeared in the doorway.

'Good morning,' she said, greeting them warmly, and ushering them inside to a small but cosy sitting room. 'Do sit down,' she continued indicating an enormous settee while she and her sister took the two armchairs.

'I apologize for calling so early, Miss Taylor,' Ada began, 'but it's just, well, you see . . .'

'It's our Kate,' Jim interrupted. 'Show her the letter, Ada.'

Ada laid the still sleeping baby across her lap and handed Florence the letter. Florence retrieved her glasses from the bureau in the corner and quietly read the contents of the letter.

'I see,' said Florence passing back the letter.

Ada made a slight choking sound in her throat. Henry looked anxiously at his mother and Dot pulled him up onto her knee.

'Now don't distress yourself,' Florence reassured Ada. 'This is not as uncommon a situation as you might think. Do we know who the father is?'

'No,' Ada replied mopping her eyes. 'All we know is what you've read for yourself, that Kate had to leave her employment and gave birth to a son at the Greenwich Union Workhouse infirmary in June.'

Jim sat, cap in hand, with his arms on his knees looking downwards. Dot didn't know whose face to look at and shifted in her chair uncomfortably. She settled on looking at a painting above Florence's head which showed a cottage with a latched gate. A young maid stood knitting at the cottage door and a reed basket stood ready at her feet to take to the fields.

'A beautiful painting, isn't it?' Florence said. 'The girl seems happy enough but moments after the artist put down his brush who knows what befell her?'

Motes drifted in the air in the morning light and settled silently between them as each dwelt in their own thoughts. Florence was aware of the awkwardness of the situation and said with a smile, 'But I am too maudlin. Shame on me! The point is, my dears, what can be done to help your lovely daughter?'

Jim raised his head, Dot straightened her back and Ada tucked her handkerchief up her sleeve.

'Please try not to worry,' Florence continued. 'I will do my best to help Kate. I'm sure there are plenty of things she can do here. We've been struggling since our farm hands joined up. Old Graves has always been a hard worker but there's too much for him to do by himself. When she arrives, give her time to get adjusted, find her feet. It will be hard for her. Then bring her to see me.'

Ada wrote back instructing her daughter to come home and the Truscott family waited for Kate and her child to arrive.

\* \* \*

Kate was both pleased to be returning home and sad to be leaving Edith. They had got on so well and that brief time in her life had made her realize that she was not the only mother to be left on her own. There was no certainty that Edith's husband would return to her and there were so many thousands of other women across the country who were in exactly the same position. The thought brought some comfort, but when she looked down at the sleeping face of her son and touched his delicate eyebrows, she couldn't stop the surge of pain that came over her. Ronnie's lashes were long and full like his father's and that little frown between his brows was Philip's frown when he was thinking. What thoughts could such a tiny baby have and how would she ever be able to help him see what his father was like. He would never know him.

On the train ride from London to Hook, Kate thought about Edith. She was sad to be leaving her but happy to be going home.

She recalled the number of times she had made this journey, times of joy and of sorrow. Bringing her mother a posy on Mothering Sunday; holding her new brother, Henry, on her knee; holding her mother close as she wept at the loss of her eldest son. Now she was going home for good, a very different person to the one who had left to become a nursemaid five years ago. But she would come through this.

She was sorry she hadn't been able to tell Clara the truth about Philip but what point would there be now? Her parents would never accept their grandson, they probably wouldn't even believe that Ronnie was his. She hoped that Clara and Carnforth would eventually be able to marry. She had no doubts that Clara was on the way to becoming an independent woman, who would know her own mind and not allow her father to make any decisions for her about her future.

As for her? The future was a complete blank. The only certainty was that she would need to provide for Ronnie. What to tell her parents? The best way was to say that the war had taken Ronnie's father, just like it had taken their son. That much they would understand. That much was the truth.

There were so many fatherless children. Ronnie was no different. She had survived the workhouse, she had become a mother and she knew she was loved. Her family would not shun her. They were no doubt shocked; her father might show his disapproval and the neighbours would gossip, but as soon as the initial excitement had died down they would all get back to living their lives. There was too much still going on with the war for people to dwell on the misfortunes of others for too long.

As the train pulled into Hook station, Kate became more nervous. She leaned out of the carriage window and opened the door. She turned and picked Ronnie up from the seat where she had laid him and then picked up her bag and dragged it to the door.

'Here, let me help you,' a gentleman said and she let him carry her bag for her.

As she stepped down onto the platform, the whole family were waiting for her. She felt apprehensive but her fears soon melted when she saw their beaming faces.

Dot and Henry raced down the platform to greet her.

'Let me take him,' Dot said, her arms waiting to hold her nephew.

'I guess you're a bit small to carry this,' the kindly gentleman said to Henry holding Kate's suitcase.

'Thank you, sir, I'll take it,' Kate's father said. 'Welcome home, Kate.'

Kate greeted her father and they all walked the length of the platform, where Ada was sitting holding her youngest daughter. The two mothers kissed each other, whilst holding their babes. They smiled and cried at the same time. Kate put one arm around her mother and her father put his arms around the two of them. Dot and Henry completed the family group and they all held on to each other. Kate knew at that moment that she was loved and that Ronnie was loved too.

# CHAPTER THIRTY-FIVE

*September 1917*

September in Micklewell! All things bright and beautiful! Kate couldn't believe that she was really there. Sorting through the plums with Dot to make plum jam, laying out the apples in straw in the shed, boiling up the marrows to make chutney. Baby Ronnie and little Tilly, gurgling to each other lying on a shawl on the rug, feeling the swoosh of the women's skirts as they brushed by, moving around the kitchen with a purpose.

Kate hummed hymns to herself as she chopped and sliced, bottled and boiled, heated and cooled. Occasionally Dot would join in and they would burst into song. They knew all the words by heart. All was indeed 'safely gathered in'.

'Will you come to the harvest festival at the church tomorrow?' Dot asked. 'The children from the school will be singing "We plough the fields" and they're doing a little tableau. I've been practising with them for weeks.'

'I'm not sure,' Kate replied. She was still cautious about facing people and imagining how they might be gossiping about her.

'You'll have to show your face sometime,' their mother said, as she entered the kitchen with a basket of plums.

'People are asking after you, Kate,' Dot said.

'Like who?' Kate replied.

'Miss Clarence, at the school, for one, and Mary White. Mary says you're welcome to go there with Ronnie any time. She has news of her sister, Elsie, to give you. You were good friends at school, weren't you?'

'People are just nosey,' Kate said. 'I know what they're thinking.'

'What does it matter what people think?' Dot said.

'You can't afford to shut yourself away,' her mother added. 'You'll need to find work.'

'I know,' Kate said, picking Ronnie up. 'I just need a bit more time, is all.'

She carried him outside into the back yard and watched her father loading his gardening tools into his box trailer that he pulled behind his bike. He called to Judy, his little black dog, and was making ready to wheel his bike out onto the lane. When he saw Ronnie in Kate's arms, he leaned his bike against the wall and pulled back the shawl to smile at his grandson.

'You're looking much stronger and brighter than when you first arrived, Kate,' he said. 'And how's our little Ronnie this morning?'

'I feel stronger and Ronnie is well too. It was the right thing to bring him back to the country; we're both so happy to be here.'

'And we're happy to have you,' he replied.

'You're not ashamed of me then?' Kate asked.

'How could we be ashamed of such a bonny lad and his lovely mother?'

'Can I ask you something, Pa?' Kate tentatively asked.

'Ask away.'

Kate decided to ask the question that had been on her mind since arriving home. Her mother was right; she needed to think of the future.

'Would you have married Mum if she already had a child?'

216

Jim Truscott stopped loading his tools and stood upright. He had been caught off guard. He beckoned to her to come and sit down on the garden bench with him.

'I can't answer that question, Kate,' he said, 'but what I can tell you is that you were on the way before we walked down the aisle.'

'You mean?'

'Yes, I do. There's plenty of women out there who've found themselves in your predicament, Kate.'

She interrupted him. It was about time they knew. They hadn't pushed her on the question of Ronnie's father and had left her to tell them in her own good time. It was a miracle that Dot hadn't pestered her to know. She'd probably been warned by both her parents to leave her be and Kate was grateful for their patience.

'He was a good man, Pa. He was killed in action, like Fred,' she explained, her voice faltering. 'I don't want Ronnie to be without a father, but who would marry me now?'

'Give yourself time, Kate,' her father said. 'There will be someone, I'm sure.'

He put his arm around her shoulders and she leaned her head against him. She hoped he was right. After a short while he stood up and said, 'Now, in the meanwhile, it's time you had some fun. There's to be a harvest supper on the green next weekend, after church. There'll be music and dancing and plenty of good food. We'll all go together. It's time we showed off our new additions to the family to the whole village, Tilly and Ronnie Truscott. Now get in there and tell your sister that you'll come to church and to the supper too.'

'You were listening to what we were saying in the kitchen! I didn't take you for a snoop, Pa.' Kate smiled.

'Your mother says I only hear what I want to hear and you know your mother's always right. I needed to hear that you are ready to show off that lovely boy of yours and hold your head up high. I know that you'll discover the villagers are more on your side than you think they are. They've all had their trials the last few years and welcoming a new life to the community can do nothing but good is what I say.'

Kate took her father's hand. 'I love you, Dad,' she said.

The church service didn't turn out to be as much of a trial as she'd thought it would be. The church was beautifully decorated with rosy-red apples all along the top of the rood screen, thirty in all, she counted them during the psalms which never were her favourite. Either side of the steps leading up to the altar, there were the usual two wheat-sheaves presented by Farmer Addison and everyone in the village had given the rest of the fruit and vegetables on show. They brought shape and colour to the church. Shards of light cut across the seated congregation, reds and blues playing across the wrinkled green cabbages and strings of long beans. A sack of earthy potatoes spilled out over the chancel floor and baskets of yellow mirabelles and purple damsons, huge green Bramleys and furry-skinned Russets, stood beneath the choir stalls. The sloping window ledges overflowed with rusty orange and warm yellow chrysanthemums, deep red crab apples still clinging to their branches and virginia creeper from the walls of the big houses. A tapestry of delights!

Ronnie slept through most of the service, until the rousing chorus of 'Praise my Soul the King of Heaven', when Matthew Bunce, who'd already sampled some of the cider for the harvest supper by the sound of him, roared over Kate's shoulder and woke him. When she turned and looked at Matthew, he just gave her back a toothy grin and winked. She made a mental note to avoid him at the supper, for Matthew was well known for having one over the eight and swinging a girl's arms off in the barn dancing.

Her father had been right, the villagers were, for the most part, very welcoming and cooed and sighed over Ronnie. Once the Taylor sisters had come to speak with them, then Kate didn't have a minute to herself. If the sisters were publicly accepting of her, then everything was fine. The young girls flocked around her and wanted to hold the baby and know all about London, but the young men kept their distance. Most of the men of fighting age were serving their country, of course. The ones that remained were either not fit or in reserved occupations, like the reverend and most of the farm owners. Kate learned that many families had, like their own, lost someone but they'd all turned out for the festival to show thanks for what they had and to celebrate life.

The village green was alive with a higgledy-piggledy of tables and chairs carried from people's kitchens. A long trestle was set up for the food and families ferried pies and cheeses, bread and vats of soup until it was groaning under the weight of it all. There wasn't much left at the end but a few crumbs that were thrown to the birds and, as the evening light softened features and made cheeks glow, the musicians started to play.

'Go on, Kate, you and Dot get up and show 'em how it's done,' Jim Truscott said to his daughters, holding his tankard of cider aloft. His leg was jiggling to the music.

'How about you and Mum have a dance?' Kate said.

'I've got to get these two home,' Ada replied, lifting Tilly, and taking Henry's hand.

'Your dad will hold Ronnie and you and Dot can dance. When he's finished his drink, he can bring Ronnie home for you and you stay for a bit,' she said, flicking her head at her husband and throwing him a look that was more an instruction than a request.

Kate and Dot partnered each other for the Gay Gordons, and then joined in the Circassian Circle. They giggled uncontrollably during Strip the Willow, when arms were flying and partners were lost in a muddle that no one really cared about. All the conventions of the right steps were dropped in favour of the fun of the dance.

As they collapsed onto two straw bales and bent over double with breathlessness and laughter, they both declared that it was the best fun they'd had in years.

'Some of those men have two left feet,' Kate whispered.

'And some of them think you're a sack of potatoes the way they throw you around.' Dot grinned. 'I shouldn't like to

219

be kissed by any of them, should you? They'd probably hug the life out of you with their grubby paws and then plant a slobbery one right on your lips.'

They both dissolved into giggles again and gazed around to see what other entertainments were worth watching.

'There's someone over there keeps looking at you,' Dot said.

'More like he's looking at you,' Kate replied.

'No, I've seen him give you the eye earlier on this evening,' Dot insisted. 'He's a tall one and his shoulders look like they could carry more than a sack of potatoes. He's probably strong enough to lift that anvil in the blacksmith's, don't you think?'

'Stop staring at him, Dot. It's rude to stare,' Kate scolded her sister.

'I've not noticed him about the village,' Dot said. 'Perhaps he's an incomer?' Then she gave a sudden gasp.

'Ooo . . . watch out! He's . . . he's coming over,' she stuttered.

'Would you dance with me, miss?' the stranger asked Kate. 'It's the Dashin' White Sergeant, the only one I know.'

Kate looked up at him and felt as if she was peering up at a mountain of a man. His chest swelled through his waistcoat and his broad hands swung on the ends of arms covered in dark hair. His sleeves were rolled to his elbows and, around his thick neck, he wore a blue kerchief. His face had a smudge of stubble around the chin and his hair was trimmed short about the ears. It was his shy smile, though, that intrigued her most and his firm stance while he waited for her answer.

He was not what you'd call a handsome man, but there was something in the way he stood four square and a kindly confidence in his manner that made Kate say yes. She extended her hand and he pulled her to her feet. He held her in a firm but gentle hold and they danced, barely exchanging a word. He was a good six foot tall and she was only five foot four, so he stooped a little to look at her. When their eyes met, he let his gaze rove over her face and then looked away.

Kate noticed that one of his eyes was different. Then, as they danced, she realized. He had a glass eye. She took occasional glances at his face and saw that the hair grew less thickly on that side of his head and there were wrinkled scar marks. He had been badly wounded. When the music stopped, he thanked her and turned to go.

'My name's Kate,' she said.

'Albert,' he replied, 'Albert Locock, pleased to meet you.'

# CHAPTER THIRTY-SIX

*November 1917*

Florence Taylor decided that the best way she could help Kate was to give her some work on the farm. By the time November came, Ronnie was in a good routine and the agreement was that she should start work in the mornings, straight after feeding Ronnie, then go home at midday to feed him again. It would not be long before she could wean him and then everything would be easier. Kate was to help with the work in the barns and animal pens and around the yard. There were chickens to be fed and stables to be mucked out. Fresh straw was to be laid and the hay mangers topped up. She should expect the list of tasks to change every day, the Taylor sisters said, and Mr Graves, the farm manager, had overall responsibility, so if she was unsure of anything she was to ask him.

She and Nora were not the only women working on the farm. The usual farmhands, who had enlisted, had been replaced by two Land Army girls. They had also recently taken on a young man. That young man was Albert Locock.

Kate's first morning at the farm was a wet one. The runnels in the lane joined forces with one another and became a second stream, flowing parallel with the brook. She'd borrowed

222

a pair of her father's work overalls and rolled up the legs and the arms to fit her small frame. As she walked, the water ran down her face and into her eyes but she resisted wiping it away with a wet sleeve. The trouser legs began unravelling themselves and dangling in the mud and one boot was letting in water.

When she arrived at the farm, Nora Taylor was waiting for her in the barn.

'Well, we said you'd get covered in mud,' Nora laughed, 'but we didn't mean before you started work. You're drenched. You'd best get out of those clothes and I'll fetch you something from the house.'

Nora left Kate shivering in one of the horse stalls and returned with a towel and some dry trousers, a cotton twill shirt and a long work coat.

'The shirt and trousers are Mabel's, she's in Egypt of all places, nursing. The coat belonged to our stockman, Doug. He's somewhere in France. Ypres, I think,' Nora said. 'I'll leave you to get changed. Just hang your wet things up on that nail and I'll take them into the kitchen later to dry out.'

Kate shuddered as she heard the name of that place. Philip was there but he would never return. Images of his broken body formed, despite her trying to banish them. She saw him being laid to rest in some strange place, where no one who loved him could visit his grave. She tried to think instead of their most tender moments together. The sweet beads of sweat on his back, the saltiness of his taste, his fingers playing over her skin and the way his breath caressed her cheeks. She hoped, for the sake of those he loved, that Doug would be one of the ones who came safely home.

'Beg pardon, miss. I didn't realize anyone was . . .' a voice said.

Kate whipped around, her arms across her chest for modesty. She had stripped down to her underwear and her skin was all goose bumps.

She let out such a loud cry of surprise that the young man turned rapidly away. He walked out of the barn apologizing profusely as he went.

'Sorry, sorry. I didn't mean to . . .'

Kate pulled on the dry clothes as quickly as she could to avoid any further embarrassment and then went outside to look for the owner of the apologies. He was nowhere to be seen. She hadn't got a good look at him but she was sure that it was the young man she had danced with at the harvest supper. A pity he ran off in such a hurry.

The best part of the morning was spent leading the two remaining horses out onto the field. The strongest horses had been taken for war work. The shire, Sampson, and two other horses, Starlight and Sunny, had been requisitioned. At least they were left with old Barney to pull their riding trap plus the brood mare and the skittish yearling. They had been managing the plough with their ageing draft horse, Rex, until the tractor arrived. The government had decided that farming should be mechanized and here it was! Old Graves had been mystified by it when it arrived, said it was a new-fangled thing and give him horses any day. Thankfully the Land Army girls had soon got the measure of it and it was proving useful.

'Except on days like this,' Nora said, 'when they will probably have to abandon it in the field if it gets bogged down.'

Kate looked out for Albert every morning but he was always out in the fields before she got there or repairing fences or off taking things to market. It was sometime before they bumped into one another again. They exchanged a few words while he was sawing wood and she offered to bring him a hot drink and a chunk of bread pudding for his break. He drank it down, almost without pausing and consumed the bread pudding with such speed that you'd have thought he'd not eaten in a week.

She asked Nora about him, when they were feeding the pigs.

'That's Albert,' Nora said. 'He's been medically discharged as a result of his injuries. He got shrapnel in the eye apparently. He cycles every day from Hambleden and he's never late, whatever the weather. He's got just the sort of build and temperament for farm work, he's strong and calm with the animals. His hands are the size of dinner plates and he has shoulders that carry a hay bale with ease. His shirts are clean and his trousers patched. He works long hours and is always ready to take on more to keep his younger sisters and brothers fed. He's a fine young man and can turn his hand to anything. The builders' yard is always trying to steal him from us for his strength and diligence is second to none. On top of all that he is as honest as the day is long and completely dependable.'

'You give him a very good reference,' Kate said.

'We're lucky to have him,' Nora replied.

# CHAPTER THIRTY-SEVEN

*January 1918*

By the beginning of January, the weather was so bad that much of the work was indoors cleaning, repairing and patching. Kate and the land girls were kept busy tending to the animals, cleaning tack and mucking out. Albert was given the job of repairing some of the fabric of the barn and rebuilding part of the chicken coop. Lunchtimes were spent inside the large farm kitchen where the workers could all warm themselves in front of the range and be heated from the inside with warming soups. At these times, Kate had more opportunity to talk with Albert and the land girls, who were very entertaining with their talk of the London dance halls and how they would dance the night away. They all avoided wishing aloud that the war would end and tried to keep the numbers of dead, which were rising every day, out of the conversation.

Kate and Albert were often in and around the barn together and Kate noticed that when Albert was working with the horses he spoke to them kindly. He sometimes had a carrot in his pocket for each of them and when he put on their head collars to move them to muck out the stables, he nuzzled them behind their ears. When Kate was grooming

them, he offered to help and if old Rex was stubbornly refusing to lift his feet and let Kate pick his hooves out, then
Albert would use his bulk and strength to lean into him and
get him to cooperate. He was always ready to help. Albert was
a gentle giant and he never complained about the weather,
the cold or the difficulty of any job. He just got on and did
whatever was required of him. Kate grew to like him more
and more.

One day when Kate was going to retrieve wood for the
range, she heard a banging noise and shouting coming from
inside the wood shed. She discovered Albert beating his arm
against the wall and wondered whatever had got into him.
As she moved closer, she could see that he was holding one
arm out and blood was dripping from it.

'Albert, you're injured,' she said.

'Oh, 'tis nothing. Just a scratch. He's worse off than me,'
he replied nodding his head towards a dead rat lying on the
wood shed floor.

Kate was not the squeamish sort but she was glad that it
was Albert who had encountered the rat and not her.

'I don't think he'll be causing any more damage,' Albert
said.

* * *

It was one afternoon when the first of the snowdrops came
peeping through the cold dark soil to light the winter days
that Albert was summoned to the farmhouse by Nora Taylor.
As he collected kindling from the woodland floor, to dry out
in the barn, the delicate white flowers nodded at him as he
passed by. He took a moment to take in their delicate beauty,
their sweet heads bowed down against the freezing winds.
He looked across the fields to the leaf-bare woodland on the
eastern boundary of the Taylor land and thanked God for
bringing him here.

'Ah! There you are, Albert. My sister wishes to see you
on a matter of utmost importance,' Nora explained. 'I'm not

permitted to give the details but, suffice to say, the matter is a delicate one.'

He threw down the bundle of kindling inside the barn and followed Nora to the kitchen door, his heart beating enough to scare the crows. All manner of ideas went through his head. He couldn't recall having missed any instructions that day. The farm manager had complimented him on the quality of his work, said he never saw a man move so many potato sacks before tea break.

Albert removed his cap and stood on the mat looking down at his boots which carried all the evidence of a day in the muddy yard. He just hoped that the odour of his sweaty shirt didn't reach the delicate noses of the sisters.

'Never mind the muddy boots, Albert. The kitchen flags will clean up well enough. Would you like to wash your hands and take some tea with us? There's Nora's fruit cake too.'

Albert thanked Florence and cleaned himself up at the deep kitchen sink. She poured him a cup of tea and passed it to him across the scrubbed kitchen table. Albert's hand shook as he took it and Florence smiled to set him at ease.

'Now, Albert, Ted Graves tells me what a good worker you are, says you learn quickly and put in more than a day's work in the time you're here.'

'Thank you, Miss Taylor. I'm obliged to him,' Albert replied taking his cake but leaving it on the plate.

'No, Albert, we are obliged to you for being such a reliable worker on our farm. Where would we be without you? You will make some lucky young woman a very good husband one day. Is there anyone special, Albert, a sweetheart perhaps?'

'No one, Miss Taylor. I've not long been discharged from the army. I've been too busy earning for courting. Besides there's my . . . er . . . disability,' Albert said lifting his left hand to his cheekbone.

'Your injury is a badge of honour that you wear to show you've fought for your country and it certainly doesn't impair your ability to work, Albert. We can all testify to that,' Florence said. 'Now, do eat your cake, Albert, please or there'll not be time for a second slice before you need to get back to work.'

Albert nodded. The cake was very nice but rather stuck in his throat, for Miss Taylor had not yet told him of the purpose of this exchange. He knew it couldn't be purely to commend him for his hard work. They asked politely after his parents and how he was adjusting to being back home.

He realized that the two women were staring and smiling at him with fixed expressions. What did they want of him? What could it be?

'I expect you're wondering why we've asked you here to take tea with us,' Florence finally said.

'Yes . . . yes, I was,' Albert fumbled.

'Albert, no doubt you have spoken to Kate, our young helper who has returned to the village after some time away. She's a very pretty girl from a good family but has fallen upon difficult times and needs a friend. I won't go into any details. It is for her to explain things to you, when she's ready,' Florence announced.

'Ah . . . yes, Kate and I have met and talked a bit. She has two sisters and a brother, I believe, likes to read and sew and such like, when she has time. Used to be in service, she tells me. People talk, I know, and I don't usually listen to tittle-tattle, but there's a child, I believe.'

'The child's father was killed in battle,' Florence said. 'It's hard for women during a war, Albert. Hard for the soldiers too, I'm sure. You would know all about that.'

'She's a very hard worker, like yourself, Albert,' Nora interrupted.

Florence gave her sister a firm stare.

'Do you like her, Albert?' Florence asked.

'Yes, I do, she seems a kind person,' Albert replied.

'And you have no sweetheart at all?' Florence probed.

'No, Miss Taylor,' Albert said fumbling with his cap on his knee.

'Good. Well, we were wondering if you would consider inviting her to walk out with you? She's such a lovely girl and she needs a friend. You do seem to get along quite well,' Florence said.

'I don't know what to say,' Albert replied. 'It's, it's a bit . . .'

'Irregular? Yes, I know but I have every confidence that you two will enjoy one another's company, otherwise I wouldn't have suggested it. Will you think about it, Albert?' Florence replied.

Albert didn't know what to think. The Misses Taylors did a lot in the village but as far as he knew, matchmaking was not one of their usual tasks. He wasn't sure how to answer them and wondered just what he was getting himself into, but nodded his agreement which delighted the two women.

He thanked them for the tea and cake, took his cap and bid them good evening. As he wheeled his bike out of the yard, he heard the song of a robin spinning through the evening air. He found himself whistling an answer to its call and then let a sigh of pleasure rest quietly on his lips.

Albert and Kate met many times over the following weeks and months, under the steady but encouraging eye of the Taylor sisters and Albert grew to value Kate's company and bask in the warmth of her smile. She was very beautiful, he thought, but he really didn't know her that well. The first time the evenings were warm enough for them to spend more than an hour or so in one another's company, it was well into April.

# CHAPTER THIRTY-EIGHT

*April 1918*

Spring had arrived in Micklewell. The lanes were sprinkled with the yellow and green of primroses and the cow parsley forced its long stalks skyward, not yet revealing its white umbrella blooms. The wood anemones carpeted the copses so thickly that there was not a bare stretch of soil to be seen and the pastures hid small pink secrets amongst the grass, the delicate pyramids of wild orchids. The air tingled with the smell of wild garlic. Kate was so happy to be out in her beloved Hampshire countryside and walking with a man who was so kind to her. She really was extremely lucky that Albert wanted to get to know her better. He had been somewhat flustered when he'd asked her to walk out with him, but she was delighted he had finally got around to it.

Kate and Albert walked across the fields that Sunday afternoon to St Swithun's Church at Nately. Albert helped her over the stiles and, each time he looked at her face, he let his eyes rest upon her until she blushed with his attentions. His hands fitted comfortably on her waist as he helped her jump down and he commented on her delicately patterned floral dress.

'You seem to grow right out of the meadow, Kate,' he said.

'All cornflowers and cotton grass, edged with forget-me-nots,' Kate laughed.

They walked on, arm in arm, until they came to the church. The sun was losing its warmth but the brightness reflected in the windows threw back a glow that Albert felt deep inside him. They walked around to the main entrance and he paused to look at a strange carving on one of the pillars of the doorway.

'What's a mermaid doing here?' he said. 'We're far from the sea.'

'The legend goes,' she said, 'that a sailor from Micklewell met and flirted with a mermaid but would not stay with her despite her pleadings. He returned home, where he met and fell in love with a girl from Nately.'

She took his arm and turned him around to see the long approach to the church from the road. 'Imagine this, Albert. The wedding day arrives and the joyful procession of the bridal party moves towards the church door. There, sitting outside it, is the mermaid.'

She pulled him forward. 'Look closely and you'll see there is a tiny figure on the mermaid's back. That is the sailor, for she snatched him away from his bride-to-be and plunged with him into the stream. She swam with him into the Lyde and the Loddon and from there into the Thames and out to sea. They were never seen again.'

She pulled away from him and smiled. 'Now let that be a lesson to you, Albert, this is the fate of the feckless and the unfaithful.'

Albert stared at Kate, his face suddenly serious. 'I would never abandon you, Kate,' he said.

'You might,' she replied. 'We can never know what the future holds.'

'No, never. I will never leave you. Kate . . . will you . . . ?'

Kate placed a finger over his lips.

'Just listen to me,' she whispered. 'Sit down with me here and listen to me and then we'll see.'

She told him more of her employment in Andover, of moving to London and how she had conceived and given birth to a son. She explained how difficult life was for a young woman away from her family and with no one to call upon to help her in such a time of great need. She described the drudgery of the workhouse and how Ida and Mrs Bowden had helped her escape.

'When the mistress found out I was pregnant, I was dismissed,' she said looking down at her hands which plucked the blades of cotton grass. 'The workhouse was the only refuge for me.'

Albert sat in silence, so much to take in. Kate waited. Eventually he broke the fine thread of connection between them.

'I knew you had a child,' Albert said. 'People talk. But it makes no difference. His father was killed in battle, as so many have been.'

'That much is true,' Kate said. 'But we were never married. He didn't even know of Ronnie's birth. Now he will never see him. It's so hard for me to talk about it . . . I hope you understand, Albert.'

Albert took Kate's hand. She could see the deep concern in his eyes. This was a man who understood. He had been there and fought beside men like Philip. He was not one for deep conversation but he had a strength about him that she liked. The way he looked at her betrayed his feelings. She could see that he cared about her.

'Kate, if you'll let me, I'd like to come and meet Ronnie so that he can begin to know me and be happy in my company.'

Kate kissed him gently on the cheek, her lips revealing all he needed to know.

'I can love again, Albert,' she said, 'and I can't think of a better person to give my love to than you, if you'll have me, that is?'

'Is that a proposal, Miss Kate Truscott?' Albert laughed. 'I thought it was me supposed to do the proposing!'

'Times are changing, Albert. There're women doing all manner of things these days, driving tractors, making weapons in factories. Next thing you know we'll be serving in parliament,' Kate joked.

'You'll have to get the vote first,' Albert said.

'What is it they say, stranger things have happened . . .'

'At sea, yes,' Albert added, 'but maybe not in Micklewell yet.'

'Well, let's just wait and see, shall we?' Kate replied, smiling at him and taking his hand.

They walked back to Micklewell together as the sun lengthened their shadows and the memories of the past moved away.

# CHAPTER THIRTY-NINE

*September 1918*

Kate and Albert were married in Basingstoke Register Office. At the time they were taking their vows, the American Army were taking their first stand against German troops in St Mihiel, southern France and the first reported cases of the Spanish Flu had already reached England.

On a clear, bright September day, Kate and Albert and the Truscott family walked down the lane to Taylor Farm, where Florence and Nora were waiting for them. Ted Graves was sitting on the cart, wearing a well-worn top hat and long jacket with a red scarf knotted at his neck. And the cart! How it was transformed! Nora had enlisted the help of the two Land Army girls to scrub it clean and festoon the sides with greenery, gathered from the local woods and gardens. There was scented pine for long life, myrtle for love and rosemary for remembrance.

Rex had been groomed and his mane plaited. Woven into his mane were purple rosemary flowers. Kate wore a lilac dress with a shawl collar and a buttoned sash, which Dot had made for her, with material supplied by Miss Florence. She carried blue delphiniums, picked that morning from the garden and she looked pretty as a picture. Albert looked the smartest he'd ever been, clean-shaven and wearing his best jacket, complete with buttonhole. Kate just couldn't stop smiling all the way as they paraded through the village and were waved at by well-wishers all the way to the station at Hook.

After the ceremony they made the long journey back again but this time as man and wife. The Taylor sisters had gathered together some willing helpers and there was a wedding day supper ready for them on their return. Dot moved out of the bedroom she shared with Kate, so that the couple could spend their first night together and although it was not luxurious or very private, Kate gave herself to Albert willingly. She'd never stop loving Philip but theirs was a love that just could not be. As she laid her head gently on the warm space between his chin and his chest, she felt that his strong arms would always be there to protect her. When Ronnie whimpered in his sleep in the next room and Albert raised himself up on one elbow, his head turned to listen, she knew he would love Ronnie too and be a good father to him.

There was not the room in the small family cottage for Kate, Albert and Ronnie to stay for very long. So, Albert had made plans for them to lead a more independent life. The prospects for Albert in Micklewell were limited and the work at the farm, though enjoyable, had only ever been a means of adapting to life outside the army and bringing in a little money in order to get by. Now he had a family to support. He needed a better paid job. He turned to Florence Taylor for some guidance.

'I do enjoy working on the farm, Miss Taylor,' he said, 'and the pay has been enough when it was just me but . . .'

'It's quite all right, Albert, I understand,' Florence said. 'You're a family man now. Why don't you go and talk to Tucker, the landlord at the Queen's Head? He keeps his ear to the ground. He'll know if there are any opportunities for you elsewhere.'

Tucker turned out to be a very useful source of information.

'They're recruiting on the railways at the moment. All part of the war effort. They're building branch lines all over, to assist the transport of ordnance from factories throughout Hampshire down to the docks in Portsmouth,' he explained. 'You're a strong bloke,' he continued, looking Albert up and down. 'If I had the money I'd employ you here to save me humping those barrels about, but I can't take on any more workers at the moment.'

Albert acted immediately and got himself over to Hook station to ask about the possibility of employment on the railways.

'Got any experience?' the station master asked.

'No, but since I was discharged from the army, I've been doing heavy work on a farm the past year and there's not much I can't turn my hand to. I'm a fast learner,' Albert replied.

'Well, I can't do anything for you here, you'll have to get yourself over to the main station at Basingstoke. That's where they do all the signing on,' the station master said.

Albert got straight back on his bike and cycled the seven miles to Basingstoke where he was asked to wait until the station manager could see him. An hour later he was called into an office painted green and cream with an enormous oak wooden table, covered in various papers and files. There was a map of the rail network in the south of England on the wall and a poster that encouraged people to travel to Lyme Regis and Its Bay (delightful climate all year round). Albert allowed himself a moment's daydream about how wonderful it would be to take Kate there, but that was all it was, a dream. He needed well paid work and then they must find a place to live.

Albert was offered work as a railway plate-layer down near the docks in Fareham, Portsmouth. There was a need for maintenance and repair of the lines between the army supplies and armaments stores at Gosport and the docks. He paused for a moment before accepting. Fareham was a long way from Micklewell and Kate would perhaps be concerned about being so far from her family. On the other hand, she had worked in service for many years and had been through a great deal with birthing Ronnie on her own and surviving the workhouse. She was made of stronger metal than many young women. It would be all right, he told himself.

'You could be sent anywhere along those lines,' the manager said. 'So I suggest you find yourself some lodgings in Fareham. That's midway between the two depots.'

Albert cycled back to Micklewell with a broad grin on his face. The pay was good and they could afford to rent somewhere, a place they could call their own. He burst into the kitchen and announced his success with pride.

'Fareham?' Kate exclaimed when Albert told her about accepting the job. 'I don't even know where Fareham is.'

'It's down near the docks, Portsmouth way,' Pa explained. 'You'll be doing important work, Albert, keeping those lines open. The supply lines to the docks are essential for our boys over there.'

'It's good money, Kate,' Albert said. 'You and I and young Ronnie will be able to have our own space. There'll be enough for us all to live on. I thought you'd be pleased.'

Kate looked at his downcast expression and her tone softened.

'Of course I'm pleased,' she said. 'It's just that I've got used to being back in Micklewell, is all. I'm going to miss everyone,' she said, looking round at the family gathered in the kitchen.

Ronnie and Tilly were playing happily together on the floor sorting a box of old buttons and swopping them with each other. They laughed when Jimmy, the cat, jumped in amongst them and started padding them with his paws.

'Tilly will miss Ronnie,' Kate said.

'But they will still be able to see one another from time to time,' Albert said. 'I get special rate fares on the railways now I'm working for them.'

'Yes, and think what fun it will be for me to come down and see you.' Dot smiled.

238

'It's a good opportunity for you both,' Ada said, joining in the general encouragement.

The family's support for Albert and Kate's new venture did not stop there being a tearful farewell. There were hugs and handshakes and promises to write. Ada had packed them a lunch for the journey and Dot had made Ronnie his own little drawstring bag to put a few of his special toys in. They were waved off enthusiastically by neighbours and were soon on their way to Fareham. The manager in Basingstoke had told Albert of a lodging house where many of their railway workers lived.

'It's not much to write home about, apparently, but it's a roof over our heads until we can find somewhere else,' Albert explained.

They struggled from the station to Queen's Road with Albert carrying their bags and Kate holding a sleeping Ronnie.

'It's not far now,' Albert said. He stopped to put down the bags and rest his arms.

'I shouldn't have brought my mother's bowl,' Kate said. 'It's awkward to carry.'

'We haven't brought much that's our own,' Albert said. 'I couldn't deny you that. Your mum gave it us on our wedding day.'

Kate smiled at him. He was a good man, her Albert.

Mrs Morton, the lodging house owner, was a kindly soul. She'd made them feel very welcome. The old lady made a fuss of Ronnie and gave him some biscuits she'd baked. The two rooms at the top of the house were small and sparsely furnished but they were all they could afford until Albert got paid. There was a sitting room with a fireplace, two armchairs and a wooden table with two ladder-back chairs. The tiny bedroom had a double bed and a cot for Ronnie. Bed linen was provided in the cost of the rooms and they could use the communal kitchen downstairs.

'Best time to cook is before all the workers get home,' Mrs Morton said. 'After five o'clock it gets busy down there.'

When Kate kissed Albert goodbye on his first morning, she didn't know how she would spend the day, but with the little money they had saved, she needed to find the nearest shops where she could get some food to last a few days. Mrs Morton kindly offered to look after Ronnie for an hour while she got some essentials. She pointed Kate in the right direction and she found the grocers and the hardware store. She came back with bread, butter, cheese, porridge, potatoes, minced beef, tea and a tea towel.

'Oh, I forgot the milk,' Kate said on her return.

'I can let you have some,' Mrs Morton said.

Kate felt that she would get on well with Mrs Morton, she had all the qualities of a good country woman even though she lived in the town.

When Albert arrived home, he needed a good wash before eating his dinner. Railway plate-laying was dirty work. Kate was pleased with the cottage pie she'd made. It tasted good and they spent their first evening in 51, Queen's Road telling each other of their first impressions of Fareham and its people.

Albert's strong physique and attention to detail made him an efficient worker. He could work longer hours and lift heavier loads than most of the other plate-layers, making him a valued member of the team. The ganger often chose Albert to do the more difficult jobs. When other men failed to shift stubborn fixing bolts or heave a sleeper into place, he would call for Albert. But the ganger was not a soft-hearted man. He could be ruthless in dismissing men who didn't pull their weight.

The first signs of Kate being unwell came after only four weeks of them arriving in Fareham. Kate had decided to take Ronnie down to the waterfront to look at the boats. She wrapped him up warmly, criss-crossing a scarf around his chest to protect him from the winds that often swept up the river and wound their way up and down the streets.

It was late October and, although the sun shone brightly, Kate couldn't get warm. After just a short while of walking up and down the quay and throwing some bread to the swans, she began to shiver. The voices of the men, calling to each other on the boats, echoed in her head and Ronnie's squeals of delight at seeing the fishing boats unload their catch made her ears ring and her head pound. She suddenly came over hot and felt the sweat pooling under her arms. Her mouth was dry and she felt the need to sit down. She leaned on a low wall and tried to breathe deeply but the air felt sharp in her lungs.

'Ronnie, come here,' she said. 'We must go now.'

Kate reached out her hand and Ronnie took it but began pulling in the direction of the crates.

'No, Ronnie, we have to go now, Mummy's sick,' Kate tried to explain to him.

They managed to walk back home but every step leached more strength from Kate's body. Every so often Ronnie stopped and held his arms up to Kate. 'Carry, Mamma, carry,' he pleaded. But Kate did not have the energy.

Once inside the house, the two of them climbed the stairs. Kate lay down with her son on the bed and they both drifted off to sleep. Ronnie's hands on her face were what woke her and she realized that she needed to get down to the kitchen and cook their dinner.

Mrs Morton was in the kitchen baking. She took one look at Kate and said, 'You look dreadful, Kate. Get yourself back to bed and Ronnie here can help me with this cake mix. Are you good at stirring, Ronnie?'

'But I need to make Albert's dinner,' Kate replied.

'You leave that to me,' Mrs Morton said. 'I'll just add a few more carrots and swede to the meat stew.'

When Albert arrived home that evening, he was shocked to see the shivering form of his dear wife under the bed-clothes. He came straight to her bedside and placed his arm gently over her shoulders.

'Kate,' he whispered. 'Kate, what's wrong?'

When she rolled towards him he could see that his lovely Kate was racked with pain and she had a fever.

'Everything aches,' she said, and began to cough at the effort of speaking. Albert kissed her gently on the forehead and asked if he could get her anything.

'Some water,' she whispered, her voice weak.

'Where's Ronnie?' he asked, bringing her the water.

'With Mrs Morton,' Kate replied. 'She's made your dinner too, bless her.'

Albert asked if he could bring her some, but she said she couldn't stomach it.

'She looks really poorly,' Mrs Morton said. 'I can look out for them both tomorrow if you like. You need to go to work.'

Albert thanked Mrs Morton for her understanding. He couldn't risk asking for time off to look after his wife. He had to report for work as usual, despite his worries for his Kate. He couldn't be late either, the ganger was a stickler for punctuality. What should he do? There was talk of the Spanish Flu at work. Might she have caught that from somewhere?

After a very restless night with Kate tossing and turning and her body burning against his, Albert reluctantly decided he must leave her. He kissed his wife gently on the forehead and roused himself to prepare for the day and walk the two miles to work. He made himself a cup of tea and took one to Kate in bed. Ronnie was still sleeping and he carefully pulled the blankets up over him. He sliced the bread slowly and carefully. It had to last two more days. Taking his bread and cheese, he closed the door quietly.

He hated leaving her but he needed to keep this job. There were plenty of other men who would step into his shoes if he didn't show willing. He was desperately worried about Kate and leaving her on her own. All he could do was pray for her recovery.

The call came halfway through the afternoon. He was in the plate-layer's hut, taking a well-earned break when he heard the news.

'Albert,' the ganger said. 'There's a message for you arrived back at the depot. Your wife's been taken bad and you need to get home in a hurry.'

Albert left his bread and cheese on the bench and ran as fast as his legs would carry him, his heart pounding and sweat forming on his forehead. She had to be all right.

# CHAPTER FORTY

*October 1918*

When Albert arrived home, Mrs Morton was watching over Kate, placing cold compresses to her forehead. Kate was racked with coughing and finding it difficult to breathe. Albert went straight to her bedside but she barely opened her eyes when he spoke to her.

'I heard Ronnie crying,' Mrs Morton said. 'I waited but he didn't stop, so I came upstairs. I found her like this.'

'I don't know what to do. What should I do? Should I call a doctor?' Albert gasped.

'You stay with her. I'll fetch something to help her breathe,' Mrs Morton said.

She returned with a bowl of steaming water which gave off a pungent smell.

'I've put come camphor oil in to help clear her lungs,' Mrs Morton said. 'We'll rub some on her chest too. Now, you sit her up and support her and I'll hold the bowl. Come on now, Kate, deep breaths.'

Albert and Mrs Morton both encouraged her to inhale the vapours and Ronnie joined in too. He made loud sucking noises and repeated, 'Come on, Mumma.'

Kate managed to take in some of the vapours and then dropped off to sleep, exhausted with the effort. When Mrs Morton left saying she would bring a plate of something up for Albert, Ronnie wouldn't move from Kate's side. He stood beside the bed, holding his mother's hand until his own eyes started to close.

'Come on, little man,' Albert said, picking him up, 'time for you to sleep too.'

Albert settled Ronnie down, then sat looking at Kate's chest rising and falling, and listened to her struggling to find air. Mrs Morton brought him plate of stew.

'Do you think it's the Spanish Flu?' Albert asked her. 'I've heard tell of the hundreds who've got it and some who have . . .' His voice trailed off as he struggled with the possibility that Kate might be suffering from such a deadly disease.

'There have been some cases around here, so I've heard. It could be just a chill, let's hope so. She's sleeping quite peacefully now,' Mrs Morton replied.

'Should I call a doctor?' Albert asked again, his face creased with tiredness and worry. 'I don't know how we'll pay for one though. I have no savings. We spend everything I earn. What should I do?'

Mrs Morton placed a hand on Albert's shoulder and tried to reassure him that Kate seemed to be breathing easier.

'Perhaps give it 'til morning,' she said. 'Just in case, though, I'll give you the address of Dr Clift, he won't charge you the earth and he's a good doctor. Good night, Albert. I will come up first thing to see how she is.'

Albert pulled the chair close to the bed to watch over Kate. He tried to keep awake but his head gradually settled on his chest and he too fell asleep. An hour or so later he woke with a stiff neck and back, undressed himself and crept quietly under the blankets. Kate's breathing was still laboured but she was, at least, sleeping. He turned towards her and kissed her gently on the lips.

'My beautiful Kate, my lovely wife,' he whispered.

As he lay beside her, he stayed awake for a long time, worrying that he should have called the doctor and praying that she would survive the night. He thought of all the men he'd witnessed die in front of him, of bodies blown apart, of brains spilling over the mud, blood seeping into the ground, men's intestines — worm fodder. He thought of the lives he'd taken and how precious life was. What he would give now to exchange his life for hers!

He reached across, took her hand and turned her wedding band with his broad fingers, a circle of gold that bound his heart to hers. He felt his own chest tighten. He couldn't lose her. He listened to the rhythms of her struggling body, willing her to take the next breath and the next one and the next.

He caressed her fingers, one for each week they'd been married. If only those fingers could touch his face, entwine gently with his own, be there to hold the hands of more children, brothers and sisters for Ronnie. If there was a God, then let him be satisfied with all the lives he'd taken already and spare hers.

Time passed so slowly. Albert struggled to stay awake and all he could hear in the darkness was the deep rattling sound in Kate's chest, a sound he'd heard so many times before. The gurgling of gas in a man's lungs was a sound he would never forget. He got out of bed, reached for the matches and lit the lamp, the sulphurous smell filling the air. Taking the lamp to the bedside, he raised the yellow light to her face. Her eyes were closed and her mouth open, her skin pale. He placed the lamp on the table and sat beside her. She was slipping away from him. All he could do was hold onto her and hope that she could feel him, hear him. He bent to whisper in her ear, all that he wanted to say to her, his love, his joy, his Kate. He wrapped his arms around her, his warm breath settling on her, trying to breathe life into her. The night hours closed around them and sleep eventually came.

When night turned to day, Albert's eyes sprang open, a sudden feeling of panic constricting his throat. He'd turned away from Kate in his sleep and he feared to turn back and look at her, that he would see what his heart could not bear to see. Slowly he shifted his body to face her. Her eyes were still closed but she was no longer struggling for breath. Her skin still looked pallid but the wheezing from her chest had lessened. He held his face close to hers. The whisper of breath that emitted from her lips came as such a relief to him, that tears flowed down his cheeks. She was still alive. He allowed himself to feel a sweet moment of hope. Could the crisis have passed?

Ronnie murmured in his sleep. Albert carefully folded back the bedclothes and went to him. The child opened his eyes and immediately said, 'Mumma?' Albert lifted him and carried him to Kate's bedside. Ronnie looked down at her and then back at Albert. 'Mumma sleeping?' he asked.

'Yes, Mumma is sleeping,' Albert said with a deep sigh of relief, 'but she will wake soon. She needs to rest. Come, let's make some breakfast together.'

'Can we have porridge?' Ronnie asked.

'Yes, son, we can,' Albert replied. 'But let's get dressed first. We must be as quiet as we can, so as not to disturb Mumma.'

As Albert sat Ronnie on the chair to fasten his shoes, there was a quiet tap at the door. It was Mrs Morton.

'How is Kate?' she asked, a look of concern on her face.

'Come in, please,' he said holding the door open. 'I think she's a little better, her breathing is easier.'

Mrs Morton walked across to Kate's bedside and felt her forehead. 'She's less clammy,' she said. 'The camphor seems to have helped. Rub some more on her chest, Albert, and make sure she takes some water. Fetch a cup and I'll show you how.'

At Mrs Morton's touch, Kate stirred, her eyelids flickering. She murmured something that made no sense but she was beginning to come around.

Mrs Morton sat on the bed and gently moved her arm behind Kate's back.

'Bring another pillow,' she said. 'We need to get her more upright.'

Together the two of them raised Kate up, enough for her to sip some water.

'Little sips, Albert. Not too much or she'll choke. Whenever she stirs, try to get her to take some more.'

Albert moved through the days that followed with one mind only, to make sure Kate recovered. Mrs Morton cooked and looked after Ronnie when she could, while Albert carried out Mrs Morton's instructions, watched and waited and prayed.

On the third day, the morning light travelled through the window and touched Kate's eyelids. She was aware of sounds and movement in the room. She tried to lift her head off the pillow. Her neck was stiff and her whole body ached but she wasn't coughing as much and the air filtered in and out of her lungs more easily. Her eyes were heavy as she tried to look around her. The room wavered in and out of focus, until the familiar sight of the dresser and the bowl that her mother had given them as a wedding present, came into view. She heard the faint singing of the kettle and the chink of cups, then the splash of water as the teapot was filled.

'Albert?' she whispered.

Her voice was faint but Albert heard her immediately. Ronnie heard her too and rushed to the bed. He clambered up and threw his arms around his mother.

'Gently, son, gently,' Albert said. But then he couldn't stop himself from holding her too. The three of them lay on the bed together, wrapped in each other's arms for a while, until Kate said, 'I'm thirsty. Could I have some water?'

'Of course. What am I thinking of?' Albert replied. 'I'll get you some and there's tea too.'

'And porridge,' Ronnie said.

Kate gave a weak smile and then lay back on the pillow. After she'd taken some tea and a little food, Albert said, 'I should go and tell Mrs Morton you're over the worst. She helped me nurse you and looked after Ronnie while you were sick.'

'How long have I been ill?' Kate asked.

'Several days,' Albert replied.

Kate could see how worried he'd been and took his hand. This was her gentle giant. The man of iron who could carry half a tree on his shoulders, who could lift bales above his head and hold back the power of horses, spooked by a storm. This was the man who could work twelve-hour days, laying railway sleepers and miles of metal track to bring in the money to support his family. And this was the man who loved her and she loved him. She thought of the first time they'd walked together to Nately church and how he'd said he would never leave her. She'd come so close to leaving him though, she knew that now.

Albert smiled at her and squeezed her hand. She smiled back at him. She was so glad that he'd found her. Taking on another man's child was not something that every man would do, but he had, willingly. She looked at Ronnie, playing with his toy car on the floor. Her father had made it for him. She recalled how happily Ronnie and Tilly played together and realized how much she missed her family and the country lanes of Micklewell. Being here, in Fareham, had brought in more money but Albert was a man who belonged amongst the fields and the trees with the grass beneath his feet, not the concrete of the streets and the steel of the railways. He was a country man and she was a country girl, a woman who needed the smell of freshly turned earth and the sound of bird song. They should go home, the three of them, home to Micklewell and the life they loved.

* * *

A week later, Kate was strong enough to travel. They packed their few belongings, including the pink and white bowl, thanked Mrs Morton for all she had done for them and made their way to the station. When they arrived at Hook, they waited for the cart. As they climbed on board, Kate smiled at the thought of the first journey she'd taken on her own, to go to Andover and begin her life as a nursemaid. That life seemed so far away now. Here she was, so many years later, returning again but this time with a husband and a child.

As the horse trotted down the country lanes, drawing ever closer to her beloved Micklewell, she thought about the turning of the seasons. Soon the frosts would come and the fallen leaves would have a silver edging. The winds would whip across the barren fields and the clouds turn heavy with snow. Villagers would appear with shovels to clear the roadways and the birds would seek refuge in the hedgerows.

Then, when the snows melted, the snowdrops would nod their welcome to the coming spring. The sweet smell of witch hazel would drift on the winds and the earth give up new life. Children would return to the village pond with their jam jars, running home with the sticky, glutinous masses from the shallows. The stream would fill with watercress and the laughter of children splashing each other would ring around the village. The cycle of life would begin again.

**THE END**

# ACKNOWLEDGEMENTS

My thanks to:

My partner, Andrew, my family and friends for the encouragement to keep writing.

My first readers Margaret Colyer, Sheila Kelly and Angie Reid.

My late Aunt Bettine, who gave me a copy of what has proved to be an excellent resource, *Hampshire Harvest — A Traveller's Notebook by Robert Potter.*

The Writers' Company, particularly Petra McQueen and Elizabeth Ferretti.

My agent, Kate Nash and the team at the Kate Nash Literary Agency.

Kate Lyall Grant and the editorial and publishing team at Joffe Books.

# THE JOFFE BOOKS STORY

We began in 2014 when Jasper agreed to publish his mum's much-rejected romance novel and it became a bestseller.

Since then we've grown into the largest independent publisher in the UK. We're extremely proud to publish some of the very best writers in the world, including Joy Ellis, Faith Martin, Caro Ramsay, Helen Forrester, Simon Brett and Robert Goddard. Everyone at Joffe Books loves reading and we never forget that it all begins with the magic of an author telling a story.

We are proud to publish talented first-time authors, as well as established writers whose books we love introducing to a new generation of readers.

We have been shortlisted for Independent Publisher of the Year at the British Book Awards three times, in 2020, 2021 and 2022, and for the Diversity and Inclusivity Award at the Independent Publishing Awards in 2022.

We built this company with your help, and we love to hear from you, so please email us about absolutely anything bookish at: feedback@joffebooks.com.

If you want to receive free books every Friday and hear about all our new releases, join our mailing list: www.joffebooks.com/contact

And when you tell your friends about us, just remember: it's pronounced Joffe as in coffee or toffee!

Ingram Content Group UK Ltd.
Milton Keynes UK
UKHW012245130423
420127UK00007B/633